JUST THE

No Mission
Is Impossible

ONE

會展英語

一本在手 MICE English So~ EASY

MICE是
- Ⓜ Meeting 會議
- Ⓘ Incentive Travel 獎勵旅遊
- Ⓒ Conferences 大會
- Ⓔ Exhibitions 展覽會

MICE 是什麼？

CE English?

陳志達◎著

本書詳實記錄MICE情境
是同時兼顧**MICE技巧+英文實力**的超級好幫手

Special Highlights

- **情境對話** 透析MICE各種狀況，MICE四大流程一學就會，英文辦展不卡卡
- **單字解析** 精準掌握MICE**關鍵字**用法，辦展一路闖通關
- **同義字** 吸收MICE English也不忘累積**英文好實力**
- **句型解析** 好用句型加強MICE English**記憶力**
- **雙料職場補給+達人提點** 從沒看過這麼詳細的**超寫實職場實錄**，最貼心的MICE不出錯提醒

PREFACE

作者序

在接受邀請撰寫本書時，適逢本人奉派代表公司參加杜拜汽車零配件暨汽修展（Automechanika Middle East 2014），執行與台灣車輛公會及模具公會共同合作出版會員名錄之發行工作。本次國際展會我國約有 150 家汽配與手工具廠商參展，與全球近 30 國，數千家廠商躬逢其盛，每天在平均攝氏達 40℃炎熱高溫下，戮力堅守崗位接待來訪買主，洽商訂單。

各國展會代表普遍對 Made in Taiwan 的產品讚譽有嘉，使本人深感與有榮焉，同時也相當敬佩台灣參展廠商所表現出來的精神與競爭力；且部分台商之攤位佈置精緻，甚至有凌駕歐美代表國家館的態勢，屢獲國際買主青睞及造訪，儼然成為另類的『台灣之光』。

本人職場生涯有幸曾參與、規劃並執行多檔跨國會議及大型宴會活動，包括：和信集團宴請出席國際貨幣基金（IMF）、世界銀行（World Bank）、亞洲開發銀行（Asian Development Bank）會議中外代表，中國信託華府雙橡園晚宴（Chinatrust Twin Oak Banquet, Washington, D.C.）及中美／美中經濟合作會議（ROC-USA & USA-ROC Economic Councils）等。上述國際性活動，從研擬／寄發邀請函、會議議程／主席、專題主講人定案、往返班機（含私人飛機）行程、飯店住宿預約、餐飲

／座位安排，晚會表演節目，以及到當地交通（禮車租賃）等諸多事項，皆須精心規劃及反覆演練；並要隨時注意內容修正及臨時變動，尤其掌握有關受邀特別貴賓（VVIP）進出會場／安全隨扈配合，或特別交辦事項。

　　MICE 的核心精神--發揮團隊最高戰鬥力，達成既定工作目標。基此歷練，今摘錄各式情境模擬，對話例句援用，及單字、句型分析等謹供卓參。期盼本書讀者或可藉此舉一反三，自我衍生更佳學習效果。倉促成書，野人獻曝，力有所未逮之處，尚祈各方行家不吝斧正，感激不盡。

　　學海無涯，唯勤是岸。在此也特別感謝力得文化提供出版本書的機會，及編輯部與相關同仁的大力協助。願教學相長，自強不息，共勉之！

陳志遠謹誌于台北
8/18/2014

目錄

❷ Incentive Travel 獎勵旅遊

❸ Conference 大會

3-2 主持報告會 To Preside Over a Presentation ·······················242

④ Exhibition 展覽會

Meeting
會議

1-1 腦力激盪會議
Brainstorming Meeting

情境 1 Meeting with Your Boss 與自己老闆開會

情境設定

This is a brainstorming meeting presided over by the boss in person with the purpose aiming at strengthening the coordination works among departments of the company. Attendees of the meeting include executives of both sales and administration.

這是由老闆親自主持之腦力激盪會議，主要目的乃為加強公司各部門之溝通工作。本次與會者包括業務及管理部門主管人員。

角色設定

Boss：老闆
Sales Executive (SE)：業務主管
Administration Executive (AE)：管理部主管

給力對話

Boss ▶ The company has become increasingly successful in recent years, but the coordination among individual departments is not yet smooth as expected. Through the

老闆 ▶ 我們公司近年來越發成長，可是各部門間之協調仍然不如預期般順利。透過今天舉行

brainstorming meeting held today, I hope to solicit for your true comments and or opinions on this regard.

之腦力激盪會議，我想徵詢各位在這方面確切之批評或卓見。

SE ▶ My department spares no efforts to reach the sales target each year. This needs the assistance from other associates, of course.

業務主管 ▶ 我們部門為達成每年銷售目標不辭辛勞。當然，這也需要其他同仁支援。

AE ▶ We always offer the most appropriate assistances to sales but my department has to look after our own jobs at the same time.

管理部主管 ▶ 我們一向對業務單位提供最恰當之協助，可我們部門也須同時要照顧好自己的工作。

Boss ▶ That explains the reason behind this brainstorming meeting. What I concern is how our colleagues have a better understanding of priority in work and if they could tackle the problem all together?

老闆 ▶ 這正是說明本次腦力激盪會議之理由。我所關心的是同事如何了解工作之優先順序，以及大家是否可共同把問題處理好？

SE ▶ In line with the incoming sales promotion, the new product brochure must be printed and mailed to our clients by the administration department no latter than the first week of next month. Previously, we lost several sales opportunities due to the delay of delivery.

業務主管 ▶ 配合即將到來之促銷活動，我希望新產品型錄最慢在下個月的第一星期前，由管理部印製完成並寄發給客戶。之前由於交貨延誤，我們損失不少銷售機會。

17

AE ▶ The printing can be getting started as soon as the draft is finalized, and the sales department is informed about the deadline already. Due to the tight printing schedule, the delivery was unable to meet on punctual date last time, and in the future we'll pay much more attention on this issue.

管理部主管 ▶ 只要確認最後完稿，型錄印刷即可開始；業務部門已經被告知截稿日期。上次茲因印刷時間太緊迫，以致無法如期交貨，未來對此事件我們會特別加以注意。

Boss ▶ I'll also demand all coordination works be noted with a specified completion date. Maybe we need a new timesheet which has to be countersigned by executives of individual departments.

老闆 ▶ 我也要求所有協調工作必須有詳細指明完成日期加以註記。或許我們需要一張新的時間控管單，並由跨部門主管互相連署。

AE ▶ My department will soon design a new form for this function, and we plan to use it after submitting for approvals.

管理部主管 ▶ 本部門會針對該功能立刻重新設計一份新表格，並且在呈請核准後開始使用。

SE ▶ I would appreciate it very much if the new form would emphasize on checking points of any delays. This avoids any responsibilities in departments.

業務主管 ▶ 如果新表格能在有關延誤檢查點上多做些強調的話，我會很感激，這樣可避免部門之間所應負之責任。

給力單字

1. **brainstorming** (*n.*)　腦力激盪
The boss held a brainstorming session to improve the company's coordination work.
老闆召開腦力激盪會議以改善公司之協調工作。

2. **solicit** (*v.i.*)　請求；懇求
The executive solicited supports to reach the sales target.
該主管請求支援以達到業績目標。

3. **comment** (*n.*)　意見，評論
The boss made comments on proposals submitted by each department.
老闆對每個部門提出的建議作評論。

4. **effort** (*n.*)　努力
We are asked to spare no efforts to get the work completed.
我們被要求要不遺餘力把工作完成。

5. **associate** (*n.*)　夥伴；同事
We have many outstanding and competent associates at the company.
我們公司有許多傑出及勝任的同事。

6. **appropriate** (*adj.*)　適當的，相稱的
An appropriate proposal was discussed and made conclusion in the meeting.
一個非常適當的建議在會議中被提出來討論並達成結論。

7. **look after** (*v.t.*)　照顧，管理
Each department has to look after its own jobs and offer other supports, if needed.
每個部門都必須管好自己的工作，但有必要時也需要提供其他支援。

8. **colleagues** (*n.*)　同事，同僚
Most of colleagues are getting along very well in the office.
辦公室裡的大部分同事都相處得很好。

9. **priority** (*n.*)　優先，重點
The team coordination work has high priority in the company.
團隊協調工作為公司的優先重點。

10. **tackle** (*v.t.*)　著手對付（或處理）
The boss tackled the difficult problem and solved it.
老闆處理過這一難題並且解決了它。

11. **brochure** (*n.*)　小冊子，目錄
A brand new brochure is compiled by the sales department for the exhibition purpose.
為了參加展會，業務部門編撰一份嶄新的行銷小冊子。

12. **delay** (*n.*)　延遲；耽擱
The sales department suggests a marketing brochure be printed out without delay.
業務單位建議必須及時印好行銷目錄。

13. **finalize** (*v.t.*)　最後定案，確定
This brainstorming meeting finalized the details of the department coordination work.
這次腦力激盪會議確定了部門協調所有的細節。

14. **punctual** (*adj.*)　準時的，守時的
It is expected that the delivery of brochures will be on punctual.
期待目錄製作能夠準時交貨。

15. **specified** (*v.t.*)　具體指定；詳細指明
The delivery date is specified on next Wednesday.
交貨日期詳載是在下星期三。

Meeting

16. **countersign** (*v.t.*)　連署

The timesheet must be countersigned by executives of each department.

這張時間控管單必須由各部門主管連署。

17. **submit** (*v.t.*)　提交，呈遞

The boss has not yet approved the resignation submitted by the sales executive.

老闆尚未批准業務主管所提出之辭呈。

18. **appreciate** (*v.t.*)　感謝，感激

I highly appreciated his kindness and support.

我對他的好意及支持深表謝意。

給力句型

1. a brainstorming meeting + 過去式動詞 or 過去分詞

（召開）腦力激盪會議。

A brainstorming meeting is held by the boss, who asked executives to discuss mutual coordination of departments.

老闆召開腦力激盪會議，並要求主管討論各部門互相協調之工作事宜。

For the new product launch, the executive is asked to attend a brainstorming meeting.

為了新產品上市，主管依要求需參加腦力激盪會議。

The marketing team brainstormed for hours in designing the new product campaign.

為了設計新產品的行銷策略，行銷小組腦力激盪多時。

2. effort (n.)　努力，盡力，努力的成果；成就[C]

Each salesman is asked to make more efforts on his target.
每位業務人員都被要求在業績方面再多加努力。

The boss made a fine effort on the coordination work of each department.
老闆在各部門溝通工作方面有很好之作為。

3. delay (v.t.)　及物動詞＋名詞（耽擱；延誤）

The delivery of brochure delayed for one day.
宣傳手冊的運送耽擱了一天。

(v.i.)　不及物動詞＋時間副詞（拖延；耽擱）

He has delayed so long for attending the next meeting.
他拖了很久才去參加下個會議。

4. emphasize (v.t.)　強調，著重[+that][+wh-]
The boss emphasized what he was saying by writing on the white board.
老闆強調他所說的話並將它們寫在白板上。

Every colleague should attend the meeting on time, the boss emphasized.
老板強調，每一位同仁都必須準時與會。

The boss emphasized the importance of meeting.
老闆強調了本次會議的重要性。

Internal Coordination 內部溝通

Meeting

角色設定

Executive：主管
Colleague：同事

情境對話

E ▶ As the boss requires the strengthening of the company coordination, I suggest a department meeting be convened for this purpose soon.

主管 ▶ 由於老闆要我們加強公司內部溝通，我建議儘快召開部門會議來討論此事。

C ▶ I will notify other people of this meeting, and book a conference room with the administration department.

同事 ▶ 我將通知其他同仁有關此會議，並且會跟管理部預訂會議室。

E ▶ It will be suitable for me if the meeting can be held within this week as I have an important business trip next Monday, and I have to leave the office for abroad on Friday.

主管 ▶ 該會議可否在本週內召開，那樣對我比較適合。因為我下週一有重要業務出差，必須於本週五離開公司出國去。

C ▶ Most of our colleges are in office except both David and Allen who are out of the town for business. I can arrange them to attend a video conference, if necessary.

同事 ▶ 目前除了 David 與 Allen 因公出城，大部分同仁都在公司裡。如果有必要，我可以安排他們參加視訊會議。

23

給力單字

1. **strengthen** (*v.t.*)　加強；增強；鞏固
   We are required to strengthen the competitive ability.
   我們被要求必須增強競爭能力。

2. **notify** (*v.t.*)　通知
   The meeting is notified to start at 10 o'clock.
   會議通知在十點召開。

3. **suitable** (*adj.*)　適合的，適當的；合適的；適宜的[（+to/for）]
   The meeting time is not suitable for the boss according to his tight schedule.
   該項會議召開時間不太適合老闆繁忙的行程。

4. **video conference** (*n.*)　視訊會議[U]
   The video conference has become increasingly popular in multinational enterprises.
   視訊會議在跨國企業裡已逐漸流行。

給力句型

1. suggest　建議，提議[+v-ing][+（that）][+wh-]

   I suggest that a meeting be held immediately.
   我建議立刻召開一個會議。

   He suggested that the meeting (should) be held another day.
   他建議改天再開會。

2. notify sb. of sth. 將某事通知某人

Please notify the boss of the meeting time.
請通知老闆開會時間。

Please notify us of when you may come here.
請通知我們你何時能來這裡。

3. suitable 適當的；合適的；適宜的[（+to/for）]

The meeting time is very suitable for me right before my departure for a business trip.
該會議的時間對我而言相當合適，剛好就在我要去商務旅程之前。

I am trying to find a suitable meeting room for the boss.
我正設法能找到一個合適老闆開會的會議室。

The meeting room is not really suitable for the boss and his guests.
這間會議室不太適合老闆與他的客人。

idiom 慣用語 **suitable to do sth**

Would this meeting room be suitable to offer to the boss?
這間會議室適合提供給老闆（開會）嗎？

職場補給 **Department Leadership 領導統御**

　　一般公司或企業（enterprise）如果是老闆親自主持會議，大部分僅由各部門主管(executives)參加，當然也有時候會邀請相關專業人員（professionals）同時列席。除固定業務彙報外，老闆有可能臨時會針對某些事項，另召開特定（special purpose）會議，以便馬上交辦或進行處裡公司事情。

　　有規模之公司組織，其各部門雖職司不同工作，有時也要肩負支援跨部門之任務；此時彼此互相溝通（communications）或協調工作就變得十分重要。如果不特別注意甚或忽略這方面工作，大家僅是埋頭苦幹，結果卻是做白工，有時也可能讓公司蒙受不必要之損失。這個時候大家再去追究或檢討哪個部門應該負責任，已經沒有多大意義了。

　　所謂腦力激盪會議，顧名思義就是大家集思廣益，尋找出一套可行做法，擬定共同之目標，並於預定時間內達成任務。此時部門主管之領導統御（leadership）就顯得十分重要，例如：如何接受特定工作或是完成老闆交辦事項（assignments）。

　　開會時，主管（或部屬）先衡量自已之工作負荷（working loads）外，才可答應另提供特定之人員及物力等支援。畢竟原先屬於自己分內之工作，最後還需由自己負責，別人也幫不上忙。但如果評估除可以完成份內工作外，也盡力配合並完成老闆或部門交付之額外工作。如此增加自己成就感外，另年底加薪（raise in pay）或年終獎金（bonus）則有機會水漲船高。

　　記得筆者之前服務報社時，有設計部門小主管對於老闆或其他報系部門要求的配合事項，幾乎凡事有求必應，無怨無悔，並如期達成任務。歷經不斷磨練，在短短數年之後，已被拔擢（promote）擔任報系總經理要職。對比當時其他有能力之主管，甚至有被譽為明日之星者，因為只會管理自己部門工作，對於跨部門協調或額外工作，未曾作出任何貢獻。老闆在幾經審核與整體考績後，當然會比較傾向指派（appoint）前者，並委任以重要職務。

　　參加公司會議，算是一項重要工作，也是要考驗（test）各部門或同仁展現能力之時機。另平時如有機會，可多了解其他部門同事之工作內容，以免彼此開會時，不知所云，甚或雞同鴨講（talking in different things）。

　　工作是一種責任，也是一門藝術。平時上班認真份內工作，盡心盡力。對於部門間協調溝通事項，有所準備，如期交差，正所謂：『戲棚下站久就是你的。』（if you stay long enough）

達人提點 **Fulfill Assignments** 使命必達

1. 如果是在大公司上班，老闆大多是神龍見首不見尾，難得驚鴻一瞥，更遑論有機會一起開會。有幸參加此類會議，務必要準時（be punctual）出席，切忌遲到（除非有正當理由，另要事先告知或請假）。最好提前 3-5 分鐘就抵達會議室就定位，並先將手機關機或設定為無聲—這是一種基本禮貌和尊重。

2. 預先檢查並攜帶好當天開會主題之資料，包括有關道具（fixtures or fittings），或樣品（samples）等。儘量避免於開會中途，跑進跑出會議室。

3. 專心並記錄老闆交辦事項，如有不清楚（vague）之事項，另找機會詢問。對於其他部門要求配合協辦之事項，須具體回覆或表明實際工作上等問題。

4. 如果是自己部門會議，可儘量安排每位同事有機會上台或輪流（take turns）發言。報告個人工作狀況外，或有需要請求部門或公司協助之處，並適時處理。

1-2 視訊會議
Video Conference

情境 1 Exchange Views 意見交換

情境設定

Two colleagues of the company exchanged views on the latest technologies and functions of the video conference in their conversations, as following excerpts：

位公司同事對於目前最先進視訊會議之科技及功能等，彼此交換看法，如以下對話摘要：

角色設定

Colleague A：同事 A
Colleague B：同事 B

情境對話

A ▶ Regarded as a virtual meeting of its kind in website technology, video conference has now played an important role in enterprises, providing distance exchanges of images, voices, and messages. What are your views on this regard?

同事 A ▶ 視訊會議被認為是網路通訊技術中一種虛擬會議，在目前企業裡已扮演重要之角色；它可以提供遠距離圖形，聲音或信息之交流。對此方面，您有何高見？

B ▶ As I know, video conferences can offer real time voice and picture services for two or more users in multiple places. Big-sized video conference systems are now used in military, government, trade, and medical care functions, for example.

同事 B ▶ 就我所知，視訊會議可同時提供兩個或多點即時語音和畫面服務。例如，大型視訊會議系統目前也廣泛運用在軍事，政府，商貿，及醫療保健等功能。

A ▶ Some video conference systems are designed to allow few groups of people to attend a meeting in different places. Other designs only allow a few individuals to talk on the desktop of their computers, however.

同事 A ▶ 有些視訊會議系統設計可以允許多組不同地區人員同時參加一個會議。可是其他有些則設計僅讓幾個人在他們的電腦桌面上討論。

B ▶ This is because that attendees can clearly see pictures and hear discussions of each other, and feel just like they "face to face" and stay together.

同事 B ▶ 這是因為出席者能夠清楚地看到活動圖像，聽到別人討論，感覺就像」面對面在一起。

A ▶ Besides, video conference creates a good environment for quick decision-making and strong team work, transmitting thought, knowledge, and encouragement among

同事 A ▶ 此外，視訊會議創造一個優質環境，更快地下決策，更強大的團隊工作；以及同事

colleagues.

間想法、知識，以及鼓
勵之傳遞。

B ▶ Above all, one remarkable advantage of video conference represents no need of business travels.

同事 A ▶ 最重要的，還有一個值得注意的優點是不用出差。

給力單字

1. **virtual** (*adj.*)　虛擬的
   The video conference adopts many high-tech virtual functions.
   視訊會議運用許多高科技虛擬功能。

2. **distance** (*n.*)　距離；路程[（+to/from/between）]
   The long distance meeting becomes very popular in the video conference nowadays.
   遠距會議在當今視訊會議裡已經非常流行。

3. **real time** (*ph.*)　即時的，連線立即反應的
   The TV station offers the real time news report.
   該電視台提供即時新聞報導。

4. **medical care** (*ph.*)　醫療保健
   The medical care system on this island has greatly been improved.
   這個島上的醫療保健制度已有大大地改善。

5. **allow** (*v.t.*)　給與，提供；容許[（+for）]
   The video conference allows delegates to attend the meeting from different countries.
   視訊會議讓來自不同國家之代表在一起開會。

6. **desktop publishing**　桌面出版

The book was compiled by the latest desktop publishing software.

這本書使用一套最新的桌面出版軟體編撰而成。

7. **attendee** (*n.*)　出席者

Attendees of this meeting come from many different countries.

出席本次會議者來自許多不同國家。

8. **discussion** (*n.*)　討論，商討；談論[（+about/on/over）]

Through the video conference, we had a discussion on the communication issue.

透過視訊會議，我們討論溝通方面之問題。

9. **environment** (*n.*)　自然環境；生態環境

It is highly important to preserve the environment.

維護自然環境至關重要。

10. **transmit** (*v.t.*)　傳（光、熱、聲等）；傳動

A better way of transmitting the video conference will be revealed soon.

一種更好的輸出視訊會議方式即將被揭示。

11. **remarkable** (*adj.*)　值得注意的；不尋常的，奇特的

The telecommunication industry has made remarkable progress on video conferences.

電信業界在視訊會議方面有很了不起的進步。

給力句型

1. allow　容許[（+of）]；考慮[（+for）]

The situation allows of no delay.

情況不容許有任何延誤。

The video conference allows the meeting to be held in different time and places.

視訊會議可在不同時間及地點裡舉行開會。

2. environment　環境，周圍狀況

Enterprises can now use the good environment of video conference to speed up their policy-making paces.

企業界目前已經可運用良好的視訊會議環境以加快他們的決策步伐。

The company expects to build up a more competitive environment for its business.

公司期望對於其業務能建立一個更有競爭力的環境。

3. transmit　發送，播送，播放〔電子信號、信息等〕

The conclusion of board directors meeting has been transmitted by the video conference.

董事會議之決議已經由視訊會議傳遞出去。

The shareholders' meeting will be transmitted live via satellite.

股東會議將通過衛星現場直播。

4. remarkable　值得注意的；非凡的；卓越的[（+about）]

The video conference has many remarkable advantages.

視訊會議具有許多值得注意的優勢。

It is particularly remarkable about the technology of video conference.

有關視訊會議的科技方面特別地引人注目。

Meeting

情境 2 Further Discussions 深入探討

情境設定

The two colleagues continued their discussions, as the following dialogue. They probed into relevant contents of video conference, and more.

該兩位同事持續他們的討論,如以下對話。他們深入探討視訊會議及更多相關內容。

角色設定

Colleague A:同事 A
Colleague B:同事 B

情境對話

A ▶ You may know that hardware video conference requires specialized camera installations, decoders, specified lines, and a meeting room. Thus, the amount of investment totals a lot and reaches up to million of dollars.

同事 A ▶ 您或許知道硬體視訊會議需要專門攝影裝置,解碼器,專線和一間專屬會議室。因此,投資金額花費很大,甚至高達數百萬元。

B ▶ Yes, it is also expensive in both updates and maintenances of hardware facilities. Most small and medium enterprises can not afford the cost.

同事 B ▶ 是的,在硬體設施的更新和維護費用也很高昂。大部分中小企業很難負擔的起。

A ▶ Compared with hardware video conference, the system of software video conference is lower in cost however. Users can directly conduct a video conference on the web page.

同事 A ▶ 軟體視訊會議系統則較硬體視訊會議系統費用來得低。使用者可以直接在網頁上進行視訊會議。

B ▶ But there are abnormal situations and troubles in process of software download for video conference. To protect the security of computer, major anti-virus and firewall software are needed, incurring certain problems in such kind of video conference.

同事 B ▶ 但是在下載軟體進行視訊會議過程中，會出現異常情況及麻煩之事情。為了保護電腦安全，需要各大防毒軟體及防火牆；也因此導致這類視訊會議有些問題。

A ▶ Many internet video conference companies have now offered the service for free of charge. Compatible with all browsers, the pure web page video conference requires with not any downloads of extra modules and avoids the risk of viruses.

同事 A ▶ 現在許多網路視訊會議公司已提供免費服務。純網頁視訊會議與所有瀏覽器相容，無須下載任何外掛模組，並且避免各種病毒風險。

B ▶ For your information, the NetMeeting from Microsoft serves the function mentioned above. Through the internet, this telephone conference can transmit documents such as Powerpoint or Excel and use computer microphone for voices, but face expressions and body languages of

同事 B ▶ 僅供您參考，微軟公司的 NetMeeting 可達到上述提及之功能。透過網路，此類網路電話會議可用 Powerpoint 或 Excel 進行互動簡報，並用電

attendees are not available, however.

腦麥克風傳輸音訊，只是看不到與會者的臉部表情或身體語言而已。

給力單字

1. **require** (*v.t.*)　需要
   This video conference project will require less money.
   這項視訊會議工程所需的投資較少。

2. **investment** (*n.*)　投資；投資額；投資物[（+in）]
   The enterprise made a large investment in the video conference facilities.
   該企業在視訊會議設施方面作了大量投資。
   Its investments amount to one million U.S. dollars.
   它的投資額高達美金壹百萬元。

3. **expensive** (*adj.*)　高價的；昂貴的；花錢的[+to-v]
   Facilities of the video conference room must have been expensive.
   視訊會議室一定會要花很多錢。
   It is expensive to build up an advanced video conference room.
   打造一間最新穎的視訊會議室很貴。

4. **afford** (*v.t.*)　買得起；有足夠的（去做…）[+to-v]
   The company did not consider whether it could afford the expenditure or not.
   公司沒有考慮是否有經費。
   The company can't afford to pay such a price for the video conference room.
   公司付不起視訊會議室的價錢。

5. **conduct** (*v.t.*)　進行調查/實驗/調查研究等

The company conducted a survey to find out the requirement to the video conference.

公司進行了一次調查，研究對視訊會議需求的反應。

6. **abnormal** (*adj.*)　不正常的，反常的；變態的

Due to wrong software download, there are abnormal situations in video conference.

由於軟體下載錯誤，視訊會議出現不正常狀況。

7. **incur** (*v.t.*)　〔因自己的舉動而〕招致〔不愉快的事〕，招惹，遭受

The company incurred losses of over \$300,000 in the first half.

公司上半年蒙受損失三十多萬美元。

He incurred the displeasure of everyone in the meeting.

他在會議上引起眾怒。

8. **avoid** (*v.t.*)　避免，防止

The video conference room is well-equipped to avoid any risks of virus.

該視訊會議室有全套防毒設施。

9. **mention** (*v.t.*)　提到，說起

Certain software is mentioned in the video conference for free service use.

有些特定的軟體被提及可免費使用於視訊會議。

The installation mentioned about the use of several software in the video conference.

該安裝說明有許多軟體可使用在視訊會議。

10. **available** (*adj.*)　可用的，在手邊的；可利用的[（+for/to）]

The company's video conference room is available in most of the time.

本公司視訊會議室大部分時間均可以使用。

給力句型

1. require　需要[+v-ing] or [+that]

The company's video conference system requires repairing.

公司的視訊會議系統需要修理了。

The video conference always requires several equipment and installations.

視訊會議通常需要許多設備與裝置。

The company requires a new video conference system, which expects to offer the real time meeting service for our departments both home and abroad.

公司需要安裝一套新視訊會議系統，可以提供我們國內外部門之即時會議服務。

2. compared to/with　與…相比

Compared with the business trip, the video conference saves much of time and cost.

跟商務旅行比較，視訊會議比較節省時間及成本。

Statistics show a 20% reduction in revenue compared with last year.

統計數字表明，與去年相比，營收下降了 20%。

3. protect sb/sth from sth　保護某人或某物之安全；防衛、防護

Anti-virus and firewall software are a must to protect the security of computer.
防毒軟體及防火牆對保護電腦安全是必要的。

Try to protect your computer from the virus.
儘量保護你的電腦不受病毒侵入。

The video conference room should be protected from all that malfunctions.
應保護視訊會議室免受故障。

職場補給　Distant Meeting Weapon 遠距會議利器

　　目前由於大環境經濟不景氣（economic recession），許多企業大幅縮減出差預算。除實際需要面對面洽商外，有很多方式可以利用虛擬會議，以避免不必要之商務旅行。

　　另隨著網際網路及高科技（high end technology）不斷發展，包括視訊訊會議，電話會議，及線上共同作業等工具已可全面滿足遠距離開會，資料共用，異地（exotic）商務，或培訓等需要；因此更有效降低公司營運成本並提升工作效率。

　　運用視訊會議創造了一個更快下決策及強大的工作團隊。研究顯示，高達 60%的有效信息（effective message）是依賴面對面的視覺效果（vision effect），33%左右是說話者的語音，7%才是靠內容。傳統通信（如電話或傳真等）無法達到一群人面對面聚集在一起的溝通效果。

　　視訊會議對於緊急事件（emergency case）之時間爭取、即時商討，與貫徹指示方面更具明顯的優越性（benefits）。與會者彷彿坐在同一個會

議室內，同一個會議桌前交流；另外也可以同時處理其他日常工作，不必因為出差而苦惱。

　　一般而言，硬體式（hardware style）視訊會議視聽效果良好，唯價格較高並需要專線等特殊需求，僅有政府部門才會採購。目前純軟體的視訊會議已具有低價格，高適應性與即時使用等優點（advantages），在網路會議市場上已另形成新生力量。

　　視訊會議的好處及其進行活動，可歸納如下：
*發表各自意見，使用自己電腦與其他用戶通話。
*觀察對方形像，動作，表情等。
*共用文件：所有用戶能同時瀏覽某用戶電腦內的共同文件。
*協同工作：可利用各種軟體工具，標示文件重點，共同編輯。
*共同瀏覽圖像或顯示於屏幕白板上之文字。

達人提點 **Installation & Budget 裝置及預算**

　　目前可以利用免費或低成本軟體進行視訊會議。例如 Microsoft 的 NetMeeting 可以安裝在 Windows XP 及 Windows 2000 系統上使用，以降低視訊會議成本。

　　另外 NetMeeting 需要電腦音效卡，麥克風與喇叭，還要有視訊擷取卡及攝影機去支援視訊會議。針對承租視訊會議系統，有些供應商會按小時計費，使用前公司要事先評估會議總共佔用時間，並抓好預算；以免事情尚未談完，還要擔心是否會增加其他有關費用。

1-3 新產品開發專案會議
New Product Development Meeting

情境 1 ▸ A Panel Discussion 小組討論

情境設定

In a panel meeting, two executives discussed on new product development projects to be launched by the company, and their conversations are excerpted as follows：

在一個小組會議裡，兩位主管討論公司即將開始之新產品開發事宜，摘錄彼此對話如下：

角色設定

Executive A：主管 EA
Executive B：主管 EB

情境對話

EA ▸ In an effort to further expand its market share, the company plans to develop several competitive products beginning in the second half.

主管 EA ▸ 為了進一步擴大市場占有率，本公司計畫從下半年起會陸續開發許多具競爭性的產品。

EB ▶ The development of new products will no longer be limited by ideas and innovations of engineers or designers but also includes the participation from sales, marketing, R&D, finance, administration, and legal departments.

主管 EB ▶ 新產品開發不再是侷限於工程與設計人員的突發奇想或是創作，而必須是包含市場銷售、行銷、研發、財務、行政與法律支援等等的全員參與。

EA ▶ Thus, the company needs a good process that is suitable for the new product development. This, together with actual performance and revision, expects to help new product be marketed quickly and successfully.

主管 EA ▶ 因此，公司更需要有一套良好且適合企業的新產品開發流程。並透過確實的執行與不斷的修正，這樣才可讓新產品能快速而順利上市。

EB ▶ Statistics shows that about 38% of revenue and 42.4% of profit came from sales of new products in the top 20 enterprises in the U.S., an indication that innovation serves as an important strategy to overpass other counterparts.

主管 EB ▶ 調查顯示全美排名前 20 的頂尖企業，其營收有 38%、利潤有 42.4%是來自新產品的銷售，顯示出創新為超越同業之重要策略。

EA ▶ The average failure rate of new products reaches up to 41%. The development of new products is important but it still requires support and assistance, especially in integration and management.

主管 EA ▶ 新產品的平均失敗率卻達到41%。可知新產品的開發雖然重要，但仍需要如整合、管理的支持與協助。

EB ▶ Discovery, development, and commercialization are three major phases in new products. Each phase is systemized with clear job descriptions, upgrading the success of new products and market time significantly.

主管 EB ▶ 創新發現、開發、商業化為三個主要階段發展程序。各個階段都有系統地條列出清楚的工作描述），大幅提高新產品成功率與上市時間。

給力單字

1. **expand** (*v.t.*)　擴大；增加
   Water expands as it freezes.
   水結冰時會膨脹。
   The population of the town expanded rapidly in the 1960s.
   這個鎮的人口於 60 年代迅速擴張。

2. **competitive** (*adj.*)　充滿競爭的
   The hotel offers a high standard of service at competitive rates.
   酒店以優惠的價格提供高標準的服務。

3. **limited** (*adj.*)　有限的，不多的
   The amount of money we have is limited.
   我們的金錢有限。

4. **innovation** (*n.*)　革新，改革，創新
   The innovation of air travel during this century has made the world seem smaller.
   本世紀空中旅行的革新使世界似乎變小了。

Meeting

5. **process** (*n.*)　在做某事的過程中，在進行…中
The company is in the process of moving to new offices.
該公司正在搬往新的辦公室。

6. **revision** (*n.*)　修訂；校訂；修正
The law is in need of revision.
這法律需要修改。
A revision of that dictionary has been published .
那本詞典的修訂本已經出版。

7. **overpass** (*v.t.*)　超越（優於）
The national defense technology of the U.S. overpasses that of many other nations in the world.
美國之國防科技已超越世界上許多其他國家。

8. **reach** (*v.t.*)　達到
These plants take a long time to reach maturity .
這些植物要過很長時間才成熟。

9. **integration** (*n.*)　結合；整合
The meeting expects to obtain a closer integration of the economies.
本次年會期望讓經濟更密切的整合。

10. **phase** (*n.*)　階段；時期
The traffic lights were out of phase with each other.
交通信號燈是不同步的。

11. **upgrade** (*v.t.*)　使升級；提高；提升
When several offers came in, the house owner upgraded the price.
當有幾個人要買這棟房子時，房主提高了房價。

給力句型

1. ***in an effort to do sth**　為做成某事
   *make every effort　盡一切努力

   They've been working night and day in an effort to get the new project ready on time.
   為了使新計畫案能準時完工，他們一直夜以繼日地工作。

   Every effort is being made to deal with the issues you raised at the new project meeting.
   我們正盡一切努力處理你在上次新專案會議上提出的問題。

2. ***plan ahead**　事先計劃

   Now that you're pregnant, you'll have to plan ahead.
   你既然懷孕了，就必須預先把事情都安排妥當。

   *plan to do sth 計劃作某事

   Josie planned to work until she had saved enough money to go to nursing school.
   喬茜打算先工作，等儲足錢了再去上護士學校。

3. not only...(but) also　不僅…而且…

   Mr. Johnson is not only a good teacher but also a famous poet.
   強森先生不僅是一個好老師，而且是一個有名的詩人。

4. together with + n.　連同；和

   He sent me the book, together with a letter.
   他把書寄給我，還附上了一封信。

*get together with sb.　開會討論某事

The management should get together with the union.
勞資雙方應該開會。

5. indicate　指示;指出[+(that)][+wh-]

The light above the elevator indicated that the elevator was then at the fifteenth floor.
電梯上方的燈指示那時電梯在十五樓。

6. ***it is significant that**　非常重要的

Police believed it was significant that he had recently opened a bank account abroad.
警方認為,他最近在國外銀行開賬戶的事很重要。

情境
2

PACE — the Classic Process 經典開發模式『PACE』

情境設定

Prospects for the new product development are bright. The two executives talked with each other, especially in the PACE, a classic and standard process for the development new products.

產品開發前景佳。兩位主管針對經典開發模式—PACE 提出看法。

角色設定

Executive A:主管 EA
Executive B:主管 EB

情境對話

EA ▶ The company is now in a best position in developing a wide variety of 3C, machinery, and household appliances, plus exterior, structural, and sample designs. It also offers the service on the basis of mass production.

主管 EA ▶ 本公司目前在開發各類 3C、機械類，及家電產品方面，包括外觀、機構，及樣品設計已佔極佳之地位。我們也同時提供根據量產計算之服務。

EB ▶ A perfect product design must be very touched by clients and it has to take cost, details, and quality control into consideration at the same time. The presentation expects to decrease disputes between the company and clients.

主管 EB ▶ 一個完美的設計必定會讓客戶非常感動，同時也必須考慮到成本，細節及品管。它的呈現期盼降低公司與客戶彼此之爭議。

EA ▶ Our ideas are unique. This plays an important concept to lead the brand in the market.

主管 EA ▶ 我們有獨特之構思。此重要理念使我們能在市場中領導品牌。

EB ▶ The market demand and production cost are relative to the commodity value.

主管 EB ▶ 市場需求及製造成本與商品價值有相對的關係。

EA ▶ There is a classic and standard process called PACE (Product and Circle-time, Excellence) in the product development. After years of improvement, many well-known conglomerates, such as IBM,

主管 EA ▶ 產品開發流程有著經典的標準過程參考模型 PACE（Product And Cycle-time Excellence，產

Motorola, Dupont, and Huawei have put all concepts of PACE into practice and gained huge profits.

品及週期優化法）。經過多年改善，包括 IBM、Motorola、杜邦，華為等在內的許多知名大型企業已把 PACE 的各種理念方法付諸實施並獲得重大利益。

EB ▶ It is no doubt that PACE has proved verification after practices from many companies. The difference lies on the determination by the introducer and consultancy company's techniques.

主管 EB ▶ PACE 經過諸多公司的驗證，其實用性已毋庸置疑。差別僅取決於導入者的決心與協助導入顧問公司的技巧。

給力單字

1. **position** (*n.*)　地位，身分；位次[（+in）]
   He has a high position in society.
   他社會地位很高。

2. **on the basis of**　以…為基礎
   We have worked out a plan on the basis of recent research findings.
   我們根據最近研究的發現擬定了一個計劃。

3. **touch** (*v.t.*)　觸動，感動
   I was touched beyond words.
   我感動莫名。

4. **dispute** (*n.*)　爭論；爭執；爭端[（+about/over/with）]

The dispute was settled last week.

爭端在上週解決了。

5. **unique** (*adj.*)　唯一的，獨特的[（+to）]

The custom is unique to the region.

這種風俗是這一地區特有的。

6. **relative** (*adj.*)　與…有關係的，相關的[（+to）]

He asked me some questions relative to the subject.

他問了我一些有關這個題目的問題。

7. **classic** (*adj.*)　經典的

The Coca-Cola bottle is one of the classic designs of the last century.

可口可樂瓶是上個世紀的經典設計之一。

8. **conglomerate** (*n.*)　大型聯合企業

Many world-known conglomerates are based their headquarters in the U.S.

許多世界知名的大型企業總公司都設立於美國。

9. **no doubt**　無疑地，確定地

No doubt Michael was the smartest boy in his class.

麥克在他班上是公認最聰明的男孩。

10. **lie on**　取決於

Whether we succeed lies in our effort.

我們能否成功取決於我們的努力。

給力句型

1. on a (or the) basis 根據

   *on a daily/weekly etc basis 按天／週等計算

   All new product development projects are reviewed on a weekly basis.

   所有新產品開發案每週要檢討一次。

   *on a voluntary/part-time basis 自願性質／以兼職的形式等

   This new product development project has been conducted on a trial basis.

   這項新產品開發案是試驗性的。

2. ***it is important to do sth**

   It is important to complete the project as the scheduled date.

   按照既定日期完成該項計畫是很重要的。

   *it is important that

   It's vitally important that you understand the danger.

   了解危險所在是極為重要的。

3. dispute 爭論；爭執 [（+about/on/over/with/against）]

   The two executives disputed over a small problem of the product project.

   這兩個主管為了產品計畫上一個小問題爭執不下。

4. relative merits/cost/value etc 相對優點／成本／價值等

   They discussed the relative merits of new product developments.

   他們討論各種產品開發的相對優點。

5. no doubt 表示毫無疑問地，當然

This project will no doubt be successful if everything goes smoothly.
如果一切進行順利的話，本計畫將會很成功。

職場補給 Six Process Steps 六階段流程

產品開發流程（Product Development Process）

產品開發流程是指企業用於想像、設計和商業化一種產品的步驟或活動的序列。流程就是一系列步驟，它們把一系列投入變成一系列產出。

基本開發流程的六個階段是：

階段 0，計劃（Step 0，Planning）

規劃經常被作為"零階段"是因為它先於項目的達成和實際產品開發過程的啟動。這一階段始於公司策略，並包括對技術開發和市場目標的評估。

階段 1，概念開發（Step 1，Concept Development）

概念開發階段的主要任務是識別目標市場的需要，產生並評估可替代的產品概念，為進一步開發選擇一個概念。

階段 2，系統水平設計（Step 2，System Level Design）

系統水平設計階段包括產品結構的定義以及產品子系統和部件的劃分。生產系統的最終裝配計劃也通常在此階段定義。

階段 3，細節設計（Step 3，Detail Design）

細節設計階段包括產品的所有非標準部件與從供應商處購買的標準部件的尺寸、材料和公差的完整細目，建立流程計劃併為每一個即將在生產系統中製造的部件設計工具。該階段的產出是產品的控制文檔（Control

Document）──描述每一部件幾何形狀和製造工具的圖紙和電腦文件、購買部件的細目，以及產品製造和裝配的流程計劃。

階段 4，測試和改進（Step 4，Testing & Improvement）

測試和改進階段包括產品的多個生產前版本的構建和評估。早期 α 原型通常由生產指向（Production-intent）型部件構成，即那些和產品的生產版本有相同幾何形狀和材料內質，但又不必在生產的實際流程中製造的部件。要對 α 原型進行測試以決定產品是否如設計的那樣工作，以及產品是否能滿足主要顧客的需要。後期 β 原型通常由目標生產流程提供的部件構成，但不必用目標最終裝配流程來裝配。

階段 5，產品推出（Step 5，Product Launch）

在產品推出階段，使用規劃生產系統製造產品。試用的目的是培訓工人和解決在生產流程中遺留的問題。有時把在此階段生產出的物品提供給有偏好的顧客並仔細對其進行評估，以識別出一些遺留的缺陷。

達人提點 Curriculum & Certification 課程及認證

對新產品研發、企劃、專案管理有興趣者，可報名參加例如中國生產力中心（China Productivity Center, CPC）主辦：新產品開發流程管理等課程。由源流管理改善流程品質，創新產品，協助企業建立開發流程，縮短新產品開發時程，強化企業接案能力，改善開發工作減少浪費，提高研發生產力。

另外資策會（Institute for Information Industry, III）也有開辦新產品開發管理師（New Product Development Process, NPDP）國際認證班⋯NPDP 是全球獨一無二的新產品開發證照，在全球重視產品或服務的創新開發趨勢下，亦為歐美公認之最高等級產品開發專案管理證照。

1-4 用英語談授權案
Authorization Contract

情境 1 A Dialogue of Boss & Sales Executive 老闆與業務主管對話

情境設定

The company plans to sign an authorization contract with foreign distributors, and the boss is soliciting opinions from his sales executive, as in the following conversation：

公司打算要跟國外經銷商簽訂授權合約，老闆正詢問業務主管相關意見，雙方會談如下：

角色設定

Boss：老闆
Sales Executive (SE)：業務主管

情境對話

Boss ▶ We plan to authorize the foreign distributor for sales and promotion of our new products in the global marketplace, and the terms and conditions are not yet formally contained in the contract by both sides, however. How do you comment on this

老闆 ▶ 我們公司正在計劃授權國外經銷商，以銷售並推廣新產品到全球各地市場；唯雙方尚未將有關條件和條款正式包含在合約裡。您如

trade?

何看待此項交易？

SE ▶ The distributor has to agree and faithfully observe the agreement, and to exert its best endeavors for sales of products in the market. This is the point of my opinion.

業務主管 ▶ 該經銷商必須承諾並忠實地遵守條約，另發揮最大之努力在市場上銷售產品。這是我對此事的看法。

Boss ▶ The company insists that the distributor shall not sell products to existing customers, unless authorized in writing by the company, for the duration of the contract.

老闆 ▶ 本公司堅持經銷商不得販售銷售貨品給原有客戶, 除非在合約有效期內得到書面授權。

SE ▶ As I know, the distributor has a strong opinion and is controversial about this issue. Thus, the company may suspend its authorization soon after an assessment is finalized by the sales department.

業務主管 ▶ 就我所知，經銷商在這問題表達了強烈意見並且引起爭論。因此，公司有可能在業務部做好最後評估後即暫緩該項授權。

Boss ▶ Meanwhile, the company shall in no manner whatsoever modify the price for the duration of this agreement. The market price is subject to change with prior notice, a policy which is practiced by the company since its establishment.

老闆 ▶ 同時，在該項協議的期限內公司不得以任何方式修改價格。市場價格可以依照事先通知而修訂，這是公司自成立以來之政策。

SE ▶ We'd better notify the distributor of the company decision as they have the right to

業務主管 ▶ 我們最好要儘快通知該經銷商本公

know any changes especially in the authorization, according to the memorandum of cooperation.

司之決定，因為根據當初合作備忘錄，他們有權利知道任何改變，尤其是授權事宜。

給力單字

1. **authorize** (*v.t.*)　授權給，全權委託
   The manager was authorized to act for the boss during his absence.
   該經理被授權當老闆不在時可代理他的職務。

2. **contain** (*v.t.*)　包含；容納
   The contract contains important authorization terms, especially in the price setting.
   合約書裡包含許多重要授權條款，尤其有關價格訂定方面。

3. **observe** (*v.t.*)　遵守，奉行
   This authorization contract must be strictly observed by both sides.
   這項授權合約必須由雙方嚴加遵守。

4. **exert** (*v.t.*)　用（力），盡（力）
   The company exerted all its efforts in signing up the contract.
   公司在簽訂該項合約已竭盡全力。

5. **insist** (*v.t.*)　堅決主張；堅決要求 [+（that）]
   The company insisted that distributors sell no products to existing customers.
   公司堅決主張經銷商不得銷售產品給現有之客戶。

6. **duration** (*n.*) （時間的）持續，持久；持續期間
The duration of the authorization contract is three years.
合約授權時間為三年。

7. **controversial** (*adj.*) 引起爭論的，有爭議的
The meeting settled down a controversial plan from the sales department.
該會議讓業務部一個有爭議的計畫得以定下來。

8. **suspend** (*v.t.*) 暫緩作出（決定等）
The company decides to suspend the authorization until all the terms are finalized.
該公司決定暫緩授權，直到所有條款都被確認。

9. **modify** (*v.t.*) 更改，修改
We have to modify our authorization contract.
我們必須修改授權合約。

10. **be subject to** 受…控制；有…傾向; 依照
We have made contract terms, but they are subject to the approval of distributors.
我們已經作好合約條款, 但還需要須得到經銷商的認可。

11. **notify** (*v.t.*) 通知，告知；報告[+that]
Distributors notified us that they would accept the contract.
經銷商通知我們願意接受這份合同。

12. **memorandum** (*n.*) 備忘錄，記錄
They sent us a meeting memorandum about the contract.
他們寄給我們一份合約之會議備忘錄。

給力句型

1. insist 堅決主張；一定要[（+on/upon）] + V-ing

   The boss insisted on the signing of the authorization contract.
   老闆堅持要簽訂授權合約書。

   He insists on seeing the contract.
   他一定要見到合約書。

2. suspend 停止，懸吊
   *suspend sb from sth

   The company suspended the sales contract from validity for one year.
   公司終止該項銷售合約有效期一年。

3. subject 易受…的 [+to]

   Our contracts are subject to the distributors.
   我們的合約尚有待經銷商決定。

   The authorization is subject to change due to the hectic market demand.
   該授權隨時可能因市場熱絡需求而有所變動。

4. had better 最好，必需 [+ v.t.]

   You'd better to finish the contract as scheduled.
   你最好在預定時間裡完成合約事宜。

   We had better to sign the contract by the end of this month.
   我們最好在本月底前簽約。

Meeting

In Consultation with Legal Executive 諮詢法務主管

情境設定

The conversation between the boss and an executive from the legal department, as follows:

以下為老闆與法務部門主管對話。

角色設定

Boss：老闆
Legal Executive (LE)：法務主管

情境對話

Boss ▶ The duration of the authorization is one year after the execution hereof, and each party has the right, upon giving notice to the other party, to terminate the contract without judicial recourse.

老闆 ▶ 該授權在簽訂後的一年內有效，任何一方均有權不經司法程序通知另一方解除本合約。

LE ▶ Except for otherwise expressly provided herein, the company shall have no right to receive from the distributor's customers any payment for the goods.

法務主管 ▶ 除另有明文規定外，公司沒有權利收受來自經銷商客戶的任何貨款。

Boss ▶ The distributor shall have no rights in any trade names or trade marks used by the company in relation to the products, and the

老闆 ▶ 經銷商沒有利用製造商產品的商品名稱或商標以及與商譽相關

distributor acknowledges that it shall not acquire any rights and all such rights and goodwill are vested in the company.

聯的權利，並在此承諾不應得到任何關於歸附於製造商所有權和商譽的權利。

LE ▶ Neither party shall have the right to assign the benefit of this contract (or any part of it), without the prior written approval of the other party.

法務主管 ▶ 沒有另一方事先書面授權，任何一方無權轉讓本合約項下的利益（或其任何部分）。

Boss ▶ This Distribution Agreement shall be construed in all respects in accordance with the law of the Republic of China and the company agrees to submit to the jurisdiction of the Court of the domicile of the foreign distributor.

老闆 ▶ 這項經銷協議應視為在所有方面均按照中華民國法律，且本公司同意服從國外經銷商所在轄區法院的許可權。

LE ▶ The Appendices are the integral part of this Agreement. The Appendices and this Agreement have the same effect.

法務主管 ▶ 附錄是本協定的組成部分。附錄和本協議具有同等效力。

給力單字

1. **terminate** (*vt.*)　使停止，使結束；使終止
   They have terminated the contract.
   他們已終止了合同。

2. **judicial** (*adj.*)　司法的；審判的
   The court will take judicial proceedings on the violation of the contract.
   法院準備對違約正式提起訴訟。

3. **payment** (*n.*)　支付，付款[U]，報償；懲罰
   Full payment must be made after the contract is signed by the distributor.
   在合約簽訂後，經銷商必須付清全部款項。

5. **acknowledge** (*v.t.*)　承認〔政府、法庭、領袖等〕的合法性
   Both sides acknowledged the authority of the contract.
   雙方都承認合約之權威性。

6. **assign** (*v.t.*)　把〔財產、設備等〕轉讓與…
   According to the contract, the distributor is not allowed to assign its authorization to other counterparts.
   根據合約，經銷商不得轉讓授權給其他同業。

7. **construe** (*v.t.*)　解釋；理解為[（+as）]
   His signature was construed as agreement to the contract.
   他的簽名被視為是同意本合約書。

8. **jurisdiction** (*n.*)　權限，管轄範圍
   That case is under the jurisdiction of this court.
   那宗案件屬本法庭受理範圍。

9. **integral** (*adj.*)　構成整體所必需的，不可缺少的

The signature or a seal is an integral part of the effective contract.

簽名或蓋章是有效合約書中不可缺少的。

A good contract is integral to the performance of distributors.

一個好合約對於經銷商表現是不可或缺的。

10. **effect** (*n.*)　效果，效力；作用；影響 [（+on/upon）]

The contract had a great effect upon the sales of distributors in the future.

這合約對經銷商未來銷售有很大的影響。

給力句型

1. terminate (v.i.)　終止

The authorization contract will be terminated by the end of the year.

本授權合約書將於今年底終止。

The contract signing ceremony terminated yesterday.

簽約儀式於昨天結束。

The meeting terminated its first session in the morning.

第一階段會議於早上結束。

2. payment (n.)　付款

*make a payment

The company made a payment of interest by quarterly.

公司按照每一季計算利息。

*in payment of　支付

Enclosed please find my cheque in full payment of my debts.
請查收附上付清我全部欠款的支票。

*on payment of　支付…之後

In the internet business, any item can be transacted on payment of money.
在網路商業上，只要付錢後就可以交易任何物品。

3. acknowledge (v.t.)　承認
   *acknowledge that

   The company acknowledged that the contract with the distributor was still valid.
   公司承認與經銷商的合約仍然是有效的。

   *acknowledge sb as

   The company acknowledged the distributor as its exclusive agent in the region.
   公司承認該經銷商是當地唯一的代理。

   *acknowledge receipt of

   Please acknowledge receipt of this document by signing the enclosed form.
   請在附表中簽收這份文件。

4. assign (v.t.)　派定，指定，選派
   *assign sb a job/duty/task

   I've been assigned the job of negotiating a new contract.
   我受指派的工作是洽商一份新的合約書。

5. integral (adj.) 構成整體所必需的，不可缺少的

Effective communication is an integral part before signing a contract.

有效的溝通技巧是在簽約前不可缺少的部分。

Distributors are integral to the company's sales expansion.

經銷商對於公司的擴大銷售是不可或缺的。

6. effect (v.t.) 實現，達到

Distributors effected several important sales in the market.

經銷商在該市場上完成了幾項重要的銷售。

職場補給 Contract vs. Reputation 合約 v.s. 商譽

在正式簽訂任何有關授權合約書（authorization contract）之前，任何一方均有權利不經過司法程序，通知另一方解除合約。以本文[情境 1]為例，因為公司堅持經銷商不得販售銷售貨品給原有客戶，除非在合約有效期內得到書面授權。又在協議（agreement）的期限內經銷商反對任何方式修改價格，而公司認為市場價格可以依照事先通知而修訂。

雙方如遇有爭議之處，或有不符公司現階段政策等，必須仔細釐清後並儘快發文通知，以免造成彼此損失，更有可能損及公司商譽（reputation）。所謂『生意不成仁義在。人情留一線，日後好相見』。

在授權時，經銷商多半會爭取對自己有利條件（favored conditions）。例如給他自己客戶的銷售合同，應只由經銷商自己與其客戶獨立簽訂，並應具有唯一權提供和/或接受這類合同的條件。另外同意授權之公司應有義務（obligations）及時回應經銷商的信件，傳真，通知，電話及其他需求。還有在授權期間內之相關權利與義務，也需要一併列出。

達人提點 **Clauses Ignored? 被忽視之條款？**

1. 授權公司不得銷售或以其他方式提供此類貨物，或有可能銷售那些貨物給經銷商的客戶或任何人。

2. 沒有另一方事先書面授權（written approvals），任何一方無權轉讓本協議項的利益（或其任何部分）。

3. 附錄和本協議具有同等效力，可以在後面附加一些雜項（miscellaneous）條款。

1-5 產品企畫會議
Product Proposal Meeting

情境 1 Market Analyses & Implementation 市場分析與有效執行

情境設定

In a product proposal meeting, the planning executive and his colleague made the following dialogue. Both sides opined and reached conclusions on the company's upcoming product proposal.

在一次產品企劃會議中,企劃部主管與其同事有了如下對話。雙方表示意見並對公司即將進行的產品計畫達成結論。

角色設定

Planning Executive (PE):企劃主管
Planning Specialist (PS):企劃專員

情境對話

PE ▶ The planning department is commanded to complete a new product development proposal to contain all implementation measures, resources and, time deployments. As the company has valued the development of the new product this time, the proposal

企劃主管 ▶ 企劃部被要求儘快完成新產品開發計劃案,包括各項實施步驟、資源和時間的利用分配等。由於公司非常重視本次新產品開

expects to be construed as a key element to the future survival of the enterprise.

發，因此企畫案將被認為本企業未來生存的關鍵因素之一。

PS ▶ Ideas of the new product proposal will mainly come from inside the enterprise and also include counterpart product researches of competitors, an effort to improve its existing products. Meanwhile, relevant information from both sales distributors and governmental agencies would serve as another importance resource for the proposal.

企劃專員 ▶ 新產品企畫主要來源來自企業內部想法，同時也要研究競爭對手的產品從而改進企業現有產品；另可採集經銷商建議或政府機關相關的信息，作為產品企畫的重要來源。

PE ▶ Each new product development must ensure its market target and gain the approval of market analyses. This premise is necessary and important for every project planner.

企劃主管 ▶ 每一件新產品開發必須確立目標市場並且通過市場分析。這是企劃的必要前提，也是企劃人員要特別重視之項目。

PS ▶ In somewhat extent, the market position decides whether a new product development is successful or not. The correct market position indicates an overture for the success of new product development.

企劃專員 ▶ 市場定位在某些程度上決定了新產品開發的成功與否？正確的市場定位可謂是新產品開發成功的序曲。

PE ▶ The new product strategy covers "product strategy" and "manufacturing strategy" The former identifies the product

企劃主管 ▶ 新產品的開發策略主要包括產品策略及製程策略。前項要

category while the latter pays much attention on manufacturing analyses, controls, quality management, technology introduction, machinery, ingredient improvements and applications.

確立新產品開發的種類；後項則是注意製程分析、製程控制、質量管理、技術引進、機器設備、配料技術之改善與應用等。

PS ▶ A good product project takes into account of diversification and R&D; it also thinks about other factors such as application of patent rights, project improvement, and cooperation possibilities with individual research institutes.

企劃專員 ▶ 一個好產品企畫案考慮到多角度經營、發展研究；同時也包括如專利權申請、提案改善以及與各研究單位合作等方面的因素。

PE ▶ Above all, the new product proposal has to deliberate on basic factors such as pricing, costs, profits, and market target. The person who is responsible for the task must implement the aforesaid factors thoroughly.

企劃主管 ▶ 最終要深思熟慮的是新產品定價、真實成本和利潤、以及市場營銷目標等基本因素。承辦人員對上述因素負責執行周全。

PS ▶ One thing worth mentioning is that an effective organization plays the most decisive role in the development of new products. This factor realizes the new project and makes smooth the job during the process of development, too.

企劃專員 ▶ 另外值得一提是，有效的企業組織扮演新產品開發工作的關鍵因素。此因素推動且實現新的產品開發企劃書，也使新產品在開發過程之工作得以順利進行。

Meeting

給力單字

1. **command** (*v.t.*)　命令[+that]
The executive commanded that the product project to start at once.
該主管命令立即進行本項產品計畫。

2. **proposal** (*n.*)　計劃；建議
The planning department is facing a battle to get the boss to accept its product proposal.
企劃部為使老闆接受它的產品方案正面臨着一場論戰。

3. **deployment** (*n.*)　部署；調度
The company has completed its global deployment for sales expansion networks.
公司已完成全球佈署擴大銷售網路。

4. **survival** (*n.*)　繼續生存；倖存
The competitiveness serves as an important weapon for the survival of enterprises.
競爭力是企業生存之一項重要武器。

5. **counterpart** (*n.*)　與另一方面地位職務相當的人[物]
The colleagues of sales department are discussing this issue with their counterparts from other companies.
我們業務部同仁正與其他公司相對人員正在討論這個問題。

6. **relevant** (*adj.*)　有關的，切題的
For further information, please see the relevant chapters in the users' manual.
詳情請查閱使用說明中的相關章節。

7. **ensure** (*v.t.*)　保證；擔保[+that][+v-ing]

I can't ensure the success of this product proposal.

我不能保證此產品計畫會成功。

I can't ensure that the product proposal will be successful or not.

我不能擔保此產品計劃成功與否。

8. **premise** (*n.*)　假定，假設；前提[+that]

The product proposal acted on the premise that the market information was right.

本產品計畫的行動是以正確市場訊息為前提的。

9. **extent** (*n.*)　程度；限度；範圍

The executive is responsible for the failure of product proposal to a certain extent.

主管對產品開發失敗在一定程度上負有責任。

10. **overture** (*n.*)　前奏曲，序曲

The market information acts as a success overture for the new product proposal.

市場訊息為新產品開發計畫拉開一個成功的序幕。

11. **strategy** (*n.*)　策略，計謀[（+for）][+to-v]

With careful strategy, the proposal was passed through in the meeting.

由於審慎策劃，該建議在會議中獲得通過。

12. **identify** (*vt.*)　確認；識別；鑑定，驗明[（+as）]

The proposal identifies a new product category in the market.

該計畫確認出一項市場新產品類別。

13. **take into account** (*ph.*)　考慮到；體諒

The company had to take the cost into account when launching new product proposals.

每當要開始新產品計畫時，公司總得考慮有關成本事宜。

14. **patent** (*n.*) 專利；專利權
Did the product obtain a patent on the design?
該項產品是否有取得設計之專利？

15. **deliberate** (*vi.*) 仔細考慮，深思熟慮 [(+about / on/ upon)]
We deliberated on possible solutions to the product proposal.
我們一起洽商關於產品計畫可能的解決方法。

16. **implement** (*vt.*) 執行計劃／政策／建議等
The company has decided to implement the suggestions in new products.
公司已決定實施針對新產品提出的建議。

17. **effective** (*adj.*) 生效的，起作用的
The product proposal becomes effective after the meeting is held soon.
該產品計畫在即將召開的會議後會立刻生效。

18. **realize** (*vt.*) 實現；使成為事實
The proposal to launch new products was finally realized.
發表新產品的計畫終於實現了。

給力句型

1. ***command sb to do sth**

The manager of planning department commanded his colleagues to report to the meeting room.
企劃部經理命令他的部門同仁到會議室集合。

*command that

The general manager commanded that the new product development start at once.

總經理下令立刻進行該新產品開發案。

2. ***proposal that**

The company had to put forward a proposal that layoffs be considered.

該公司不得不提出考慮解雇員工的建議。

*proposal to do sth

The proposal to lay off employees is meeting with stiff opposition from the union.

裁員的提議遭到工會強烈地反對。

3. ***make overtures to**

We began making overtures to the planning department in the hope of gaining their support.

我們主動向企劃部門表示友好，希望獲得他們的支持。

4. ***identify sb/sth**

The product proposal from the planning department was identified as an old project.

那份企劃部提出的計畫被認出是老方案。

Meeting

情境 2 Proposals & practices 企劃與實施計畫

Discussions between other two planning specialists are made in the following dialogue, and they offered different aspects on the product development.

以下是企劃部門其他兩位專員對新產品開發的對話,他們也提供了不同觀點。

角色設定

Planning Specialist A:企劃專員 PSA
Planning Specialist B:企劃專員 PSB

情境對話

PSA ▶ Do you know how many kinds of new product development can be divided?

企劃專員 PSA ▶ 您知道新產品開發可劃分成多少種類嗎?

PSB ▶ Yes, there are about nine kinds of new product development, as follows:(1) brand-new products with full functions; (2) products with improved functions; (3) current products with new usages; (4) new products with auxiliary functions; (5) new products with improved models; (6) developing new markets for existing products (7) products with reduced costs to solicit more clients; (8) integrating current products to become high

企劃專員 PSB ▶ 是的,大約可分為九種不同種類,如下說明:(一)全新功能的新產品。(二)現有功能上進行改進的產品。(三)具有新用途的現有產品。(四)具有附屬功能的新產品。(五)改進式樣的新產品。(六)開

grade products; (9) relist existing products to become new items.

開新市場的現有產品。
（七）通過降低成本，招攬更多客戶的產品。
（八）通過現有產品的整合，形成高檔產品。
（九）重列現有產品品項，形成新產品。

PSA ▶ The market acceptance level decides whether the new product development is successful or not. To meet the market demand also represents a key factor in mapping out the new product development proposal. Do you agree to this comment?

企劃專員 PSA ▶ 市場接收度決定新產品開發成功與否，滿足市場需求也象徵新產品開發企劃案制定的要點。您同意此評論嗎？

PSB ▶ In my opinion, a real good new product development proposal needs to stress the following points : (1) a complete market survey and analyses of feasibility; (2) benefits of new products to consumers; (3) proof of new product effects; (4) illustrations; of new product in structure, functions, and effects (5) a brief implementation plan.

企劃專員 PSB ▶ 我的意見是，一個真正好的新產品開發企劃書，還應強調以下要點：（一）完整的市場調查，分析新產品開發的可行性。（二）新產品給消費者帶來的益處。（三）新產品的效果經過論證。（四）說明新產品的結構、性能、效果等。（五）簡要的實施計劃。

給力單字

1. **divide** (*vt.*)　分，劃分[（+into/from）]
The company divided our planning department into four divisions.
公司把我們企劃部分成四個小組。

2. **brand-new** (*adj.*)　全新的，嶄新的
The R&D had a new brand-new design on our product series.
研發部門已設計好我們全新商品系列。

3. **auxiliary** (*adj.*)　輔助的
The company hires auxiliary staff for extra works.
公司雇用輔助員工去做額外增加的工作。

4. **reduce** (*vt.*)　減少；降低
The company is trying to reduce expenses.
公司正試圖減少開支。

5. **integrate** (*vt.*)　使成一體，使結合
The marketing unit is expected to integrate into the sales department.
行銷單位預定會併入業務部門。

6. **represent** (*vt.*)　象徵；表示
The sales department represents revenue of the company.
業務單位象徵公司營收部門。

7. **stress** (*vt.*)　強調，著重
The planning department stressed the importance of sales strategy.
企劃部門強調了業務策略的重要性。

8. **feasibility (study)**　可行性（研究）

A feasibility study for developing new product lines is under the way by the planning department.

一項新產品線開發計畫由企劃部正在進行中。

9. **illustration** (*n.*)　說明；圖解

The process for the new product development will use a diagram for illustration.

有關新產品開發流程會有一張圖表解說。

給力句型

1. divide 分,劃分[(+into/from)]

   ***divide sth into**

   The planning department divided the new product project into four development steps.

   企劃部把新產品計畫分成四項開發步驟。

   ***divide sth from**

   The planning department is divided from the rest of other divisions by different functions.

   企劃部門因有不同功能,須與其他單位區隔開來。

2. **integrate [(+with/into)]**

   I integrated your suggestion with my plan.

   我把你的建議採納到我的計畫中來。

   He integrated all their activities into one program.

   他把他們的活動都併入一個計劃。

職場補給 Market Elements 市場要素

新產品已成為決定企業生存的關鍵因素之一。隨著知識經濟（knowledge-based economy）時代的到來，技術創新使產品的更替速度變得更快，任何企業要想在競爭的市場中立於不敗之地，力求能夠實現企業效益的增長和可持續發展，必須十分重視新產品的開發問題。

新產品開發企劃書的重要組成部分是新產品的可行性分析、定位設計、品牌策略、促銷策略、營銷渠道策略、廣告方式、風險預測（risk predictions）控制、產品定價等要素。

新產品定價的選擇必須考慮真實成本和利潤（costs & profits）、產品或服務的顧客認知價值（recognition value）、細分市場差別定價（pricing differences）、可能的競爭性反應（competition response）、市場營銷目標（sales targets）五個基本因素。價格企劃對各因素一定要進行周全的考慮。

另外，市場導人（market leaders）策略企劃首先是渠道（channels）問題，良好的營銷渠道和周全的維修服務是新產品成功導人市場的保障；其次是市場導人手段、銷售促進策略、廣告策略、公共關係等因素的設計。這些因素對新產品開發全過程的最終實現起到關鍵作用（critical functions）。

Meeting

達人提點 **Proposal Engineering** 企劃工程

- 新產品開發是一項複雜的工程，涉及的因素（involved factors）較多。因此，新產品開發企劃書與一般的企劃書相比，內容更加豐富，製作起來難度更大。

- 新產品概述要對所開發產品的名稱、商標（logo, trade mark）、包裝、用途、功能等內容進行簡要說明，以便起到對其產品有一個感性認識的作用。

- 新產品開發企劃書的寫作除了要關注內在因素（internal factors）外，也要考慮到外在因素（external factors）的存在，要注意書寫格式的條理性、內容的全面性。

- 新產品的外在因素分析是指企劃者對新產品與消費者、競爭者等之間關係進行分析，這能有利於新產品市場競爭力（competition）的提升。

- 新產品的開發推進，這一部分是關於新產品開發中具體實施計劃方面的內容，其內容一定要考慮到新產品設計、試製、原材料等具體的生產管理計劃和研發（research & development）經費預算一系列的實施計劃。

1-6 績效考核會議
Performance Assessment Meeting

情境 1 Performance Report 重要報告

情境設定

The company expects to conduct its performance assessment for the second half. The personal executive and his colleague reiterated the importance of report in the meeting.

公司即將進行下半年度績效考核。人事部主管與人事專員強調該報告之重要性。

角色設定

Personal Executive (PE)：人事主管
Personal Specialist (PS)：人事專員

情境對話

PE ▶ The performance assessment is an important content for personnel management in the enterprise and also serves as a powerful measure regarding management. It mainly aims at upgrading the efficiency of individuals and finally

人事主管 ▶ 績效考核是企業人事管理的重要內容，更是企業管理強有力的手段。其目的是通過考核提高個體的效率，而最終實現企業的

reaching targets set by the enterprise.

目標。

PS ▶ Indeed. An effective performance assessment can improve the working efficiency and stimulate the morale of employees. With more fair and reasonable references, the company can also use the result to reward its staff.

人事專員 ▶ 確實如此。有效的績效考核提高員工的工作績效,更可激勵士氣;公司亦可作為公平合理地酬賞員工的參考依據。

PE ▶ Do you know the performance assessment originate from which country, and the feature of this system?

人事主管 ▶ 您知道績效考核發源於哪一個國家嗎?以及此制度的特色?

PS ▶ To my acknowledge, the success of civil official system in Britain offers an experience and example for other nations and the U.S. set up its own performance assessment system in 1887. This system has a common feature which reviews the working performance as its most important content in promotion.

人事專員 ▶ 就我所知,英國文官考核制度的成功實行,為其他國家提供了經驗和榜樣,而美國也於 1887 年也正式建立了考核制度。這種制度有一個共同的特徵,即把工作實績作為晉升的最重要的內容。

PE ▶ Meanwhile, the civil official system in western countries has proved that the assessment system is a significant content to link with the upgrading efficiency of the government. Based on the performance, the rewards and penalties are decided for the promotion of civil officials.

人事主管 ▶ 同時,西方國家文官制度的實踐證明,考核是公務員制度的一項重要內容,是提高政府工作效率的中心環節。並根據工作實績的優劣,決定公務員的獎勵懲罰和晉升。

PS ▶ It is correct that most enterprises followed suit and carried out the application especially in the early years of the century, trying to evaluate its employees through the performance assessment.

人事專員 ▶ 事實上，大部分企業也於本世紀年初採用此做法，並藉由表現評估評定員工的能力。

PE ▶ Each department expects to complete the second half performance report by the end of December, and the personal department has to make a summary for approval.

人事主管 ▶ 各部門要在 12 月底前完成下半年績效報告，另由人事部總結呈核。

PS ▶ I will relay this information to all executives, and prepare assessment documentation needed.

人事專員 ▶ 我會將此信息轉達給各部門主管，並準備好所需要之考核資料。

給力單字

1. **performance** (*n.*) （工作或活動中的）表現
The boss was disappointed at/by the performance of the Sales Department.
老闆對業務單位的表現感到失望。

2. **measure** (*n.*) 措施；手段
The Sales Department was urged to take measures to combat the sales decline.
業務部門被敦促要採取措施以防止業績下滑。

Meeting

3. **stimulate** (*v.t.*)　刺激；促使 [（+to/into）]
The boss will do everything in his power to stimulate sales growth.
老闆將竭盡全力去促使業績成長。

4. **reward** (*n.*)　報答；報償；獎賞
The employee gets good rewards for his hard work.
員工以辛苦工作去獲得優渥報酬。

5. **originate** (*v.t.*)　發源；來自[（+ from/with）]
The modern performance assessment system originated from the Western world.
現代之考績評審制度發源於西方世界。

6. **example** (*n.*)　範例；榜樣[（+to）]
The good performance of Sales Department was an example to all of us.
業務部門的優異表現是我們學習的榜樣。

7. **feature** (*n.*)　特徵，特色[（+of）]
The performance assessment has many features of its system design.
考績評估在制度設計上有許多特色。

8. **significant** (*adj.*)　重要的；值得注意的
The significant purpose of the performance assessment aims to upgrade efficiency. .
考績最重要目的在於提升效率。

9. **link** (*n.*)　環節；聯繫
A link to upgrade the work efficiency is now established.
目前已建立起一個提升工作效率間之聯繫。

10. **penalty** (*n.*) 處罰；刑罰[（+for）]
Like rewards, penalties are an important measure in the performance assessment.
如同獎勵，處罰也是考績評估裡一項重要之措施。

11. **follow suit** (*ph.*) 跟著做, 照別人的方式去做; 學樣
Many enterprises are expected to follow suit the latest system.
許多企業預計會參照最新的系統來製做。

12. **evaluate** (*v.t.*) 評估，評價
The company is reviewing the system of performance evaluation.
公司正在檢討考績評估制度。

13. **summary** (*n.*) 總結，摘要[（+of）]
We made a summary of the evaluation system.
我們為這個評估制度做了一個總結。

14. **relay** (*v.t.*) 轉達；轉播
This information was relayed to executives of each department.
這個消息已轉達給各部門主管知悉。

同義詞

· **measure** 措施；手段
→size→grade→rank→compare

· **stimulate** 刺激；激勵
→spur→stir→move→motivate

· **reward** 報答；酬謝
→compensate→pay→remunerate→award

· **example** 例子；樣本
→sampleà specimen→illustration→model

Meeting

- **feature**　特徵，特色
  → show → headline → star → mark

- **significant**　有意義的
  → momentous → eventful → fateful → historic

- **link**　環節；紐帶
  → unite → connect → join →combine

- **penalty**　處罰；刑罰
  →punishment →sentence→condemnation

給力句型

1. performance　演出；表現

   The Personnel Department is expected to complete the performance assessment of each department soon.
   人事部門即將完成各部門之績效考核。

   The performance of Sales Department was better than expected.
   業務單位的表現比預期好。

   The boss expects the performance of Sales Department is better for the year.
   老闆期待業務部門今年業績會更佳。

2. measure　衡量

   * measure sth by sth

   The Sales Department shouldn't be measured purely by sales results .

業務部門不應該純粹用業績來衡量。

3. stimulate 刺激增長/需求/經濟等

*stimulate sb to do sth

An inspiring executive can stimulate employees to succeed .
一個富有啟發性的主管可以激勵員工取得成功。

4.. for example 例如; 譬如

The British's civil official system is older than that of the U.S. for example.
譬如說，英國文官制度比美國更悠久。

The civil official system of British is better than the U.S. for example.
例如，英國文官制度優於美國。

5.. morale 士氣，鬥志

*keep up/maintain morale

The Sales Department keeps up high morale for its sales performance.
業務部門在業績表現方面一直保持高昂士氣。

6.. feature 特徵

*common feature

The work performance is a common feature of evaluation.
工作表現是評估的一個共同特徵。

The evaluation system has so many other features.
該項評估制度另擁有許多其它特色。

情境 2 ▶ View-Sharing 觀點分享

情境設定

Regarding the performance assessment system, two senior executives expressed their views in the meeting. And they shared the same experience for a better and reasonable change of the system in the future.

對於公司績效考核制度，兩位資深主管在會議中表達了他們的觀點。同時分享相同經驗，為此制度將來有一個更好及合理的改變。

角色設定

Senior Executive A：資深主管 A
Senior Executive B：資深主管 B

情境對話

SEA A ▶ Our company's performance assessment is now conducted on the basis of one month, one quarter, half year, and one year.

資深主管 A ▶ 我們公司目前進行績效考核，依照時間可區分成：一個月、一季、半年、及一年。

SEB ▶ Yes, I am reviewing the performance of the department for the second half, and I expect the result to be finalized soon.

資深主管 B ▶ 是的，我也正在檢討我們部門下半年的考績，有關結果希望能儘快完成。

SEA A ▶ How do you comment on the design

資深主管 A ▶ 您覺得我

of the company's performance assessment system? Does it reflect the real performance of each employee?

SEB ▶ I heard that the system imitates a well-known enterprise in the U.S., and it costs a lot in order to introduce the system into our company.

SEA A ▶ In my opinion, most assessment items are a kind of objective, but some assessment items of the system are too conventional, however.

SEB ▶ I shared the same view but this system is a stereotyped policy of the company. I highly recommend a correction in the future, if possible, thus making it more reasonable.

們公司考績制度設計如何？是否真正反映出每位員工之實際表現？

資深主管 B ▶ 我聽說該考績評審是仿照美國某知名大企業所使用之制度，我們公司為引進此制度也花了不少錢。

資深主管 A ▶ 以我個人意見，該制度大部分考核項目還頗客觀，唯有些評估項目卻流於太過形式化。

資深主管 B ▶ 我頗感同身受，只是這是目前公司之既定之政策。我強烈建議將來如有機會要做一些改變，使其較為合理化。

給力單字

1. **conduct** (*v.t.*)　進行調查/實驗/調查研究等
   The company conducted a survey to the performance assessment system.

Meeting

公司對考績評估制度進行調查研究。

2. **review** (*v.t.*)　回顧，檢討
The Personnel Department ordered an urgent review of evaluation system.
人事部命令對評估制度進行緊急審查。

3. **finalize** (*v.t.*)　最後定下，確定
Relevant details of the performance assessment are finalized.
有關考績評估的細節已經定案。

4. **reflect** (*v.t.*)　反射；照出
The still water reflected the full moon.
平靜的水面映出了滿月。

5. **imitate** (*v.t.*)　仿效〔某物〕
The U.S. imitates most of its civil official system from Britain.
美國在文官制度方面大多仿效英國。
Our methods have been imitated all over the world .
全世界都在效仿我們的辦法。

6. **introduce** (*v.t.*)　引進；採用[（+to/into）]
This system was introduced into England from the European Continent.
這套制度是從歐洲大陸傳入英國的。

7. **conventional** (*adj.*)　守舊的，傳統的
The company's assessment method is a quite conventional one.
該公司使用一種相當傳統的方法作為評估方式。

8. **stereotype** (*v.*)　對…有老一套看法; 把…模式化 [+as]
The performance assessment is often stereotyped, especially in a big company.
考績評估經常被一律看成是老套作法，尤其在大公司裡。

同義詞

- **imitate** 仿效
  →follow→trace→copy→duplicate

- **introduce** 介紹，引見
  →inaugurate→institute→launch→innovate

- **objective** 客觀存在的
  →purpose→intent→intention

給力句型

1. reflect 反映，表現

   That report reflects the performance of the Sales Department in the first half.

   那個評估報告反映了業務部門上半年之表現。

   帶給，招致[（+on/upon）]

   Such performance can only reflect poor work efficiency on you .
   這樣的表現只能說明你的工作效率差。

   思考，反省[+（that）][+wh-]

   The executive reflected that he had no right to do this.
   該主管深思後明白他無權做這件事。

   深思；反省[（+on/upon/over）]

   The Sales Department reflected on its poor performance.
   營業單位反省業績表現太差。

2. review　審查

*under review

A new performance assessment system is now under review.
一套新考績制度目前正接受審查。

*come up for review

The new performance assessment came up for review recently.
新的考績評估最近應該進行審查。

3. introduce　介紹

*introduce sb to sb

The new system was introduced to the company.
一個新制度已經被引進公司。

*introduce oneself

Allow me to introduce myself ; my name is Johnson .
允許讓我自我介紹一下，我叫約翰遜。

*introduce sth. to/into

The civil official system was introduced into North America from Britain.
文官制度是由英國傳入北美的。

職場補給 Performance Assessment 績效考核

　　公司或企業績效考核可分為定期（periodical）與不定期（non-periodical）兩種，主要考核內容又包括考核員工的個人特質，如誠實度、合作性、溝通能力等。同時也考核員工的工作方式和工作行為，如服務員的微笑和態度，待人接物的方法等，即對工作過程的考量。另外如果考核的重點是工作內容(job contents)和工作質量（job quality），例如產品的產量和質量、勞動效率（labor efficiency）等，則側重員工完成的工作任務和生產的產品。

在考績方法上，可以直接量化（quantity）的指標體系所進行的考核，如生產指標和個人工作指標（job index）。考核者也可根據一定的標準設計的考核指標體系，對被考核者進行主觀評價，如工作行為和工作結果。

確保公平性是推行人員考績制度的前提。另考績不嚴格，就會流於形式，形同虛設。不僅不能全面地反映工作人員的真實情況，而且還會產生消極的後果。考績的嚴格性包括：明確的考核標準（standards）；嚴肅認真的考核態度（attitudes）；嚴格的考核制度與科學的程式及方法等。

對各級職工的考評，都必須由被考評者的"直接上級"進行。直接上級相對來說最瞭解被考評者的實際工作表現，也最有可能反映真實情況。間接上級對直接上級作出的考評評語（statement of judgment），不應當擅自修改。考評系統與組織指揮系統取得一致，更有利於加強經營組織的指揮機能。

考績的結論應對接受考評者本人公開，這是保證考績民主的重要手段。一方面，可以使被考核者瞭解自己的優點和缺點、長處和短處，從而使考核成績好的人再接再厲，繼續保持先進；也可以使考核成績不好的人心悅誠服，奮起上進。另一方面，還有助於防止考績中可能出現的偏見以及種種誤差（tolerances），以保證考核的公平與合理。

依據考績的結果，應根據工作成績的大小、好壞，有賞有罰，有升有降，而且這種賞罰、升降不僅與精神激勵相聯繫。而且還必須通過工資（wages）、獎金 （bonus）等方式同物質利益相聯繫，這樣，才能達到考績的真正目的。

考核的等級之間應當有鮮明的差別界限（differential limits），針對不同的考評評語在工資、晉升、使用等方面應體現明顯差別，使考評帶有刺激性，鼓勵職工的上進心。

達人提點 **Assessment Methods** 考核方法

目前供採用績效考核方法，有主要以下數種：

1. 圖尺度考核法（Graphic Rating Scale，GRS）：一般採用圖尺度表填寫打分的形式進行。

2. 交替排序法（Alternative Ranking Method，ARM）：交替排序的操作方法就是分別挑選、排列的 "最好的" 與 "最差的"，然後挑選出 "第二好的" 與 "第二差的"，這樣依次進行，直到將所有的被考核人員排列完全為止，從而以優劣排序作為績效考核的結果。

3. 配對比較法（Paired Comparison Method，PCM）：它的特點是每一個考核要素都要進行人員間的兩兩比較和排序，使得在每一個考核要素下，每一個人都和其他所有人進行了比較，所有被考核者在每一個要素下都獲得了充分的排序。

4. 強制分佈法（Forced Distribution Method，FDM）：是在考核進行之前就設定好績效水平的分佈比例，然後將員工的考核結果安排到分佈結構裡去。

5. 關鍵事件法（Critical Incident Method，CIM）：是一種通過員工的關鍵行為和行為結果來對其績效水平進行績效考核的方法，一般由主管人員將其下屬員工在工作中表現出來的非常優秀的行為事件或者非常糟糕的行為事件記錄下來，然後在考核時點上與該員工進行一次面談，根據記錄共同討論來對其績效水平做出考核。

6. 行為錨定等級考核法（Behaviorally Anchored Rating Scale，BARS）：是基於對被考核者的工作行為進行觀察、考核，從而評定績效水平的方法。

7. 目標管理法（Management by Objectives，MBO）：目標管理法是現代更多採用的方法，管理者通常很強調利潤、銷售額和成本這些能帶來成果的結果指標。

1-7 品管流程會議實錄
Quality Management Meeting

情境 1 U. S."TQM" vs. Japan"TQC" 美國"TQM" v.s.日本"TQC"

情境設定

In a quality management meeting, two colleagues from the quality control department discussed the world's most famous TQM and TQC system by retrieving the historical development of the expertise in both the U.S. and Japan. The company has built up its own quality control circle, as elaborated in the following conversations.

在公司品管會議中,兩位品管部門同仁就舉世聞名的全面品管(TQM/ TQC)系統相互探討,並溯及該專門知識在美國與日本之歷史沿革。他們公司目前也建立起自己品管圈,雙方言談中多所披露。

角色設定

Quality Executive (QE):品管主管
Quality Specialist (QS):品管專員

情境對話

QE ▶ As you may know, the concept of "total quality management" (TQM) was first submitted by both Armand Vallin

品管主管 ▶ 如您所知,全面品質管理的概念,乃是由美國通用電氣公

Feigenbaum of General Electric and Joseph M. Juran, a quality specialist in the U.S. , in 1950s. This concept enables each department of enterprise to build up an effective system in researching, maintaining, and upgrading quality activities.

司的阿曼德・費根堡姆和質量管理專家約瑟夫・朱蘭於 1950 年代首度提出。此概念把企業各部門在研製質量、維持質量和提高質量的活動中構成為一種有效的體系。

QS ▶ That's why some major American enterprises have used the scientific theory of behavior management to implement the co-called "zero defects" beginning in early 1960s. Leading industries in Japan also initiated their own "quality control circle (QCC)", thus accelerating the fast development of TQM in the world.

品管專員 ▶ 也因為如此,一些美國主要企業從 1960 代初期根據行為管理科學的理論,開始在質量管理中推動所謂無缺陷運動。之後,日本之各大工業也發起「品管圈」活動,使得全面品管在全世界加速發展起來。

QE ▶ Among the quality management theories, Dr. Edwards Deming of the U.S. offered his famous four staged—Plan, Do, Check, and Action—abbreviated as the "PDCA circle", or known as the "Deming Circle".

品管主管 ▶ 在品管流程理論中,最著名的是美國的艾德華茲・戴明博士所提出的「計劃,執行,檢查,行動」四階段的迴圈方式,簡稱 PDCA 迴圈,又稱為「戴明迴圈」。

QS ▶ In order to solve the quality

品管專員 ▶ 但是解決品

management, it usually needs to collect and handle mass data, and which are analyzed systemically by scientific methods. Math statistics are used as important bases, thus offering a more objective view.

管問題時，通常需要收集和整理大量的資料，並用科學的方法進行系統的分析。同時也以數理統計為理論基礎，可提供比較客觀之看法。

QE ▶ Our company focuses quality control on products in mass production. But in singe product and small orders, the quality control switches to working procedures.

品管主管 ▶ 在大量生產中，我們公司著重產品的質量管理。然而在單件小批單生產中，重點則轉換至控制工序。

QS ▶ Each major step of the manufacture or service processes should be controlled if you want to ensure the product quality effectively. These controls are called job of quality control, which is now adopted in the company.

品管專員 ▶ 如果你要確實有效地控制影響產品品質的因素，就必須在生產或服務過程的每個主要階段加以管控。這些管控就是所謂質量管理工作，也是公司目前採用之方式。

給力單字

1. **quality** (*n.*)　質，品質
   The company's management motto: quality always matters more than quantity.
   公司管理宗旨：品質永遠比數量更為重要。

Meeting

The product quality has to be examined carefully before delivering.

產品的品質必須仔細檢查後才可出貨。

2. **submit** (*v.t.*)　提交，呈遞[（+to）]

The QC Department submitted a new quality control proposal, waiting for approval.

品管部門提出新的品質控管建議案，正等待核准中。

3. **implement** (*v.t.*)　執行計劃/政策/建議等

We have decided to implement the QC Department's suggestions in full.

我們已決定全面實施 QC 部門提出的建議。

The new quality control program costs a lot if it is implemented.

這個新品管計畫如果付諸實施將所費不貲。

4. **initiate** (*v.t.*)　開始實施; 發起

The company initiated measures in order to sharpen its quality controls.

公司開始想辦法以增強它的品管控制。

5. **theory** (*n.*)　學說；論說 [（+of）]

The most famous total quality management theory was submitted by Dr. Edwards Deming of the U.S., or known as the "Deming Circle".

最有名的品管理論是美國的艾德華茲‧戴明博士所提出，或又稱為「戴明迴圈」。

Your quality control theory is good but it seems not too practical.

你的品管理論上是很好，但在實際上卻不太可行。

6. **abbreviate** (*v.i.*)　縮寫，使省略[（+to）]

QC is abbreviated from quality control.

"QC"是"quality control "（品質控管）的縮寫。

7. **mass** (*n.*)　眾多；大量[（+of）]

There are masses of work to do in the total quality control.

在全面品管中需要作很多的工作。

8. **objective** (*adj.*)　客觀的，無偏見的

Statistics from the QC Department offers an objective opinion.

來自品管部的數據提供了客觀的意見。

9. **focus** (*n.*)　中心，集中點；重點[the S][（+of）]

The focus of the company production is the quality control.

公司生產的重點是品質控管。

The company's QC Department represents the focus of its production.

公司品管部代表生產之焦點。

10. **switch** (*v.t.*)　改變；轉移；調動

The QC Department switched the production to working procedures.

品管部將有關生產轉換至控制工序方面。

11. **effectively** (*adv.*)　有效地；生效地

We attempted to make the quality work more effectively.

我們嘗試把品質工作變得更有效率。

同義詞

· **quality**　特性；品質

→nature→kind→characteristic

· **submit**　使屈服

→yield→surrender→comply→obey

- **implement** 完成，實行
  →complete→carry out→get done→bring about

- **theory** 原理；推測
  →hypothesis→explanation→inference→conception

- **abbreviate** 縮寫，縮短，使簡短
  →shorten→curtail→condense

- **objective** 沒有偏見的，公正的
  →unprejudiced→impartial→impersonal

- **focus** 集中；調節
  →concentrate→adjust

- **major** 較大的；較高的
  →larger→greater→superior

- **effective** 有效的
  →efficient→productive→successful

給力句型

1. submit　同意服從[遵守]
   *submit sth to

   The QC Department will submit to approval of its recent proposal.
   品管部門願意接受新進提案之核准。

*submit oneself to sb/sth

The QC executive submitted himself to questioning of new quality control proposal.

該品管部主管接受被詢問有關新品管案事宜。

2. focus　中心；重點[the S][（+of）]

*the focus is on sth

The focus of the company has been on quality control issues.

最近公司的焦點是品管問題。

*the focus of attention

The quality control had now become the focus of attention.

品管控制已成為公司關注的焦點。

3. order　預定; 訂購

*order sb sth

Customers only ordered the company on a single product, but it's small orders recently.

雖然近來客戶僅向公司下單一產品，但屬於小量訂單。

*order sth for sb/sth

The company has ordered relevant materials for the new production line.

公司已經為新生產線訂購有關材料。

An Open-up Talk on TQC & Certifications 暢談全面品管及國際認證

情境設定

Two colleagues had a constructive dialogue on TQM and ISO international quality standards as well. Their conversations are consented in the following dialogue.

兩位公司同事對全面品質管理以及國際品管認證等有建設性之暢談。他們有如下之同意對話。

角色設定

Colleague A：同事 A
Colleague B：同事 B

給力對話

Colleague A ▶ Could you elaborate the difference between TQM (total quality management) and TQC (total quality control)?

同事 A ▶ 您可否詳述 TQM 和 TQC 有何不同之處?

Colleague B ▶ The main difference lies on the use of individual nations, such as the U.S. and Japan, for instance. The former uses the system of total quality management（TQM）while the latter, the total quality control (TQC).

同事 B ▶ 主要的不同則在於使用國家的區別，例如美國與日本。前者使用 TQM 系統，而後者則使用 TQC。

Colleague A ▶ ISO 9000 series are a world standard set up by the International Standard

同事 A ▶ ISO 9000 系列是國際標準化組織設

Organization (ISO). The standards are relevant to evaluation of enterprises in their quality control capabilities instead of the level of good or bad product quality.

立的世界標準。此標準並不是評估產品的優劣水準，而是攸關企業在生產過程中對流程控制的能力。

Colleague B ▶ As the application for ISO certification costs a lot, many companies employ with other standards, such as IC9700 or IC9200. However, ISO 9200 is still standards accepted widely.

同事 B ▶ 申請 ISO 認證的費用很高昂，導致很多公司使用其他標準如 IC 9700 或 IC 9200。ISO 9000 目前仍是最被廣泛接受的標準。

Colleague A ▶ TQM is now used in manufacturing, education, the government, and the third industry, as well as in the aerospace fields conducted by the National Aeronautics and Space Administration (NASA) of the U.S.

同事 A ▶ 全面品質管理目前已使用在製造、教育、政府與第三產業，以及美國國家航空暨太空總署的太空科學計畫等領域。

Colleague B ▶ It provides a protection umbrella, which makes all employees to compete within the organization. This also continues to reduce costs and upgrade customer satisfactions.

同事 B ▶ 它同時也提供了一個保護傘，使得在組織之中的所有員工都能夠競爭。並同時持續降低成本及提升客戶滿意度。

給力單字

1. **elaborate** (*v.i.*)　詳細說明；詳盡計畫[（+on/upon）]
   The executive elaborated on the difference between TQM and TQC.
   該主管詳細說明 TQM 以及 TQC 不同之處。

2. **main** (*adj.*)　主要的，最重要的
   I noted down the main points of quality control.
   我把品管的要點記了下來。

3. **standard** (*n.*)　標準，水準
   Your recent work has been below standard.
   你最近的工作一直低於標準。
   Your work is not up to (the) standard.
   你的工作未達到標準。

4. **evaluation** (*n.*)　評估
   An intensive evaluation of the quality control program has been made public recently.
   一份深入有關品管的評估已經在最近被公布。

5. **application** (*n.*)　申請，請求[（+to/for）][+to-v]
   The company made an application ISO quality certification.
   公司申請 ISO 品管認證。

6. **employ** (*v.t.*)　使用，利用
   The company employs its ISO quality certifications as exports criteria.
   公司使用其 ISO 認證以作為外銷規範。

7. **industry** (*n.*) 工業；企業
The TQC system represents a necessity in the manufacturing industry.
全面品管在製造工業上已成為必備之物。

8. **fields** (*n.*) 領域；專業；範疇
He is a prominent expert in the field of quality control.
他是品質管控的傑出專家。

9. **compete** (*v.t.*) 競爭；對抗[（+with/against/for）]
We can compete with the best companies in the field.
我們能與此行業最好的公司競爭。

10. **reduce** (*v.t.*) 減少；縮小
The company is trying to reduce expenses on the production cost.
公司正在試圖降低生產成本。

同義詞

- **main** 主要的
  chief→principal→foremost→leading

- **standard** 標準
  model→rule→pattern→criterion

- **relevant** 相關的
  pertinent→applicable→apropos→suitable

- **compete** 競爭
  rival→vie with→contend→contest

- **reduce** 減少
  lessen→lower→decrease→diminish

給力句型

1. standard practice/procedure　例行的做法/程序
   →Pursuing quality control at industries is now a standard practice.
   →To pursue quality control has now become a standard practice at industries.
   →It is now a standard practice to pursue quality control at industries.
   企業追求品管現在已成為一項例行的做法。

2. compete　競爭
   *compete to do sth

   Several advertising agencies are competing to get the contract.
   幾家廣告代理商在競爭，力求得到這份合同。

職場補給　Three "Q's"　全面品管 3Q

全面品質管理可用三個 Q（Quality）來表示：
1. 人（People）的品質
2. 系統及流程（System & Process）的品質
3. 產品及服務（Product & Service）的品質
TQM 的架構主體是品質管理發展的主流之一。

達人提點 Graphic Tools 圖表工具

另外，品管工具（Basic Tools of Quality），又稱 QC 手法，為品管上經常使用的工具。目前比較著名的工具包括：

石川圖（又稱魚骨圖 Fishbone Diagram），是用圖解展示一定事件的各種原因的方法。它常用於產品設計，來顯示某個總體效果的可能因子。

管制圖（Control Chart），也稱為修哈特圖或流程行為圖，是統計過程控制（Statistical process control）中，確定製造或業務流程是否在統計控制狀態下的一種工具。

直方圖（Histogram）是一種對數據分布情況的圖形表示，是一種二維統計圖表，它的兩個坐標分別是統計樣本和該樣本對應的某個屬性的度量。

柏拉圖（Pareto Chart）又稱排列圖法、主次因素分析法，是一種條形圖（bar chart），為品質管理上經常使用的一種圖表方法。1930 年由約瑟夫·朱蘭首次應用於品管當中。

Meeting

1-8 存貨管理會議
Inventory Management Meeting

情境 1 Fast & Precise 快速及精確

情境設定

The inventory management represents a fast and precise administration, supporting the production of manufacturing industries, and so on. Modern enterprises have now added the automation facilities in inventory, as elaborated by the two employees in the Warehousing Department.

存貨管理代表快速及精確管理，也支援製造業及有關行業之生產運作。目前自動化設施也搭配在現代企業裡，如同兩位倉儲部門同仁在洽談中提及。

角色設定

Warehousing Executive (WE)：倉儲主管
Warehousing Specialist (WS)：倉儲專員

情境對話

WE ▶ The inventory management mainly relates with the business of both planning and controls of stock materials, and aims at

倉儲主管 ▶ 存貨管理主要是與庫存物料的計劃與控制有關的業務，而

105

the support of manufacturing operation. The inventory management governs stock items, including all materials of enterprise, raw materials, parts, semi-finished/finished products, and auxiliary materials.

以支持生產運作為目的。存貨管理支配庫存項目，即企業中的所有物料，包括原材料、零部件、半成品及產品，以及輔助物料。

WS ▶ The inventory management differs from the warehouse management. The management of warehouse focuses on the deployment of warehouse, material transportation, moving, and storage automation.

倉儲專員 ▶ 存貨管理與倉庫管理有所區別。倉庫管理著重於倉庫或庫房的布置，物料運輸和搬運以及存儲自動化等的管理。

WE ▶ The major function of inventory management is to build up a buffer between supply and demand. It also helps to relax the contradictories between customer demand and enterprise production, final assembly and parts, parts processing and procedures, manufacturer demands and material supplies.

倉儲主管 ▶ 存貨管理的主要功能是在供、需之間建立緩衝區。以達到緩和用戶需求與企業生產能力之間，最終裝配需求與零配件之間，零件加工工序之間、生產廠家需求與原材料供應商之間的矛盾。

WS ▶ A good inventory makes logistics smooth and balanced. It guarantees normal production and supply, and compresses inventory capital reasonably, thus reaching a better economic effect.

倉儲專員 ▶ 一個好的庫存管理可使物流均衡通暢。它也會保證正常生產和供應，又能合理壓縮存貨資金，以得到較好的經濟效果。

WE ▸ The inventory cycle represents only eight days in certain enterprises in the U.S., compared with 51 days in mainland China. The cost of logistics structure takes 14% of total costs in China, while such costs are 3.8% in the U.S.

倉儲主管 ▸ 在美國有些企業存貨周期只佔有 8 天，但有些中國企業的存貨周期長達 51 天。從物流成本結構看，中國物流管理成本佔總成本的 14%，而美國只 3.8%。

WS ▸ The purpose behind inventory management of logistics is to reduce costs of enterprise. The logistics should be carried out from the point of view on the supply chain, no matter on conducting of inventory management or cost down.

倉儲專員 ▸ 對物流進行存貨管理，其實就是降低其企業成本。物流不管是對庫存進行管理還是要降低成本，都要在供應鏈的角度上來實行。

WE ▸ Judging from the information trend of enterprises in early 60s of 20th century, the inventory management in logistics has tended to become information, website, and highly concentrated.

倉儲主管 ▸ 從 20 世紀 60 年代以來企業信息化的趨勢來看，物流企業的存貨管理也需趨向於信息化、網路化和高度集成化。

WS ▸ Following the fast development of information technology and competition of large-scaled logistics worldwide, the inventory management—as a core of logistics management—has to accommodate itself to the era.

倉儲專員 ▸ 隨著信息技術的高速發展和國外大型物流企業的競爭，作為現代企業的物流管理的核心部分——庫存管理，也要適應時代的發展。

給力單字

1. **inventory** (*n.*)　存貨清單；存貨盤存

   The store has full inventory for sales both home and abroad.

   那家商店存貨充足可供國內外銷售。

   詳細目錄；清單

   The warehouse executive made a complete inventory of everything in the company.

   倉儲主管將公司裡的所有東西開列了一份詳細清單。

2. **aim** (*v.t.*)　以⋯為目的

   The warehouse management mainly aims at the support of manufacturing operation.

   倉儲管理主要目的在於支援生產運作。

3. **govern** (*v.t.*)　管理；統治

   Who really governs this warehouse?

   真正管理著這個倉庫的是誰？

4. **differ** (*v.t.*)　不同，相異〔（+from）〕

   The inventory management differs from warehouse management, mainly in the function purpose.

   存貨管理與倉儲管理不盡相同，主要在功能方面之目的。

   That's where they differ.

   那是他們分歧的地方。

5. **deployment** (*n.*)　部署；調度

   The company employs a very good deployment system in its stock management.

   該公司在庫存管理運用了一套非常優良的調度系統。

6. **storage** (*n.*)　貯藏，保管

   A quarter of the production may be lost in storage.

   生產的四分之一可能在貯藏過程中損失。

7. **buffer** (*n.*) 　緩衝器，減震器
The storage facility designs many buffers in its delivery devices.
本項倉儲設施在運輸裝置上設計了許多緩衝器。

8. **contradictory** (*adj.*)(*n.*) 　矛盾的；抵觸的；矛盾
The planning of the new production line is contradictory to storage functions.
新生產線的規劃與倉儲功能有所矛盾。

9. **logistics** (*n.*) 　物流，運籌
The company's storage system also supports the operation of logistics.
該公司之存貨系統同時支援物流方面之運作。

10. **guarantee** (*v.t.*) 　保障，保證…免受損失[（+against/from）]
With the policy, it guarantees us against all loss in inventories.
由於此保險契約，它保障我們所有存貨有任何損失。

11. **compress** (*v.t.*) 　壓緊，壓縮
The company's capital for inventory may compress its production use eventually.
公司在存貨方面之資金最後有可能會壓縮到生產上使用。

12. **represent** (*v.t.*) 　有代表；有代表作[H]
The inventory represents an important structure in terms of logistics costs.
存貨在物流成本方面代表一個重要結構。

13. **point of view** 　視角，角度
Judging from the inventory viewpoint, your decision is not good enough.
以存貨之角度判斷，您作的決定還不足堪稱是最好的。

14. **tend to** 傾向，易於

The inventory management has tended to be popular over the past decade.

存貨管理在過去十年來愈來愈受到重視。

15. **accommodate** (*v.t.*) 使適應；使相符 [（+to）]

Enterprises will have to accommodate themselves to the changed situation.

企業界必須自我適應變化的形勢。

同義詞

· **inventory** 存貨

→stock→collection→list

· **govern** 統治

→control→regulate→curb→command

· **guarantee** 保證

→promise→secure→pledge→swear

· **represent** 代表

→portray→depict→illustrate→symbolize

· **tend** 傾向於

→(be) inclined to

· **accommodate** 使適應，能容納

→supply→have room for→oblige→conform

給力句型

1. aim   致力，意欲[（+at/for）][+to-v]

   We aim at doubling our production.
   我們的目標是將生產增加一倍。

   We aim to double our production.
   Our production aims to be doubled.

2. differ widely/greatly   相差懸殊

   Opinions on the inventory and warehouse management differ widely.
   有關存貨及倉儲管理上有很大之意見分歧。

3. tend to do sth   易於；往往會做某事

   Automation tends to be an important tool in inventory management in recent years.
   近年來自動化在存貨管理方面已經成為一項重要工具。

   The automation as well as robots tends to be popular in the inventory management.
   在存貨管理方面，自動化及機械人確實變得很流行。

4. relax   放鬆

   *relax sth/sb

   A good inventory management relaxes contradictories between the company and its customers.
   一個好的存貨管理會幫助緩和公司與其顧客之間的矛盾。

5. guarantee (be under guarantee)   在保用期內

   All inventories are under the guarantee of the logistics operation.
   所有存貨在物流操作裡完全得到保證。

*give sb a guarantee (that)

The company gave me a guarantee that the logistics will be arrived on time.

公司向我保證物流一定會準時抵達。

6. accommodate　向…提供 [（+with）]

The company accommodates customers with logistics as its extra services.

該公司對客戶提供物流當作額外之服務。

情境 2 Constructive Talks 建設性談話

情境設定

Two colleagues had a constructive dialogue on inventory, and consented this conversation as follows：

兩位公司同事對品管有建設性之暢談，也同意有如下對話。

角色設定

Colleague A：同事 A
Colleague B：同事 B

情境對話

A ▶ What is inventory and could you briefly define it?

什麼是庫存？可否請您簡短地定義之？

B ▶ The inventory is defined as the storage of all materials to support manufacturing, maintenance, operation, and customer services. It covers all raw materials, maintenance parts, production consumptions, finished products, and spare parts.

存貨一詞的定義可謂：「以支持生產，維護，操作和客戶服務為目的而存儲的各種物料，包括原材料，維修件和生產消耗品，成品和備件等」。

A ▶ The 1.5-fold principle is a significant content regarding inventory management, representing a safe mode concluded by sales of multiple companies.

1.5 倍原則是庫存管理主要內容之一，是經過很多公司的銷售實踐總結出的安全存貨模式。

B ▶ The 1.5-fold principle is based on scientific data but it still has to be flexible in applications. For example, the principle has to be adjusted under the circumstances of weather changes and holidays, for example, or the business will be affected.

1.5 倍原則也是一個科學數據，但是必須靈活掌握和應用。比如，如果遇到特殊情況應適當變化（如天氣、節假日等），否則會影響生意。

A ▶ What are major inventory management problems existing in the manufacturing industry?

您知道目前製造業在存貨管理方面普遍存在哪些問題？

B ▶ The first is unavailable of inventory information in real time. The second is information is not precise as expected. And the third is unavailable of material delivery and relevant production situations.

(1) 不能及時獲得存貨信息。(2) 存貨信息不夠準確。(3) 無法及時了解發送原料和生產用料情況。

給力單字

1. **briefly** (*adv.*) 簡潔地，簡短地
   The colleague briefly explains the meaning of inventory.
   該位同事簡短地解釋庫存的意思。
   He told me briefly the meaning of so-called inventory.
   他簡略地對我說所謂庫存的意思。

2. **define** (*v.t.*) 解釋，給…下定義
   Do you know how to define the meaning of inventory?
   你知道如何定義存貨的意思？

3. **principle** (*n.*) 原則；原理[C]
   There are many important principles in the inventory management.
   在存貨管理方面有許多重要原則。

4. **significant** (*adj.*) 有意義的；重要的
   What are other significant inventory contents in addition to the 1.5-fold principle?
   除了1.5倍原則外，在庫存上還有其他重要內容?

5. **flexible** (*adj.*) 可變通的；靈活的
   The company needs more flexible inventory management methods.
   公司需要更有彈性的庫存管理方法。

6. **circumstances** (*n.*) 在這種情形下；情況
   The inventory management has to be adjusted to meet different circumstances.
   庫存管理必須調整以應付各種情況。

7. **existing** (*adj.*) 現存的；現行的[B]
   The existing inventory system is not sound as expected.
   現行庫存制度並未如預期之完善。

8. **delivery** (*n.*)　發送的東西
Material deliveries should be made at the specified elevator.
材料運送應該用指定之電梯。

9. **precise** (*adj.*)　精確的；明確的
The inventory information and situations were not very precise.
庫存信息及相關情況並不太明確。

同義詞

· **principle**　原則
　→rule→law→standard→belief

· **significant**　有意義的
　momentous→eventful→fateful→historic

· **device**　裝置；設備
　→machine→apparatus→tool→instrument

· **delivery**　發送
　→transfer→transference→transmission→dispatch

給力句型

1. define　定義；解釋

   *define sth as

   He defines inventory as an important support to the production.
   他把存貨解釋為對生產上的一項重要支援。

   *define sth clearly/precisely

   確定⋯的界線；使⋯的輪廓分明

   He did not further define the inventory clearly.
   他並未進一步確定庫存的意義。

2. it is significant that　非常重要的

   It was significant that an inventory management meeting be held within this week.
   在本週內召開一個存貨管理會議的事很重要。

職場補給 Inventory Management & Enterprise Operation 存管與企業營運

目前由於全球性金融自由化（finance liberation）、企業國際化（enterprise internationalization）及證券市場多元化（securities diversification）等趨勢影響下，財務管理（financial management）已成為企業營運需求上的重要一環，也是管理者極為關心的課題。

財務管理的範疇極廣，主要為投資管理、融資管理、營運管理等，營運管理中的流動資產（floating asset）管理包括現金管理、應收帳款（factoring）管理及存貨管理，其中以存貨管理為目前企業最為重視；依著名的摩爾定律（Moore's Law），電子運算之元件會集中縮小於晶片中，因科技之進步，使得運算能力每 18 個月會加倍，故導致高科技產品生命週期過短，一項新產品的銷售熱潮經常僅在 3~9 個月，因此存貨管理就顯得更為重要。

存貨在資產負債表（balance sheet）上屬於流動資產，然而就存貨管理的觀點而言，存貨並非資產而是成本的積壓，存貨不足（inventory shortage）雖然可能無法滿足客戶需求，流失部分訂單；然而過多的存貨（over storage）亦會積壓公司資金，另依國內會計準則 35 號公報資產減損評估，若為呆滯品則會立即影響公司當期損益（profit and loss）。

和存貨有關的成本大致可被歸納為下列三種類型：

1. 持有成本（carrying cost）
2. 訂購成本（ordering cost）
3. 短缺成本（shortage cost）

達人提點 **Effective Technology** 有效技術

為了使存貨總成本極小化，有以下幾種存貨管理技術：

1. ABC 法：依存貨的價值來分類，通常 A 類存貨的價值最昂貴，管理上最為嚴格，再依序為 B、C 等。

2. JIT 法：及時生產系統，將存貨維持在最低水準。

3. EOQ 法：經濟訂購量，在考量訂購成本及持有成本下，求取存貨成本極小化。

4. MRP 法：物料需求規劃，以資訊系統管理存貨之訂購與管制。

為有效控制存貨，公司應定期計算存貨週轉率（revolving rate）或存貨週轉天數，並編製貨齡分析表，用以檢討存貨狀況，才能達到有效監控存貨的目的。

NOTE

Incentive Travel

獎勵旅遊

2-1 旅遊計劃
Travel Program

情境設定

Starting the talk from a successful travel program of the company, two colleagues shared their experiences in the enjoyment of the trip. In this conversation, they were impressed and appreciated by the service and relevant know-how offered by the travel agent.

從公司最近舉辦的獎勵旅遊談起，兩位同仁分享了該次旅遊樂趣。在交談中，他們對於旅行社提供之服務及相關專業也留下深刻印象。

角色設定

Colleague A：同仁 A
Colleague B：同仁 B

情境 1 Travel Pleasures & Service Expertise 旅遊樂趣與專業服務

情境對話

A ▶ Regarded as a success of travel program of its kind in recent year, the company held a 5-day-4-night itinerary to Japan for over 100

同仁 A ▶ 被視為是近年來一個類似成功的旅遊計畫，本公司最近舉行

122

top performers' enjoyment of sightseeing and shopping. The tour is one of the most important events honoring and rewarding the top performers in the areas of productivity and business quality.

超過 100 人到日本遊覽五日四夜的獎勵旅遊，行程包括觀光及採購等樂趣；以獎勵在生產力及業務品質方面表現傑出的同事。

B ▶ You are right. The travel brought an amazing and unforgettable travel experience, and an excellent activity to maintain loyalty and good relationship with them and the company.

同仁 B ▶ 有道理。本次獎勵旅遊帶來了一個令人驚奇及難忘的旅遊經驗，並促進及維繫公司與員工之間的忠誠度及良好關係。

A ▶ From the initial project planning to specific execution, the travel agent created an incentive travel with benefits for expanding sales and activities with originalities.

同仁 A ▶ 旅行社從策劃方案到具體實施，為公司創辦有利於擴大銷售，且充滿原創性活動的獎勵旅遊。

B ▶ I shared the same view with you. The travel agent has offered several exquisite services, including the airport pick-ups, accommodations and transportations, amiable guides, and experienced translators, for example.

同仁 B ▶ 我跟您的看法一致。該旅行公司以細緻的服務提供許多幫助。例如，從機場迎接、住宿交通，到派遣和藹可親的導遊、經驗豐富的翻譯等。

A ▶ In cooperation with U.S.-based SITE (Society of Incentive & Travel Executives), a

同仁 A ▶ 他們是與美國著名的展覽組織者 SITE

Incentive Travel

famous exhibition organizer, and MPI (Meeting Professional International), a specialized trade fair company, and services with expertise angles, they support travel assistances and help customers to introduce their own technique and knowledge.

和交易會策劃運營專業公司 MPI 合作，從專業服務角度為獎勵旅遊提供支持，並幫助客戶介紹自己的技術和知識。

B ▶ I was told that Hong Kong, Macau (Aomen), Singapore, South Korea, Thailand, and Malaysia have offered liberal benefits in incentive travels, and their hardware and software facilities have led the fashion especially in large-sized teams. Maybe we could make preparations of another incentive travels in these destinations next time.

同仁 B ▶ 我聽說香港、澳門、新加坡、南韓、泰國、馬來西亞等國家，在舉辦會展暨獎勵旅遊的優厚條件，尤其接待大型團隊的軟硬體設施方面一直引領著時代的潮流。也許我們下次獎勵旅遊可在這些目的地籌辦。

給力單字

1. **itinerary** (*n.*)　旅程；路線
   This incentive travel plans several places to visit on the itinerary.
   本次獎勵旅遊路線計畫要遊覽許多地方。

   旅行計畫；預訂行程
   Please leave your itinerary so we can contact you in case of any emergencies.
   請留下你的旅行計畫，以便有任何緊急事情時可聯絡上你。

2. **enjoyment** (*n.*)　令人愉快的事
Travel is one of my enjoyments.
旅遊是一件令我愉快之事。

享有[the S][（+of）]
The enjoyment of travel is one of the best things in life.
旅遊是人生最享受之一樂事。

3. **bring** (*v.t.*)　使產生，引起
The incentive travel always brings employees great satisfaction.
獎勵旅遊總是為員工們帶來極大的滿足。

4. **amazing** (*adj.*)　驚人的；了不起的
The recent incentive travel was an amazing experience to employees.
最近的獎勵旅遊對員工們可說是一次相當驚奇的經驗。

5. **specific** (*adj.*)　詳細的，明確的
The travel agent arranged a specific plan for the upcoming incentive travel.
旅行社對即將舉辦的獎勵旅遊安排了非常詳盡的計畫。

6. **expand** (*v.t.*)　擴張；發展；增長
The incentive travel expects to expand the company's sales by 20% in 2015.
該獎勵旅遊預定將公司2015年的業績成長擴張至百分之二十。

7. **exquisite** (*adj.*)　細緻的，敏感的
Many exquisite services are offered in the incentive travel this year.
今年的獎勵旅遊安排許多精緻的服務。

Incentive Travel

8. **amiable** (*adj.*) 和藹可親的；厚道的
Our colleagues are amiable people .
我們的同事都是和藹可親的人。
The guide in the incentive travel was an amiable young man .
獎勵旅遊的導遊是位和藹可親的年輕人。

9. **exhibition** (*n.*) 展出，展覽 [+of]
The travel agent is very experienced in accommodations for trade exhibitions.
旅行社對展覽會住宿安排等方面非常有經驗。

10. **trade fair** (*ph.*) 交易會；展覽會
The annual auto and parts trade fair held in Dubai was a success this year.
今年在杜拜舉行的年度汽車及配件展覽會相當成功。

11. **expertise** (*n.*) 專門知識；專門技術[+in]
He had expertise in the field of incentive travel.
他擁有獎勵旅遊方面的專業知識。

12. **liberal** (*adj.*) 豐富的，充足的
To stimulate local tourism, many countries offer liberal benefits for incentive travels.
為了刺激本國觀光事業，許多國家對獎勵旅遊提供優渥待遇。

13. **fashion** (*n.*) 流行
The travel program such as incentive travels used to be fashion in Europe and the U.S.
獎勵旅遊這一類的旅行計畫曾經在歐洲及美國蔚為流行。

給力句型

1. bring 帶來

   Remember to bring me a gift of your travel.
   記得旅行後要帶給我一份禮物。

   *bring sb sth

   Would you bring me a gift?
   你會帶一份禮物給我嗎？

2. go into specifics 詳談

   I can't go into specifics for this issue now, but I have an arrangement.
   對此問題我目前尚未能詳談，但是我已經有了安排。

3. expand sth. 擴大

   Incentive travel packages designed to expand sales of the enterprise.
   此為擴大企業銷售而設計的獎勵旅遊方案。

4. on exhibition 展出中

   In the world travel show, several attractive trade packages are on exhibition.
   本次世界旅遊展，許多具有吸引力的旅遊配套正在展出中。

5. be in fashion 流行

   Incentive travels are in fashion again for the year.
   獎勵旅遊今年又開始流行了。

Incentive Travel

情境 2 U.S. / Europe Popularities & Taiwan Trends 歐美風行與台灣潮流

情境對話

A ▶ The incentive travel serves as an important management measure to upgrade working dynamics of both employees and direct sales in enterprises, which has become increasingly popular particularly in Europe and the U.S.

同仁 A ▶ 獎勵旅遊對企業來說,是提高員工和推銷員工作動力的重要經營手段之一,尤其在歐洲和美國已經非常盛行。

B ▶ Many corporations in Taiwan have offered incentive travels and attended meetings and exhibitions abroad as a fringe benefit for employees with outstanding performances in recent years.

同仁 B ▶ 台灣許多公司團體近年來也以員工出國旅遊為額外福利,或到國外舉行會議、參加展覽,以獎勵績優人員。

A ▶ Incentive travels are a weapon to boost morale among insurances, direct sales, pharmacy, and medical care industries. The arrangement of such activities is a challenge for undertakers at the same time.

同仁 A ▶ 國內一些保險、直銷、藥品、醫療用品等產業,獎勵旅遊已成為鼓舞士氣最重要的利器。而此類活動的安排,對承辦人員同時也是一項挑戰。

B ▶ In an attempt to meet demands of incentive travels, several travel agencies have built up their own departments to handle

同仁 B ▶ 因應會展暨獎勵旅遊需求,許多旅行社設立專門處理會議、

businesses of meeting, incentive, conference, and exhibitions, or abbreviated as MICE.

展覽、獎勵或員工旅遊，或簡稱 MICE，會展暨獎勵旅遊的部門。

A ▶ Incentive travels need to combine peripheral facilities such as exhibitions, meeting rooms, and banquet rooms. Usually, they invite performance teams, group activity designs, and gala dinners to display originalities.

同仁 A ▶ 獎勵旅遊需要結合展覽會場、會議廳、宴會廳等周邊設施，並且也經常邀請表演團體、團隊活動設計、並展示別出心裁的晚宴盛會等。

B ▶ The number of travel groups varies from hundreds and even up to tens of thousands of people. The demand for quality food, accommodations, and others is comparably high.

同仁 B ▶ 旅遊團人數通常少則百來人、多達數千人甚或上萬人。另外，激勵性質的旅遊團對於食、宿等各方面的品質相對地要求較高。

Incentive Travel

129

給力單字

1. **incentive** (*n.*)　刺激；動機 [U][C][（+to）][+to-v]
   The travel agent offers several incentive discounts for overseas trips.
   該旅行社提供國外旅遊優惠折扣。

2. **dynamics** (*n.*)　動力，活力
   Incentive travel is seen as a dynamic of sales growth.
   獎勵旅遊被視為促進業績成長的一種動力。

3. **fringe benefit** (*ph.*)　補貼，附加福利
   The company adds fringe benefit for the incentive travel.
   公司增加本次獎勵旅遊的津貼。

4. **outstanding** (*adj.*)　顯著的；傑出的
   She is an outstanding saleswoman in the travel agent.
   她是一個傑出的旅行社女業務。

5. **boost** (*v.t.*)　提高；增加
   The travel agent boosted its sales this year .
   這家旅行社使今年的銷售量增加了。

6. **challenge** (*n.*)　挑戰；邀請比賽[+to-v]
   The travel agent faced a challenge to the arrangement of incentive travel program.
   旅行社面對安排獎勵旅遊計畫的挑戰。

7. **travel agency** (*ph.*)　旅行社
   He owns a travel agency in both home and abroad.
   他在國內外都各擁有一家旅行社。

8. **handle** (*v.t.*)　應付，處理

The travel agent couldn't handle the pressures of new incentive travel program.

旅行社無法應付新獎勵旅遊計畫所帶來的壓力。

9. **peripheral** (*adj.*)　外圍的，周邊的

Peripheral facilities are also important when arranging large-sized incentive travels.

當安排大型獎勵旅遊時，周邊的設施同時非常重要。

10. **gala dinner** (*ph.*)　盛宴

The gala dinner is usually an eye-catching event in the incentive travel.

在獎勵旅遊裡所舉行的盛宴通常是一件吸引眾人目光的活動。

11. **tens of thousands** (*ph.*)　成千上萬

The travel agent owns tens of thousands of clients at both home and abroad.

該旅行社在國內外有千上萬的客戶。

12. **comparably** (*adv.*)　類似地；在相似程度上

Earnings have risen comparably in the travel sector .

在旅遊部門利潤也以相當的幅度增長。

Incentive Travel

給力句型

1. incentive　獎勵；優惠

   *incentive to do sth

   Aided by the depreciation of Japanese yen, people have the incentive to travel the nation.
   由於日圓貶值，人們都想去該國旅行。

   *tax incentives　減稅優惠

   The government offers tax incentives in the new free economic and trade zone.
   政府在新建立之自由經濟貿易區提供減稅優惠。

2. benefit　獲得益處

   *have the benefit of

   The incentive travel had the benefit of a discounted flight tickets.
   本次獎勵旅遊獲得折扣機票價。

   *for sb's benefit　為了幫助某人; 對某人有益

   The incentive travel is offered for the benefit of top sales and outstanding employees.
   獎勵旅遊的提供乃有助於超級業務員及優秀員工的福利。

3. boost　激勵

   *give (sb/sth) a boost

   Being chosen to attend the incentive travel gave employees a real boost.
   被挑選去出席獎勵旅遊給員工帶來很大的激勵。

4. challenge　激勵；挑戰

*challenge sb to do sth

The incentive travel challenges all undertakers to think more considerably.

本次獎勵旅遊激勵所有承辦人員更貼心地思考。

*challenge sb to sth

It challenged the travel agent to a high profile program that was never held before.

它向旅行社挑戰一次過去從未舉辦過的高格調計畫。

Incentive Travel

職場補給　Added Value 附加價值

　　獎勵旅遊不同於一般公司員工旅遊，有關獎勵旅遊行程的安排及所需的費用、目的和預期效果也完全不同於員工旅遊。

　　獎勵旅遊主要定義為達成公司個別（individuals）或總體（overall）業績目標之特定對象，包括員工、經銷商、或代理商，由企業提供一定的經費，規劃獎勵會議假期，並委託專業操作獎勵旅遊的旅遊業者，針對企業的目的量身訂製精心設計專屬的獎勵旅遊活動，以犒賞創造營運佳績的有功人員，並藉此增加參與者對企業的向心力。

　　另根據『國際獎勵旅遊協會』的定義，獎勵會議旅遊為現代管理的法寶，目的在協助企業達到特定目標，並對所有參與人士，給予一個盡情享受、難以忘懷的（unforgettable）旅遊假期作為獎勵。

　　原則上，獎勵旅遊的種類及目的可區分如下：
1. 公司年度會議（annual meeting）
2. 國外教育訓練（overseas training）

3. 獎勵營運及業績有功人員（rewards for outstanding persons in operations and sales）

除了獎勵及慰勞的目的外，獎勵旅遊還包含了許多附加價值（added value）。

一個經過規劃精心設計的獎勵旅遊假期，將會替整個企業體達到許多無形的功效，主要包括有：

1. 凝聚員工向心力（condensing employees together）
2. 加強企業文化（strengthening enterprise culture）
3. 提昇工作績效之工具（a tool to improve working efficiency）

達人提點 **Considerations 考量因素**

另外，獎勵旅遊也可運用來激勵公司員工達成公司各項管理目標，譬如鼓勵全勤、提高生產力、及降低生產成本等。

由於獎勵旅遊是以旅行來達到回饋和獎勵之目的，基本上設計此種旅遊，應該將下列各項因素列入其重要考量：

1. 充裕預算（ample budget）：獎勵旅遊之目的是一種激勵和回饋的鼓舞作用，參與者對產品之內容與方式各有預期之效應。如果經費不足，將會產生適得其反的負面效果；使得獎勵的功效失去意義。

2. 目標清晰（distinct target）：有鑒於獎勵旅遊之目的是為了提高工作績效或達到產品上的銷售目標，因此應有一規劃完整清晰之目標。使參與者瞭解並盡力達到設定之目標，以擴大獎勵旅遊之效果。

3. 指派專人（assigned person）：有關獎勵旅遊的專業知識很深廣，因此委託公司和受委託之獎勵公司（或旅行業者）均應指派專人，負責協調以求任務之圓滿達成。

4. 正確旅行時間（right schedule）：獎勵旅遊的時間之選定以不影響公司的正常作業為原則，或可在業務淡季裡進行。

5. 合適目的地（suitable destinations）：合宜之旅遊目的地必須具備基本觀光條件，並且可被多數人所能接受，切忌因主事者之個人好惡而任意選定。

Incentive Travel

2-2 交通 Transportation

情境設定

Transportation serves as an important tool in the travel program. There are so many things that have to be taken into consideration, as two colleagues discussed in their conversations, as follows：

在旅遊計畫裡，交通安排可為是最重要一環工具。許多大小事情並須納入考量，如同以下兩位同仁對話。

角色設定

Colleague A：同仁 A
Colleague B：同仁 B

情境 1 Transportation Vehicles 重要交通工具

情境對話

A ▶ The transportation for the incoming incentive travel of the company is arranged by the travel agent, and the whole itinerary

同仁 A ▶ 有關我們公司即將到來獎勵旅行之交通安排，目前正由旅行

seems to be perfect to meet the purpose.

社處理中。整體行程看起來很完美，也頗符合本次之目的。

B ▶ With the travel subsidy, all of our top sales persons and outstanding suppliers are able to take business class airline flights during their trips.

同仁 B ▶ 由於有公司旅遊補助，我們全部績優業務人員及供應商在本次旅遊皆可搭乘商務艙班機。

A ▶ The transportation arrangement includes airport pick-ups and reservations of tour bus during trips in destinations.

同仁 A ▶ 該項交通安排亦包括機場接送以及預約旅遊期間往返的大巴士。

B ▶ It needs to consider special requirements of transportation, such as tour captain fees and tips for local guides and drivers.

同仁 B ▶ 我們還要考慮到特殊交通需求，例如領隊費用以及給付當地導遊及司機小費。

A ▶ Spouses of top sales and relatives of suppliers are approved to attend the incentive tour this time.

同仁 A ▶ 績優員工眷屬及供應商親戚也同時獲准可參加本次獎勵旅遊。

B ▶ In this case, we have to add shopping or other itineraries at their own expenses for the incentive trip. And relevant transportations have to be taken into consideration at the same time.

同仁 B ▶ 既然如此，我們在獎勵旅遊裡還必須增加一些買東西或是自費行程。相關的交通事宜也要同時列入考量。

Incentive Travel

137

A ▶ And the travel insurance fee for the above personnel has to be covered in the tour, according to regulations.

同仁 A ▶ 根據規定，也要涵蓋上述人員之旅遊保險費。

B ▶ Of course. We are a well-organized company and after all we are concerned with safety of our employees and their families.

同仁 B ▶ 那是當然。我們是一家有規模的公司，而且我們關心員工及其家人之旅遊安全。

給力單字

1. **incoming** (*adj.*)　正到達的；進入的
   The incoming flights will be arriving on schedule.
   航班即將於預定時間內抵達。

2. **meet** (*v.t.*)　滿足；符合
   The travel program has to meet all transportation requirements.
   本次旅遊計畫必須符合所有交通上的需求。

3. **subsidy** (*n.*)　津貼，補助金
   The transportation industry depends for its survival on government subsidies.
   交通業靠政府津貼而得以維持。

4. **business class** (*ph.*)　商務艙
   The ticket price of business is lower than that of first class but is higher than the economic class.
   商務艙的機票價比頭等艙低，但較高於經濟艙價錢。

5. **airport pick-up** (*ph.*)　機場接送
The transportation will include airport pick-up services.
交通方面有包括機場接送服務。

6. **reservation** (*n.*)　預訂；預訂的房間（或席座）
We have made reservations for three rooms at the hotel.
我們已在這個旅館預訂了三個房間。

7. **tip** (*n.*)　小費
Normally, a 10% tip is needed for dinning service at restaurants.
一般而言，在餐廳用餐服務須另加**10%** 的小費。

   tip (*v.t.*)　給小費
Did you remember to tip the waiter?
你記得給服務員小費了嗎？

8. **spouse** (*n.*)　配偶〔指丈夫或妻子〕
Spouses are allowed to join the company's incentive travel for the year.
配偶可參加公司今年的獎勵旅遊。

9. **relative** (*n.*)　親戚，親屬
Relatives of suppliers are welcomed to join the incentive travel of the company.
供應商的親屬也歡迎來參加本次公司的獎勵旅遊。

10. **in this case**　既然這樣
In this case, we need to send the invitation to them soon.
既然這樣，我們必須立刻寄發邀請函給他們。

11. **at one's own expense**　自費
They joined the travel at their own expense.
他們是自費參加旅行。

Incentive Travel

12. **insurance** (*n.*)　保險 [+on]

Do you have insurance on your travel and transportation?

你買旅行及交通保險了嗎？

13. **cover** (*v.t.*)　給…保險；使免受損失[（+against）]

Are the goods covered against transportation damage?

這批貨物保了交通險嗎？

14. **organize** (*v.t.*)　使有條理，使井然有序

The transportation of this city is very well organized.

這個城市的交通結構非常井然有序。

15. **concern** (*v.t.*)　使關心[（+about/with）]

We concerned very much about the safety of transportation in the travel.

我們相當關心旅遊之交通安全。

給力句型

1. reservation　預留，訂位

   *make a reservation

   Customers are advised to make seat reservations well in advance.

   建議顧客提前訂位。

   *have/express reservations (about)

   I had serious reservations about his appointment as captain.

   我對任命他為船長鄭重地持保留態度。

   *without reservation　毫無保留地

   We condemn their actions without reservation.

   我們毫無保留地譴責他們的行為。

2. fee　費用

*charge a fee

Some lawyers charge exorbitant fees.
有些律師收費高得嚇人。

*legal/medical fee

The insurance company paid all my medical fees.
保險公司支付了我的全部醫療費。

*entrance fee

The entrance fees have gone up by 50%.
入會費已經上漲了 50%。

3. insurance　保險

*claim for sth on your insurance　提出保險索賠

We can probably claim for the damage on the insurance.
我們可以讓保險公司賠償損失。

Specified Destinations 特定目的地

情境對話

A ▶ You have any ideas about the plan of a five-day incentive travel to Guam?

同仁 A ▶ 您對於計劃到關島 5 天的獎勵旅遊有任何主意嗎？

B ▶ I happen to know a local travel agent which is an expert in arranging such trips,

同仁 B ▶ 我碰巧有認識一家旅行社專門安排此

and a meeting can be called on this regard next week.

類獎勵旅遊，下週可以針對此來召開會議。

A ▶ As our incentive travel is a business group, I expect the transportation can be arranged in a single airline flight with all requirements included in the budget.

同仁 A ▶ 由於我們是商業團體，我希望所有交通能安排在單一航空公司班機，並包括所有需求在預算內。

B ▶ We will travel by China Airline flight No. CI026, a direct flight from Taoyuan International Airport to Gum. With a flight time of about 3.5 hours, the take-off time is 23:00 p.m. and is estimated to arrive at 04:50+1 in Guam.

同仁 B ▶ 我們將會搭乘中華航空 CI026 號班機，從桃園國際機場直飛關島。飛行時間大約需要三個半小時，晚上 11 點起飛，預估隔天早上 4:50+1 抵達關島。

A ▶ There are two hours of time differences between Taipei and Guam.

同仁 A ▶ 台北與關島有兩小時時差。

B ▶ We have arranged a city tour to downtown, plus a shopping at outlets of the mall. And a visit to Two Lovers' Point, the most famous scenic spot in Guam, is also included in the trip.

同仁 B ▶ 已有安排關島市區觀光，外加到大賣場商店購物。行程也會去遊覽關島著名景點『戀人岬』。

A ▶ People suggested that we may enjoy all facilities in the five-star hotel, which offer something like big swimming pool, tennis

同仁 A ▶ 也有人建議也可享受五星飯店度假設施，有提供大型游泳

courts, fitness centers, pool bars, beach clubs, and open-air spas. Water motorcycles, "banana" boats, and parasailing are also available in the gulf, but these have to be paid with charges.

池，網球場，健身房，池畔酒吧，海灘俱樂部及露天按摩浴池等。海灣內也可騎乘水上摩托車、香蕉船或拖曳傘，不過這些需自費。

B ▶ To have an amorous feeling of South-pacific customs, perhaps we travel around the island by renting cars. It is very convenient to rent a car in Guam without changing international driving licenses. Within one year of the valid date, Taiwanese licenses are in common use in Guam.

同仁 B ▶ 為體會南太平洋度假風情，或是可租車來趟環島之旅。在關島租車很方便，不需更換國際駕照。台灣駕照在有效期限一年內可於關島通用。

✈

Incentive Travel

🖋 給力單字

1. **idea** 主意；打算；計畫[（+of）]
   He hit upon the good idea of spending the weekend in the nearby holiday camp.
   他想到去附近度假營過週末這個好主意。

2. **happen to** (*ph.*) 碰巧
   He happened to have a vacation last week.
   他上週碰巧渡假去了。

3. **call** (*v.t.*) 召開，下令舉行
   For the emergency transportation issue, they called a meeting immediately.
   因為緊急交通問題，他們立即召開了一個會議。

4. **single** (*adj.*)　單一的，唯一的
Due to the hectic travel season, they selected the only single hotel in the region.
由於旅遊旺季，他們僅可選擇當地唯一飯店。

5. **budget** (*n.*)　預算；生活費，經費[（+for）]
It is essential to balance one's budget.
量入為出是很重要的。

6. **travel** (*v.t.*)　旅行
If I had a lot of money I'd travel.
我如果有很多的錢，就外出去旅行。

7. **estimate** (*v.t.*)　估計，估量[（+at）]
The company's incentive travel cost is estimated to be two million dollars.
公司獎勵旅遊費用估計為兩百萬元。

8. **time difference** (*ph.*)　時差
The time difference between Taiwan and the U.S. is about 13 hours.
美國與台灣時差大約 13 個小時。

9. **outlet** (*n.*)　銷路；商店
There several outlets in the shopping mall.
在購物中心裡有好幾家商店。

10. **scenic spot** (*ph.*)　景點
We visited many famous scenic spots on the island.
我們造訪島上許多著名景點。

11. **spa** (*n.*)　礦泉療養地【美】按摩浴缸
There are spa centers in the resort hotel.
在渡假旅館裡有礦泉療養設備。

12. **parasailing** (*n.*)　拖曳傘
Parasailing is a popular and exciting activity in the beach.
在海灘上拖曳傘是相當受歡迎及刺激之活動。

13. **around the island** (*ph.*)　環島
They spent seven days for a trip around the island.
他們花了七天時間去環島旅行。

14. **in common use** (*ph.*)　通用
The U.S. dollar is a world currency in common use.
美金為世界通用貨幣。

Incentive Travel

給力句型

1. idea　想法

*idea that

What do you think of this idea that we should travel by a cruise liner?
你認為大家都搭乘遊輪旅行這個想法怎麼樣？

*it is sb's idea to do sth

It was Mary's idea to travel by a cruise liner.
搭乘遊輪旅行是瑪麗的主意。

*good/great idea

What a good idea!
真是一個好主意！

2. single 一個

*not a single

We didn't get a single reply to our advertisement.
我們的廣告連一個回應也沒有。

*the single most/biggest/greatest etc

Cigarette smoking is the single most important cause of lung cancer.
吸煙是導致肺癌的一個最重要的原因。

*every single word/day etc

There's no need to write down every single word I say.
沒有必要把我說的每一個字都記下來。

3. travel 旅遊

*travel by train/car etc

We travelled by train across Eastern Europe.
我們乘火車遊歷了東歐。

4. estimate 估計

*a rough estimate 粗略估計

At a rough estimate I'd say it's about 150 miles.
粗略估計，我覺得約有 150 英里。

*a conservative estimate 保守的估計

That seems a conservative estimate to me.
我覺得那是一個保守的估計。

5. outlet 商店，通路

*retail outlet

Benetton has retail outlets in every major European city.
貝納通公司在歐洲各主要城市都有零售店。

職場補給 Qualified & Safe 合格且安全

在規劃有關旅遊交通，要選擇交通部觀光局（Tourism Bureau）核准及信譽良好的合法旅行社，應以『預算』而非用『價格』作為行程之標準。一般而言，參加低團費之團體較容易產生糾紛；因為旅行業者為彌補團費，多半會安排團員購物或強行推銷自費行程。因此出國前，要完全了解行程內容，尤其是交通、住宿，餐點、自費行程的選擇及安排。

必須要求旅行社派領有執業證書的領隊帶團，並要求旅行社安排合格安全的交通工具（transportation vehicles）及旅遊活動。參加行前說明會並與旅行社簽訂旅遊契約，同時可向旅行社索取代收轉付收據以維護自身權益。另要購買旅遊平安及醫療保險（travel and medical insurance），並詳加了解保險的項目，以確保自身的權益。

自備慣用藥品或外用藥膏，避免攜帶粉狀藥物，以免被誤為毒品，且應先到醫院索取附有中文說明的英文診斷書（diagnosis）備用。途中如身體不適，不隨便吃別人的藥，宜告知領隊安排就醫。

攜帶數張照片備用，另將機票、護照、簽證、結匯收據、簽帳卡等證件影印乙份和正本分開攜帶，以備掛失，或申請補發。準備一份旅遊地點之台灣駐外辦事處（foreign institutions）通訊資料，隨身攜帶。

達人提點 A Matter Needs Your Attention 注意事項

- 參加水上活動時，宜多備一套衣物，以防衣服濺濕時可更換。隨身攜帶水壺，以補充水份，水不能生飲，椰子汁雖便宜，不宜多喝。飲食不要過量，並注意其新鮮度，儘量不生食海鮮。不吃食保育類野生動物之食品及加工品。

從事空域及水上活動如游泳、水上摩托車和快艇、拖曳傘、浮潛等注意事項：

- 參加水上活動宜結伴同行，並了解活動場地是否合法及器材的使用操作，聽從專業教練指導，浮潛裝備不能替代游泳能力，不會游泳者，不要嘗試。

- 參加外島的活動行程，宜要求旅行社安排合法的交通船，嚴格遵守穿救生衣的規定，且應全程穿著，如未提供救生衣，則應主動要求。

- 乘坐遊艇及水上摩托車，不跨越安全海域，泳客亦不能在水上摩托車、快艇、拖曳傘等水上活動範圍區內游泳。

- 注意活動區域之安全標示、救援設備及救生人員設置地點。

- 應注意自己的身體狀況，有心臟病、高血壓、感冒、發燒、醉酒、孕婦及餐後，不參加拖曳傘及水上活動及浮潛，感覺身體疲倦、寒冷時，應立即離水上岸。

- 避免長時間浸在水中及曝曬在陽光下，亦不長時間閉氣潛水造成暈眩導至溺斃；潛入水裡時不使用耳塞，因壓力會使耳塞衝擊耳膜造成傷害。浮潛時切勿以頭部先入水，並應攜帶漂浮裝備。

● 乘坐遊艇前宜先了解遊艇的載客量，如有超載應予拒乘，搭乘時不集中甲板一方，以免船身失去平衡。

　對於旅行社安排行程之外的各種水上活動，參加前應謹慎評估其安全性及自身的身體狀況。當然還有很多的注意事項，請記得安全最重要，毒品、大麻、搖頭丸不要碰，走私販毒罪更重。

Incentive Travel

2-3 住宿
Hotel Accommodations

情境設定

The arrangement of hotel accommodations reflects the satisfaction in travel and its success or not? This, together with other issues, is discussed by the two colleagues in their dialogue, as follows：

飯店住宿安排直接反映旅遊滿意度及旅遊成功與否？這些連同其它問題經由兩位同仁以下對話：

角色設定

Colleague A：同仁 A
Colleague B：同仁 B

情境 1 Travel Satisfaction 旅遊滿意度

情境對話

A ► Compared with transportation, hotel room and board is an important issue when the company conducts the incentive travel. Relevant arrangements are expected to affect

同仁 A ► 與『交通』問題比較起來，『飯店及食宿』可謂公司在安排獎勵旅遊時極為最重要

the satisfaction of employees and the basic target of the trip.

之工作。因為有關的安排等會直接影響到員工對獎勵旅遊的滿意度及基本目標。

B ▶ I completely agree with your points. Whether the incentive travel will be successful of not depends on the orientation of above work and real experience of employees who participate in the trip.

同仁 B ▶ 我非常同意您的觀點。上述工作之定位操作是否得宜，或是參與獎勵旅遊員工的實際經驗，關係到整個獎勵旅遊的成功與否？

A ▶ We have to assign a specialist to be in charge of the work, with a preparation period of between three to six months. Meanwhile, the budget has yet to be finalized, and this will pave the way for follow-up moves.

同仁 A ▶ 關於這項工作我們必須派有專人負責，籌備時間以三至六個月為宜。另外，仍需要確定預算才有利後續動作的進行。

B ▶ I suggest that the incentive travel not be held in high season. This lowers the cost and also makes it smooth of both transportation and hotel room and board arrangements.

同仁 B ▶ 我建議公司此次獎勵旅遊的時間應盡量避開旅遊旺季。這樣不但可減少成本，同時在交通、住宿的安排也會比較順利。

A ▶ To my understanding so far, the allocation of budget in the incentive travel is as follows: airline tickets, 30%; hotel accommodations, 30%; food and beverage,

同仁 A ▶ 目前就我所知，本次獎勵旅遊預算分配：機票占 30%，住宿占 30%，食物及

20%. Transportation pick-ups and miscellaneous fee represent the share of 20%.

飲料占 20％，另外交通接送以及雜項費用占 20％。

B ▸ How do you evaluate on the local infrastructures of the upcoming incentive travel such as its airport, transportation facilities, environment sanitation, hotel, and service standards?

同仁 B ▸ 您如何評估有關此次獎勵旅遊當地的基礎設施如機場、道路交通運輸設備、環境衛生、旅館設備與服務水準？

A ▸ The incentive travel needs to hold a large sized meeting and gala banquet this time. It is a must to communicate with all authorities concerned especially the hotel, and start the coordination for this purpose soon.

同仁 A ▸ 本次獎勵旅遊也需要舉辦大型的會議及主題宴會。因此必須事先與各有關單位，尤其是住宿飯店等溝通，並儘快展開針對此項作業與協調的工作。

B ▸ I think that the after-work assessment is a best reference to the plan of incentive travel next time. To the company, the incentive travel defines as a "trip with target", and its assessment outcome is comparably important to enterprise.

同仁 B ▸ 我認為結束後的評估作業可作為下次實行獎勵旅遊計畫的最佳參考。因為獎勵旅遊對公司而言是一種「有目的的旅遊」，評估結果對企業也顯得相對重要。

給力單字

1. **room and board** (*ph.*) 【美】食宿；膳宿
We will provide room and board for them.
我們將提供他們的食宿。
I pay $100 a week for room and board.
我每週付 100 美元膳宿費。

2. **relevant** (*adj.*) 有關的，切題的
For relevant information, please see the room service manual of the hotel.
有關詳情，請查閱本飯店客房服務手冊。

3. **orientation** (*n.*) 方向；傾向性
The hotel has all facility directories for the orientation purpose.
該飯店設立所有指示性導覽以辨清方向。

4. **participate** (*v.t.*) 參加，參與[（+in）]
Not everyone can participate in this incentive travel.
並不是每個人都能參加此次獎勵旅遊。

5. **preparation** (*n.*) 準備工作，準備措施[（+for）]
We've made preparations for the incentive travel.
我們已經為獎勵旅遊作好了準備。

6. **pave the way for** (*ph.*) 為某人鋪平道路
The company had paved the way for the marketing of their new product.
這個公司為促銷他們的新產品做了安排。
His economic policies paved the way for industrial expansion.
他的經濟政策為企業的擴展鋪平了道路。

Incentive Travel

7. **high season** 【英】旅遊旺季

The high season begins in March and ends by the end of May each year.

每年旅遊開始於三月份，並於五月底結束。

8. **lower** (*v.t.*) 減低；減弱

We have to lower our expenses.

我們得減少開支。

9. **allocation** (*n.*) 撥給；分配

The budget allocation for hotel accommodations represents a lion's share for the trip.

本次旅行分配給飯店住宿之預算占了最大比例。

10. **accommodations** (*n.*) 【美】住宿膳食服務

The cost of accommodations is reasonable in this hotel.

這間飯店住宿費用很合理。

11. **infrastructure** (*n.*) 基礎設施；基礎結構

This hotel needs more room infrastructures to attract guests.

這家飯店需要更多住房基礎設施已吸引客人。

12. **facilities** (*n.*) 設施

It is a 5-star hotel with fantastic facilities

這是一間設施完善的五星級酒店。

13. **communicate** (*v.t.*) 與（某人）溝通

It is a must to communicate with the hotel for accommodations and among others.

跟飯店溝通有關住宿及其它事項是有必要的。

14. **coordination** (*n.*) 協調

Good coordination with the hotel will smooth your accommodations in the trip.

與飯店有好的協調讓你的旅行住宿事情變順暢。

15. **assessment** (*n.*) 評價，估計

The executive made a careful assessment of the proposed incentive travel.

該主管對獎勵旅遊計畫提議作了詳細的評估。

16. **outcome** (*n.*) 結果；結局[（+of）]

The company was satisfied with the outcome of incentive travel.

公司對本次獎勵旅遊的結果很滿意。

Incentive Travel

給力句型

1. room 房間，位置

*there's room to do sth

There wasn't really room to lie down comfortably.
地方實在太小，無法舒服地躺下。

*have room (for sth)

Have you got room for some dessert?
你還吃得下甜點嗎？

2. board 膳食

*full/half board

The hotel offer full board for guests.
該飯店供一日三餐膳食。

*board of directors

There is still only one woman on the board of directors.
董事會中仍然只有一位女性。

*sit on a board

He sits on the hospital management board.
他是醫院管理委員會委員。

3. preparation　準備

*make preparations

The company is making preparations for a trip of its employees.
公司正在為員工旅遊作準備。

*in preparation for

Justin had opened several bottles of wine in preparation for the party.
賈斯汀已開了好幾瓶葡萄酒為聚會作準備。

情境 2　Hotel, Restaurant, & Delicacies 飯店、餐廳、與美食

情境對話

A ▶ What are your opinions on the hotel accommodations recommended by the travel agent for the incentive travel to Guam, and how about their restaurants and food?

同仁 A ▶ 對於旅行社推薦本次到關島獎勵旅遊進駐的幾家飯店，包括各家的餐廳及美食，您有何看法？

B ▶ In fact, the hotel's room and board mainly involves the budget issue, and the recommendation is classified as very high

同仁 B ▶ 其實飯店住宿主要是牽涉預算的問題，本次旅行社所推薦

grade hotels. For instance, Hyatt Regency Hotel Guam owns 455 guest rooms and is an international first rate hotel. It takes about 10 minutes of driving to the airport, and the pick-up service is available.

的都是歸類為很優的飯店。例如關島君悅大飯店擁有 455 間客房，是國際頂級飯店。且距離機場車程僅 10 分鐘，並有機場接送服務。

A ▸ I heard that Hyatt is located in the transportation hub of Guam, and is accessible to the core areas of business, shopping, and entertainment centers. The hotel offers food and beverages mainly in western and Japanese styles.

同仁 A ▸ 聽說君悅飯店位居關島交通樞紐及鄰近商務、購物、和娛樂之核心地帶。它的餐飲主要提供西餐及日式。

B ▸ As a resort hotel, Hyatt possesses many recreational facilities, plus a 150-meter long beach. It is also equipped with a conventional center and banquet room, which are ideal for the purpose of incentive travel to come.

同仁 B ▸ 作為度假旅館，君悅擁有許多的休閒設施，包括 150 米長海灘。當然還附設有會議中心、宴會廳等，非常適合我們即將舉辦獎勵旅遊之用途。

A ▸ Is that possible to choose Outrigger Guam Resort if we want to stay in a more luxurious hotel? Most Japanese are fond of this hotel.

同仁 A ▸ 如果想要住豪華一點的話，我們是否可選擇奧瑞格飯店？日本人很喜愛住這裡。

B ▸ Since Outrigger Guam Resort is located in the center of Guam, it enjoys a convenient

同仁 B ▸ 因為奧瑞格飯店剛好位於關島中心

Incentive Travel

transportation! As for the room price, it is much expensive due to its exclusive level, of course.

點，交通很便利！至於它的房價，因為整個很高級，當然就比較貴。

A ▶ With a total of 426 rooms, Westin Hotel is another famous five-star hotel in Guam. Each room has a Jacuzzi message bathtub, and the overall quality of its facilities is just fine.

同仁 A ▶ 另外，威仕丁飯店擁有 426 間客房，也是關島知名五星級飯店。每間浴室裝有熱水按摩浴缸等特別設施；整體來說，房間設施品質還算不錯。

B ▶ In terms of general five-star hotels in Guam, I highly recommend Fiesta Hotel; very tidy and comfortable, and renovated recently. And the ocean view of its sea-front room is fantastic!

同仁 B ▶ 以一般級五星級飯店而言，我極度推薦關島悅泰飯店；很整潔又舒服，最近才重新整修過。而且面海房間海景真的是美呆了！

In related options, Hotel Nikko Guam is another good hotel. Its gorgeous restaurants offer Chinese food, Japanese cooking, tropical food, sea food, and traditional bars.

在相關選項裡，關島日航飯店也算是很好的飯店。它的豪華餐廳有多種美食，包括中式餐館、日本料理、熱帶風味餐館、海鮮屋、以及傳統酒吧。

給力單字

1. **recommend** 推薦，介紹[（+as/for）]
   Can you recommend me some new hotels in Guam?
   你能推薦一些關島的新飯店給我嗎？

2. **classified** (v.t.) 將…分類；分等級
   Hotels are classified according to facilities.
   飯店按設施大小分等級。

3. **first rate** (adj.) 第一流的，極好的
   It is a first-rate hotel in the nation.
   它是國內第一流的飯店。

4. **accessible** (adj.) 易到達的；易進入的
   The presidential suite rooms are only accessible by the penthouse.
   總統套房只有從頂樓才能進入。

5. **core** (n.) 核心，精髓[the S][（+of）]
   We would like to take a look of the hotel's core facilities.
   我們想看一下飯店的核心設施。

6. **possess** (v.t.) 擁有，具有
   The hotel possesses very beautiful sea views.
   這個飯店擁有非常漂亮的海景。

7. **equip** (v.t.) 裝備，配備[（+for/with）]
   Our hotel is well equipped in the internet service.
   我們的飯店網路裝備良好。

8. **luxurious** (adj.) 豪華的；非常舒適的
   They stayed in luxurious hotels.
   他們住在豪華的旅館裡。

Incentive Travel

The bathroom was luxurious, with gold taps and a thick carpet.

浴室很奢華，配有金水龍頭和厚地毯。

9. **be fond of**　喜歡，愛好
I am very fond of this hotel.
我非常喜歡這家飯店。

10. **convenient** (*adj.*)　合宜的；方便的[（+for/to）]
Please come whenever it is convenient to you.
方便的時候，請隨時來。

11. **exclusive** (*adj.*)　高級的；時髦的
This is the most exclusive night club in the hotel.
這是該飯店的最高檔的夜總會。

12. **Jacuzzi** (*n.*)　【商標】熱水漩水式浴缸
Most international hotels offer Jacuzzi in their bathrooms.
大部分國際飯店浴室裡都有裝設熱水漩水式浴缸。

13. **facility** (*n.*)　設備，設施[（+for）]
The hotel had no cooking facilities in the room.
飯店房間裡沒有燒煮設備。

14. **tidy** (*adj.*)　整潔的，井然的
The hotel room is always clean and tidy.
飯店的房間總是乾淨整潔。

15. **sea-front room** (*ph.*)　面海岸，海邊房間
I reserved a sea-front room in the hotel.
我跟飯店預訂一間面海的房間。

16. **gorgeous** (*adj.*)　燦爛的，華麗的
The dining-room was gorgeous.
餐廳很豪華。

給力句型

1. recommend 建議，推薦

*recommend that

The travel agent recommended that all guests should stay in the nearby hotels for the convenient coordination purpose.
旅行社建議所有客人都要住在附近之飯店，以方便聯絡之目的。

*recommend doing sth

The hotel manager recommends changing the room due to a flooding in the bathroom.
因為浴室淹水的問題飯店經理建議更換房間。

2. equip 裝備

*equip sb/sth

It cost $100,000 to equip the hotel.
裝備飯店花費了 10 萬美元。

*well/poorly/fully etc equipped

It was a modern, bright, well equipped hotel.
那是一家現代化、明亮且設備精良的飯店。

3. convenient 方便的

*convenient for sb

Is three o'clock convenient for you?
三點鐘你方便嗎？

*convenient time/moment

I'm afraid this isn't a very convenient time - could you call back later?
我想現在不是很合適，你能稍後再打電話來嗎？

Incentive Travel

*convenient for sth

Our hotel is very convenient for stores.
我們的飯店離商店很近。

職場補給 Reservations & Check-in 訂房與入住

- 有關安排飯店住宿，可自行先上網站（例如：www.agoda.com）搜尋可立即有房間入住之飯店，選擇入住（check-in）日期及退房（check-out）日期，並完成訂房交易。

- 預約或入住飯店時，務必提供與護照相同之正確英文名字。因為飯店不會臨時接受更改或變動名字，而原有之訂房（room reservations）也將被取消，也可能產生另外之費用。

- 一般之訂房網站採用線上刷卡或銀行 ATM 轉帳。未先預付款者，系統將不會進行任何預約作業。

- 訂房經過確認後，飯店會將確認（confirmation）通知單寄到個人的電子信裡。信中會詳載您的訂房資料與附住宿券（vouchers），出國前要記得先行列印出，以便持往國外使用。要特別注意，憑護照及住宿券辦理入住登記。

- 入住登記（registration）時，要正確填寫住宿者之資料；若不符合有關規定，飯店有權收取差價或當場要求全額付費。

- 另有關『旅行業代收轉付收據（receipts）』，請旅行社業者於訂購日後，儘速郵寄至您所指定之住址。如需作為公司報帳，要請註明公司抬頭及統一編號。

達人提點 **Tips 小費**

- 房價為每晚每房之售價，包含房價、稅金、服務費，唯部分城市之政府可能在不特定期間徵收非常規之人頭費（head money）或特別稅（special duties），此部分要事先問清楚，以免屆時措手不及。

- 房價不含床頭、行李小費、客房附加服務費（surcharges）或其他私人消費支出。

Incentive Travel

2-4 頒獎典禮 Awarding Ceremony

情境設定

Before the awarding ceremony is held, the ceremony worker and his colleague reviewed their preparing works, and among others. In the following conversation, certain arrangements are discussed in details.

在頒獎典禮舉行前夕，典禮工作人員與其同事共同檢視他們的籌備工作，以及其他事項。以下對話，討論到確定之安排細節。

角色設定

Ceremony Worker：典禮工作人員
Colleague：同事

情境 1 Ceremony Logistics 典禮籌備

情境對話

Ceremony Worker ▶ I expect the awarding ceremony be held with dignity and solemnity. This ensures the main purpose and

典禮工作人員 ▶ 我期望本次頒獎活動能夠以莊嚴、隆重方式舉行。這

represents the "guest of honor" for the ceremony.

Colleague ▶ Yes, I understand. For this purpose, we have already divided the ceremony into four working groups, including administrations, pre-awarding, on the day, and follow-ups.

Ceremony Worker ▶ I will confirm the list of rewarded delegates and participations of ranking officials as soon as possible. Please also inform those attendees to pay attention on their attires and demeanors.

Colleague ▶ Please be sure to prepare a manuscript of speech for the chairman, and send it to the Secretariat one week before presenting the ceremony.

Ceremony Worker ▶ No problem, I will instruct the Secretariat to do this assignment. A copy of speech will also be put in the chairman's seat for his references on the ceremony day.

Colleague ▶ Prior to the ceremony, we have to ponder over other works, such as place

也確定並表示典禮將『以客為尊』之目的。

同事 ▶ 是的，我知道。因此，我們也將頒獎工作分成四個工作小組，包括：行政作業、頒獎前準備、頒獎當天、及後續工作等。

典禮工作人員 ▶ 我也會儘快確認此次受獎代表名單及高階主管出席與否，並也請您告知所有出席者重視自己服裝及儀容整齊。

同事 ▶ 請確定要準備好董事長頒獎致詞講稿，並於典禮舉辦前一週送至秘書處。

典禮工作人員 ▶ 好的。我會交辦秘書處辦理此項差事。另外也會備一份於典禮當天放在主席位子上以供參考。

同事 ▶ 頒獎之前，我們還要考慮其他許多事

Incentive Travel

setting, seating charts, rehearsals, and receptions. By the way, photographers and a disc jockey for music have to be arranged in advance.

情，包括場地佈置、座次安排及綵排、及接待等事宜。順便提起，要提前安排好攝影師及播放音樂之工作人員。

Ceremony Worker ▶ And we almost forgot to find a competent master of ceremonies (an emcee). This is very important as all procedures and orders of the awarding are controlled in his (or her) hands.

典禮工作人員 ▶ 還有，我們差點忘記安排找一位稱職的大會司儀，因為相關流程及領獎順序都需要靠他(或她)去全盤掌握活動之進行。

Colleague ▶ Receptionists are essential too; they make the ceremony operation more smooth and let participants feel they are respected adequately.

同事 ▶ 會場接待人員也是必要的；他們會讓典禮進行更為順暢，也會令參加頒獎者有如貴賓般充分被尊重的感受。

給力單字

1. **dignity** (*n.*)　莊重，尊嚴
The ceremony is held in a dignified and honorable way.
這個典禮以尊嚴和體面的方式舉行。

2. **solemnity** (*n.*)　隆重的儀式
The ceremony was presided over by the President with solemnities.
總統以隆重方式主持該典禮。

3. **administration** (*n.*)　行政；管理
We're looking for someone with administration in international conferences.
我們正在尋求一個有國際會議行政管理經驗的人。

4. **follow-ups** (*ph.*)　後續行動；事宜
We are responsible for handling follow-ups of the ceremony.
我們要負責典禮後續工作事宜。

5. **delegate** (*n.*)　代表
They sent five delegates to the conference this time.
這次他們派了五個代表來參加會議。

6. **attire** (*n.*)　服裝，衣著
All delegates of the ceremony are required in formal attires.
所有出席典禮代表被要求要著正式服裝。

7. **manuscript** (*n.*)　手寫本，手稿
Delegates have to prepare their own speech manuscripts.
代表們必須準備自己的演講手稿。

8. **the Secretariat** (*n.*)　秘書處
The Secretariat has drafted a chairman's speech for the ceremony.
秘書處有草擬一份理事長典禮演講稿。

Incentive Travel

167

9. **instruct** (*v.t.*)　指示，吩咐

The ceremony workers are instructed to finish the assignment today.

典禮工作人員被吩咐必須於今天內完成所指派之工作。

10. **assignment** (*n.*)　分配；指派

He is responsible for the assignment of jobs .

他負責分派工作。

11. **prior to**　在…之前；首要

Prior to the ceremony, each work should take up its proper place.

在典禮舉行前，每項工作必須就定位。

12. **ponder** (*v.t.*)　仔細考慮；衡量

He pondered the problem for several days.

他對這個問題考慮了好幾天。

13. **master of ceremonies**　典禮主持人；司儀

It is not easy to find a competent master of ceremonies.

要找到一位稱職的司儀是不太容易的。

14. **procedure** (*n.*)　程序；手續

The chairman was quite familiar with the procedure for conducting a meeting.

主席對開會的程序很熟悉。

15. **receptionist** (*n.*)　接待員；傳達員

We need to hire more receptionists for the ceremony.

我們需要聘用更多典禮接待人員。

16. **essential** (*adj.*)　本質的，實質的

There is no essential difference between the two drafts .

兩份草稿沒有本質上的不同。

給力句型

1. ponder 考慮

   *ponder how/what/whether etc

   He well ponders what would happen in the ceremony.
   他充分考慮到典禮將會發生哪些事情。

   *ponder over sth

   He sat down pondering over the process of the ceremony.
   他坐下來細細地思考着典禮進行的流程。

2. instruct 指示

   *instruct sb to do sth

   Our ceremony staff have been instructed to offer you every assistance.
   我們的典禮工作人員已收到指示為您提供一切幫助。

   *as instructed 依照指示

   We'll finish the work as instructed.
   我們將依照指示完成工作。

3. assignment 任務；工作

   *on an assignment

   He was sent abroad on a special assignment.
   他接受委派出國去執行一項特殊任務。

Incentive Travel

情境 2 Working Colleagues 工作夥伴

情境對話

Ceremony Worker ▶ The company decides to invite the President and VIPs to attend the awarding ceremony, and the administration group should send out the invitation card and confirm their participation.

典禮工作人員 ▶ 公司已經決定將邀請總統頒獎及貴賓觀禮，請告知行政組要先寄上請柬並確認出席。

Colleague ▶ The Secretariat has liaised with the Presidential Palace about the invitation. If the president accepts the invitation, we will prepare a speech for his presence on the ceremony.

同事 ▶ 秘書處已聯絡總統府有關邀請事宜；如總統接受邀請，我們會幫他的出席準備一份典禮演講稿。

Ceremony Worker ▶ So far how is the preparation work for the award ceremony? Is there anything that you need me to deal with?

典禮工作人員 ▶ 目前頒獎典禮準備工作做的如何？你們有無需要我處理之事？

Colleague ▶ So far so good. Producing medals is the only thing which is yet to be waited for final approval by the chairman, however.

同事 ▶ 到為前為止尚稱順利。惟一獎牌製作方案尚待董事長做最後核准。

Ceremony Worker ▶ In terms of design, it is a must for the medal to show prominent contribution of the outstanding personnel,

典禮工作人員 ▶ 獎牌在設計上要凸顯出得獎人之傑出貢獻，也同時傳達公司形象及企業文

170

and to relay the company image and culture. Thus, I will ratify the approval immediately.

化。因此，我會立刻核准有關之提案。

Colleague ▶ Thank you so much for your instruction. I will remind the general affairs section to pay more attention on this issue when producing medals.

同事 ▶ 非常感您的指示。我將提醒總務科特別注意獎牌製作問題。

Incentive Travel

給力單字

1. **invite** (*v.t.*) 邀請，招待
   He invited several of his friends to the show.
   他邀請了幾個朋友去看表演。

2. **VIPs (Very Important Persons)** 重要人物，貴賓
   Several VIPs are invited to attend the inauguration ceremony.
   許多貴賓被邀參加就職典禮。

3. **liaise** (*v.t.*) 聯絡
   Part of his job as a ceremony worker is to liaise with the organizer.
   作為一個典禮工作人員，他的部分工作是聯絡主辦單位。

4. **presence** (*n.*) 出席，在場
   Your presence is requested.
   敬請光臨。

5. **preparation** (n.) （具體的）準備工作[（+for）]
   We made preparations for the ceremony.
   我們為典禮作準備。

6. **deal** (*v.t.*)　處理，對付[（+with）]

She is an expert in dealing with difficulties.

她是一名專門排除困難的專家。

7. **so far so good** (*ph.*)　到為前為止尚稱順利

Asked about preparations at the ceremony, he replied, "So far so good."

被問到有關典禮準備的工作，他回答：「截至目前，一切還好。」

8. **approval** (*n.*)　批准；認可

The awarding ceremony plan had the approval of the authorities.

頒獎典禮計畫得到當局的認可。

9. **medal** (*n.*)　獎章，勛章[C]

She won an Asian Games gold medal in weight lifting.

她獲得亞運會舉重金牌。

10. **relay** (*v.t.*)　分程傳遞；轉達

Please relay this important information to the ceremony organizer immediately.

請立即將此重要訊息轉達典禮主辦單位知悉。

11. **instruction** (*n.*)　命令，指示[+to]

They had carried out my instructions to the letter.

他們嚴格地按我的指示把事辦了。

12. **general affairs section**　總務科

The general affairs section is always responsible for trivial matters of the ceremony.

總務科經常要負責處理典禮中的一些瑣事。

給力句型

1. preparation　準備

   *be in preparation　在準備中

   Plans for the award ceremony are now in preparation.
   舉辦頒獎典禮的計畫則正在準備之中。

   *make preparations

   A working team is making preparations for the award ceremony.
   有工作小組正在為頒獎典禮作準備。

2. approval　同意

   *for approval

   He submitted the ceremony proposal for approval.
   他遞交該典禮企劃案希望得到認可。

   *meet with sb's approval　得到某人的批准

   The ceremony proposals met with the organizer's approval.
   典禮提案得到了主辦單位的批准。

   *seal of approval　認可，接受

   The organizer has given its seal of approval to the planning of ceremony.
   主辦單位已經認可這個典禮企劃案。

Incentive Travel

職場補給 **Ceremony Process 頒獎流程**

頒獎前要撰寫「頒獎提示稿」，供頒獎者瞭解頒獎事由。另也需要撰寫「頒獎宣讀稿（announcement）」，供司儀宣讀，以表彰受獎人。預先通知各受獎人，於頒獎典禮前提早二十分鐘到達會場。

確定受獎者頒獎前之就座位置及頒獎順序，核對受獎人及獎牌（medals）之姓名。如受獎者為係具特定事蹟、重大貢獻需特別表彰者，儘量一次排定每次一人上頒獎臺為原則。其他一般表揚，每次以不超過 10 人上頒獎臺為原則。

規劃受獎人上台、退場動線—以面向舞台（stage），由右方上台，左方退場為原則。確定「頒、受獎人位置」，並於頒受獎區貼妥標示線。指派專人負責照相事宜。

將獎牌送至會場，並預演頒獎流程。獎牌之包裝紙等物品請置於會場外，俟禮成後由引導員（ushers）帶至會場外包裝。

頒獎當天準備事宜：
1. 將獎牌事先依受獎人受獎順序整齊排放。
2. 受獎人蒞場後，請向受獎人說明頒獎流程，必要時先行演練，以確保頒獎秩序。
3. 受獎人到達時，由引導員引導接待就座；若受獎人因故缺席或臨時更換，頒獎單位應即時通知司儀，頒獎時宣讀「代表受獎人之單位、姓名」。

達人提點 **Etiquette** 禮儀

頒獎時應注意獎牌之文字方向，以示尊重受獎人。

1. 立式（vertical type）獎座：字面朝頒獎人。
2. 平面（horizontal）獎牌：字首朝傳遞人，字面朝上。

　如需照相，由引導員引導頒（受）獎人於舞台中央進行；頒獎者立於前排中央位置。會後將照片送交頒（受）獎人以為紀念。

　主辦單位仍應視實際受獎人數及頒獎場地權宜處理、實際演練，以確保流程順暢及儀式莊重。

Incentive Travel

2-5 主題晚宴
Theme Banquet

 Amway Taiwan Trip 安利台灣行

情境設定

Taiwan hosted a successful theme banquet for distinguished guests from Amway of China. In the following dialogue, two colleagues of the organizer revealed these unprecedented arrangements and the colorful contents of the activity.

台灣為來自中國安利公司貴賓主辦了一場成功的主題晚宴。以下對話中，兩位主辦單位工作人員及同事透露此次史無前例與精彩的晚宴內容。

角色設定

Banquet Worker：晚宴工作人員
Colleague：同事

情境對話

Banquet Worker ▶ People said that the arrangement of a perfect theme banquet is a vital engineering. Each detail has to be arranged skillfully, including entertainment programs, stage designs, background music,

晚宴工作人員 ▶ 有人說安排一場完美的主題晚宴可謂是一項充滿活力的工程。包括娛興節目與舞台的設計、襯場音

flower arranging, delicacies, and even theme clothing.

樂和花飾、美食、甚至是主題服飾，每一細節都需要經過巧妙地安排。

Colleague ▶ The Amway Co. of China conducted an incentive travel to Taiwan in March of 2009 and held an "Impressive Treasure Island" theme banquet in Shuinan Economic & Trade Park in Taichung. The theme banquet was successful to create a carnival-like atmosphere on that night.

同事 ▶ 2009 年三月中國安利公司到台灣中部進行寶島之旅獎勵旅遊，在台中水湳經貿園區舉辦一場「印象寶島」主題晚宴。當晚現場創造猶如嘉年華會熱烈氣氛，就是一個相當成功的案例。

Banquet Worker ▶ Taichung mayor Jason Hu was invited to address for the theme banquet. He welcomed the visit of tourists from mainland China to the city, and hoped that they enjoyed stays and shopping to the full.

晚宴工作人員 ▶ 主辦單位並邀請台中市長胡志強致詞。他歡迎大陸觀光客到台中市，希望賓客們盡興逗留、買得更高興。

Colleague ▶ With a price of NT$45,000 per table, the theme banquet served a total of 160 tables, and offered all genuine food from north to south in Taiwan, the report said. In order to control the serving speed, 80 chefs were mobilized, plus a total of over 500 waiters.

同事 ▶ 據報載該主題晚宴，席開一百六十桌，集合台灣從南到北道地的食材，每桌單價桌新台幣四萬五千元。為了掌控出菜速度，動員了八十名廚師；服務人員超過五百人。

Banquet Worker ▶ The theme banquet combined the performance of Taiwanese hand puppet show, aboriginal dancing, Taichung City Band, and string quartet, leaving an enthusiastic and unforgettable night for distinguished guests.

晚宴工作人員 ▶ 本次主題晚宴節目結合台灣本土文化的布袋戲、原住民舞蹈、台中市大樂團、弦樂四重奏等表演，給大陸貴賓留下熱情難忘的一夜。

Colleague ▶ The organizer also built up a market place outside the banquet area as an attempt to let mainland China tourists experience Taiwan's night bazaar culture. Under the one-stop shopping service, those quests are able to display their purchasing powers as well.

同事 ▶ 主辦單位為了讓大陸賓客們體驗夜市場文化，另外在宴席會場周邊同時打造一個夜市。賓客可以一次購足，也展現他們的了消費實力。

Banquet Worker ▶ Both Sheraton Taipei Hotel and the Westin Taipei offered the catering service, and they delivered all tableware from Taipei. It cost a lot in table flowers, temporary kitchens, and refrigeration equipment.

晚宴工作人員 ▶ 喜來登飯店及六福皇宮飯店負責外燴服務，所有的餐具都從台北運送下來。還有餐桌布置的花卉、臨時搭建的廚房、冷藏設備等也花了不少錢。

Colleague ▶ Executives at the hotel shared the same view. They spent NT$8 million to buy brand new porcelain tableware and five different cups are available, including each for juice, soda, wine, beer, and millet wine.

同事 ▶ 飯店主管也分享相同看法。他們花了新台幣八百萬元採購全新的瓷器餐具，光是杯子就有五種，包括果汁杯、汽水杯、紅酒杯、啤酒杯及小米酒杯。

給力單字

1. **entertainment** (*n.*) 演藝；餘興
The entertainment program serves as an important role in the theme banquet.
餘興節目在主題晚宴裡扮演非常重要的角色。

2. **stage** (*n.*) 舞臺
The organizer requires more lighting on the stage.
主辦單位要求舞臺要多打燈光。

3. **economic and trade park** (*ph.*) 經貿園區
The city government is conducting the feasibility study for the establishment of the latest economic and trade park.
市政府正在研擬興建一個最新的經貿園區。

4. **carnival** (*n.*) 狂歡; 嘉年華會
The banquet was held in a carnival atmosphere.
晚宴於狂歡氣氛中進行。

5. **address** (*v.t.*) 致詞，發表演說
He is going to address the meeting.
他將向大會作演說。

6. **stay** (*n.*) 停留，逗留
These foreign guests made a very pleasant stay in Taiwan.
這些外賓在台灣做了一個非常愉快的停留。

7. **genuine** (*adj.*) 真的；名副其實的
The food is famous for its genuine ingredients.
這道食物以使用真材實料而知名。

Incentive Travel

8. **mobilize** (*v.t.*) 調動，召集
The government mobilizes workers to support the banquet activity.
政府動員工人去支援該宴會活動。

9. **aboriginal** (*adj.*) 土著的；土生的
There are several aboriginal languages on the island.
這個島上有多種土著語言。

10. **string quartet** (*ph.*) 弦樂四重奏（曲）
For the theme banquet, the organizer invited a string quartet from abroad.
為了主題宴會，主辦單位從國外邀請了弦樂四重奏。

11. **bazaar** (*n.*) 市場，市集
A charity bazaar was held in the theme banquet.
該主題晚宴舉辦了一場慈善義賣會。

12. **one-stop shopping** (*ph.*) 一站購足
Guests can also enjoy the one-stop shopping service in the theme banquet.
賓客可同時在主題宴會裡享受一站購足的服務。

13. **catering** (*n.*) 承辦飲食服務；外燴
This catering for the banquet was recommended by the organizer.
本次外燴酒席服務是由主辦單位推薦的。

14. **temporary** (*adj.*) 臨時的；暫時的
The organizer has got a temporary place for the banquet.
主辦單位為晚宴找到一個臨時場地。

15. **share** (*v.t.*)　分享；共同使用
The banquet organizer would like to share the success experience with his colleagues.
晚宴主辦者想與其同事共同分享成功的經驗。

16. **porcelain** (*n.*)　瓷；瓷器
Made of porcelain, the tableware is easily-broken if you are incautious.
由於餐具是瓷器做的，如果你不小心會很容易打破。

Incentive Travel

給力句型

1. mobilize　爭取支持／動用資源等

   He was trying to mobilize support for the banquet activity.
   他正為一個晚宴活動爭取支持。

2. temporary　臨時工，臨時雇員

   Many temporary workers are hired in the banquet.
   晚宴聘用了許多臨時雇員。

3. share　分享；共用
   *share sth with sb

   10 persons shared one table at the banquet.
   晚宴中每一張桌子由 10 人共用。

情境 2 **Hermes Example** 愛馬仕範例

情境對話

As a success example of its kind, Hermes' annual theme banquet caused great sensation of patrons in Taiwan. Enclosed are relevant clippings of the news report from the local media.

被認為是一場成功的主題晚宴範例，愛馬仕年度主題晚宴在台灣愛用者裡造成轟動。附件為本地媒體有關報導之剪輯。

Hermes, a France-based international brand, held its annual theme banquet "Festival Des Metiers" in Taipei's most flourishing Hsinyi Shopping District, and a total of 220 distinguished quests were invited to imitate the spirit of craftsman and happiness of the cooking by themselves.

法國時尚品牌愛馬仕年度的主題宴會「與愛馬仕工匠有約」，有兩百多位賓客接受邀請在台北繁華熱鬧的信義商圈，實際仿效工匠的精神以及自己動手做菜的樂趣。

Surprise 1 ▶ The demonstration of Hermes handicrafts
Before opening the theme banquet, all guests appreciated exquisite handicrafts of Hermes in the courtyard of Bella Vita Square, where Hermes craftsmen demonstrated how they produced saddles, "Kelly" bags, diamond inlaying, movement assembling of watches, silk scarf printing, Saint Louis crystal cups

驚奇 1 ▶ 工匠示範愛馬仕工藝
所有賓客在晚宴開始前，先在麗寶廣場（貴婦百貨）中庭的工藝節展覽會場欣賞來自愛馬仕工坊工匠們示範馬鞍製作、凱莉皮包縫製、褐鑽珠寶鑲嵌、鐘錶機

Incentive Travel

framed with 24-k gold, and among other techniques. Then, the cock-tail reception is served under the opening of carnival-like party.

芯組裝、絲巾印刷、手工挑絲絨與聖路易水晶杯手繪 24K 金邊裝飾等工藝。宴會在宛如嘉年華盛會般的雞尾酒會下揭開序幕。

"We were touched to witness the handicrafts personally, understanding our daily used goods are handmade by craftsmen", said customers who visited the theme banquet of Hermes. This enables us to know more about the spirit of Hermes and change views about the value of brand, they noted.

蒞臨愛馬仕主題晚宴顧客們表示，可以親眼見證工匠製作是一種感動的心情，知道自己平常經常在使用的物品，原來都是工匠們手工製作完成。認為此舉不僅讓我們更認識愛馬仕工藝的品牌精神，也改觀了對精品的價值。

Surprise 2 ▶ Guests turned into "food craftsmen"
Hermes guided its guests to the next surprise point after the reception. Two French chefs led each guest to wear an apron specially designed by Hermes and turned all 220 guests into "food craftsmen"! A food class was getting started from the design of dishes, process to learn cooking, and to kitchenware that are used.

驚奇 2 ▶ 賓客變身料理工匠
在酒會之後，愛馬仕將所有賓客引導至下一個驚喜點；兩位遠從法國而來的主廚帶領的 220 位賓客穿上愛馬仕特製圍裙，成為「料理工匠」！並開始進行料理課程；從料理菜色的設計、學習料理的過程、到使用到的廚具。

Hermes highlighted the pleasure of "doing by oneself" and "sharing with people". Thus, all guests must not only learn cooking from the two chefs and share their handicrafts to one another. The "hands-on" activity offers the pleasure of food taste and exchange of emotions.

愛馬仕特別強調「動手做」以及「分享」的樂趣。賓客們不僅要跟著兩位廚師的指導學習做菜，還可以分享彼此的手藝。「動手做」活動不只有味覺上的享受，更有情感上的交流。

Incentive Travel

給力單字

1. **flourishing** (*adj.*)　繁榮，興旺
   The business in the Hsinyi Shopping Circle of Taipei is flourishing.
   台北信義商圈的生意很興隆。

2. **imitate** (*v.t.*)　以…做為範例，仿效
   Many companies imitate the success of Hermes.
   許多公司仿效愛馬仕成功之道。

3. **appreciate** (*v.t.*)　欣賞，賞識
   All guests appreciated the demonstration of Hermes handicrafts.
   所有來賓們都很賞識愛馬仕的工藝作品。

4. **demonstrate** (*v.t.*)　示範操作，展示
   The craftsmen demonstrated each production process of their products.
   工匠們示範操作他們產品製造的每一項加工步驟。

5. **touch** (*v.t.*)　觸動，感動

I was touched beyond words.

我感動莫名。

6. **handmade** (*adj.*)　手工做的

These are expensive handmade bags

這些是非常昂貴的手工皮包。

7. **guide** (*v.t.*)　為…領路；帶領

He guided me to the reception room.

他將我帶領到接待室。

8. **led (past tense of lead)**　引導；領（路）

She led me into the drawing room.

她帶我進入客廳。

9. **hightlight** (*v.t.*)　使顯著，使突出

The organizer highlighted the pleasure of the theme banquet.

主辦單位強調了主題晚宴之樂趣。

10. **exchange** (*n.*)　交換；交流

An exchange of opinions is helpful.

相互交換意見是有益的。

給力句型

1. appreciate　感激

   *I would appreciate it if　如果你⋯，我將不勝感激

   I would appreciate it if you would attend the banquet.
   →Please accept my invitation for the banquet, thank you.
   →Thank you so much if you join my banquet.
   如果你能來參加晚宴，我將不勝感激。

2. **demonstrate**　示範，證實

   *demonstrate that

   The craftsman demonstrated that how he made the product.
   →The craftsman showed the production of product.
   →The production is showed by the craftsman in the demonstration.
   工匠示範產品是如何製造而成。

3. **exchange**　交換

   In the theme banquet, guests exchanged food-making experiences of one another.
   →The banquet offers guests to exchange their food-making experiences.
   →Guests are able to exchange their views on food-making.
   在主題宴會中，賓客間相互交換彼此製作食物心得。

職場補給 **High Profile Reception 超高標接待**

對於此次安利中國獎勵團首發團（premiere tours）五天四夜寶島之行，許多團員都讚不絕口。台灣的美食、美景及人情味都讓他們印象深刻，回程時團員們也滿載而歸，帶回快樂記憶與採購戰利品，還獲贈台灣廠商設計的腳踏車！

中國安利集團公布對 12,000 名來台營銷菁英進行的意見調查（surveys），對台灣旅遊滿意度達 96％，也是歷年中國安利舉辦獎勵旅遊中滿意度最高的一次。此次總體消費（overall consumption）約新台幣 11 億 1,000 萬元，但最重要的是，團員們意猶未盡，未來將動員粉絲、親朋好友來台旅遊。

最滿意的活動安排是一日在地生活體驗，如透過騎乘自行車優遊台北水岸、品嚐超人氣夜市小吃、欣賞明華園表演和台灣名歌手演唱會，尤其是友善的（friendly）人民和貼心的（considerate）服務態度，留下深刻印象。

破紀錄（record breaking）高標陸客團 每人費用上看 11 萬

安利中國獎勵團的台灣之行，許多團員最讚賞的是：「吃得很好、吃得很飽！」和上次安排遊覽的行程相較，這次增加許多新路線，高雄、淡水、後慈湖等都頗受到好評。不過，最令他們感動的，還是台灣的人情味（human touch or friendliness）與台灣人的服務精神。

安利中國為了獎勵這些業績表現傑出的團員們，獎勵手段很大手筆，來台灣的這幾天每天都有禮物（present or gift），例如第一天是大禮盒，第三天送的就是第四天每個人穿在身上的鮮黃色紀念薄外套，最後一天就是一部腳踏車，團員不必自己帶回去，主辦單位已安排寄送回家。

承接這次獎勵團的旅行社業者表示，上次中國安利團的接待條件已是超高標，這次再打破中國獎勵團的紀錄，每人團費（group fees）7.5 萬，但還不包括機票、晚宴等費用，再加入的話估計每人費用上看 11 萬。

　　旅行社業者也指出，這次操作難度高，因為這次有 10 條旅遊路線可選擇，原來團員已事先報名要參加哪條路線，但他們仍允許團員在當天臨時更改，實際上約有 3 至 5％的人臨時變卦，需機動調整，他們也特設服務台（information desk）服務貴賓、解決各種問題。

　　承辦旅行社這次總共動員 500 位導遊、領隊人員，除了公司專職人員（sole duty）之外，還有長期約聘工作人員加入，及與導遊協會、領隊協會合作，每條路線都精挑出最會講解的導遊人員負責來接待中國安利的貴客們。

達人提點 Craftsman Spirit 工藝精神

　　在台北晶華酒店集團的協力之下，兩位法國大廚教導參與本次盛宴的所有賓客，搖身一變成為料理工匠，從普羅旺斯開胃小點（appetizers）、龍蝦主餐（main dish）到法式薄餅（thin pancakes）、泡芙甜點（puff desserts），賓客們捲起袖子動手烹調，並且一位接著一位共同完成料理，整場晚宴充滿在驚喜與樂趣的過程中。

　　呼應本次主題，另一方面則是將工匠的定義融入生活中，「只要有熱情，人人都可以成為工匠！」即便是捲起袖子動手燒菜，也是一名廚藝工匠。 此舉讓賓客們不只從 HERMES 的產品、展覽上感受到工匠的熱情（enthusiasm），更透過親自動手烹調的過程，體會身為工匠的工藝精神、與代表的專注內涵與情感。

2-6 宴會場地的選擇與佈置
Banquet Location and Decoration

情境設定

The organizer chief interrogates the hotel manager for many questions to make successful of the banquet. This dialogue expects to serve as a subject matter when both sides negotiating specific issues, especially for a banquet in the hotel.

為了讓宴會結果圓滿，宴會承辦主管詢問飯店經理諸多問題。本對話期待成為雙方協商特定問題之題材，尤其是在飯店裡舉辦一場宴會。

角色設定

Organizer Chief：承辦主管
Hotel Manager：飯店經理

情境 1 Ensure Banquet Success 圓滿宴會

情境對話

Organizer Chief ▶ The company is scheduled to hold a banquet in your esteemed hotel next month, and I would appreciate it very

承辦主管 ▶ 我們公司預定下個月要在貴飯店舉辦一場宴會活動，我將

much if you could introduce your location facilities and services?

很感激是否可請您先介紹有關場地設施及服務？

Hotel Manager ▶ A good place together with an excellent service team is a helper to the banquet. With a flexible room space, the hotel's ball room enables to accommodate up to 60 tables for ten persons in each table. And the ball room can be divided into two partitions for 40 tables and 20 tables, respectively.

飯店經理 ▶ 一個良好的場地加上優秀的服務團隊是宴會的好幫手。我們目前可提供彈性的宴會空間，整個大宴會廳最多可容納 60 桌，每桌坐 10 人；也可分成二個隔間，或個別分成40 桌及 20 桌場地。

Organizer Chief ▶ Roughly speaking, we require a minimum of 30 tables but the real number is yet to be calculated, and it could be more or fewer. How will your hotel accept this kind of arrangement?

承辦主管 ▶ 粗略地說，我們最少會需要 30桌，但實際數目還待估算。也有可能高出或低於此桌數。您們飯店如何接受此類之安排？

Hotel Manager ▶ The ball room will be reserved for your priority only in principle. If no other reservations are made on that day, the remaining space of the ball room is an option to use with free charges.

飯店經理 ▶ 宴會廳場地之使用優先權，原則上會被保留給貴公司。如果當天沒其他賓客預約，則剩餘之場地可以選做為免費使用。

Incentive Travel

191

Organizer Chief ▶ That would be really awesome if you provide the option. In the meantime, we still need other space for activities. Could you make further explanations on this regard, if possible?

承辦主管 ▶ 如果飯店可提供這個選項，那將會很不錯。同時，我們仍需要一些活動場地。如果可以的話，請您針對此再進一步說明？

Hotel Manager ▶ We have AV equipment for slides and projector, including a 180-inch screen and DVD projectors. Our stereo and lighting facilities are charged with controllers by hours, however.

飯店經理 ▶ 視聽設備主要有幻燈機及投影機，180 吋前投式銀幕，及 DVD 放影機。另有音響及燈光設備，控制人員是以小時計費。

Organizer Chief ▶ We need to add other equipment such as a piano for the banquet night. Are there any additional decorations, and how about these services?

承辦主管 ▶ 我們晚宴活動也要增加一些其他設備，例如鋼琴。會有哪些附加的場地布置，這些服務如何？

Hotel Manager ▶ The hotel has grand piano and/or vertical type piano but the tuning fee has to be paid. The special effect of decoration such as dry ice and paper-making machines is available with charges.

飯店經理 ▶ 本飯店有平台式或是直立式鋼琴，但需要支付調音費用。場地布置也有做特技效果服務，例如乾冰煙霧機及紙花機，會酌收一些費用。

給力單字

1. **schedule** (*v.t.*) 安排，預定[+to-v]
   Could you confirm the date of the theme banquet?
   你能確認主題晚宴的日期嗎？

2. **location** (*n.*) 位置；場所
   We must decide on the location of our banquet.
   我們要給晚宴選好一個地點。

3. **accommodate** (*v.t.*) 能容納；能提供⋯膳宿
   The hotel can accommodate 500 guests in the ball room.
   這家飯店宴會廳可容納五百名賓客。

4. **partition** (*n.*) 分隔物；隔牆
   Folding partitions separated two banquet rooms.
   摺疊式的隔板分開二個宴會廳。

5. **roughly speaking** (*ph.*) 大致上
   Roughly speaking, there are two possibilities.
   粗略地說有兩種可能性。

6. **calculate** (*v.t.*) 計算
   He calculated the costs very carefully.
   他仔細計算開支。

Incentive Travel

7. **priority** (*n.*)　重點；優先權
   Food safety has high priority in the banquet.
   宴會裡食物安全至關重要。

8. **reservation** (*n.*)　預訂；預訂的房間
   We have made reservations for three rooms at the hotel.
   我們已在這個旅館預訂了三個房間。

9. **awesome** (*adj.*)　很好的，了不起的
   Their last concert was really awesome.
   他們最後的那場音樂會真不錯。

10. **AV (Audio Visual)**　視訊
    The hotel offers the AV equipment service for free of charge.
    飯店提供免費之視訊設備服務。

11. **additional** (*adj.*)　添加的；附加的
    We needed additional facilities for the banquet activity.
    我們晚會活動需要更多設施。

12. **special effect** (*ph.*)　特技效果
    We prepared the amazing special effects in the banquet performance.
    我們晚會表演有準備特技效果。

給力句型

1. schedule 預定

   *be scheduled to do sth

   The banquet is scheduled to hold just before Christmas.
   →The banquet will be held before Christmas.
   →The banquet will be starting to hold before Christmas.
   晚宴預定於聖誕節前舉行。

2. calculate 計算

   *calculate how much/how many etc

   I'm trying to calculate how much budget we need for a banquet.
   我試着算算看我們需要多少預算去辦一場宴會。

3. priority 優先

   *give priority to

   The hotel must give priority to the reservation of the ball room to the banquet.
   飯店必須優先考慮保留宴會廳給晚宴使用。

4. reservation 預約

   *make a reservation

   Customers are advised to make seat reservations well in advance.
   顧客被建議要提前預約座位。

Incentive Travel

情境 2 Location Decoration 場地布置

情境對話

More Q& A on decorations and logistics of the banquet, as follows：

更多有關宴會場地布置及統籌事項問答，如下：

Q ▶ Is it possible to sit 12 guests in each table, and how soon should I confirm the number of total tables to the hotel?

問 ▶ 每桌可否坐 12 位客人？多久之前需要跟飯店確認總桌數？

A ▶ Yes, it will be more comfortable if each table sits 10 persons; and only the head table is able to host 12 persons due to its big size. The final table number must be advised to the hotel no later than three days ahead of the banquet.

答 ▶ 是的，每桌坐 10 位貴賓，比較舒適；只有主桌因為是大型桌子，才可以坐滿 12 位。最後總桌數最遲於宴會前三天告知飯店。

Q ▶ Any time limitations for the banquet, and what time is available to enter the ball room for the decorations?

問 ▶ 宴會廳使用是否有時間限制？多久時間前可進去會場佈置？

A ▶ The banquet time is from 6:30 p.m. to 9:30 p.m. with an extension of only half hour to 10:00 p.m. Your banquet workers are allowed to enter the arena after 5:00 p.m.

答 ▶ 晚宴時間從晚上 6：30 至 9：30；最多僅可展延半小時至 10：00。貴公司工作人員於下午 5：00 後可允許至會場進行布置。

Q ▶ Any other choices for free decoration service, and can the hotel offer free change if the organizer prepares its own tablecloths and napkins?

問 ▶ 飯店還有提供哪些免費的會場布置選擇？以及是否可免費幫主辦單位更換自己所準備之新桌布及餐巾？

A ▶ Offered as free charges, red carpets, tablecloths, and chair covers are available for the organizer to choose. If the organizer prefers its own decorations, the hotel can offer the change of new tablecloths and napkins with no charges.

答 ▶ 目前有紅地毯、桌布與椅套等可供主辦單位免費選擇。如果有準備自己喜歡的佈置，飯店可免費服務或換新桌布及餐巾等。

Q ▶ Regarding the banquet project, do you offer mineral water or beverages for free, or any corkage is charged if we bring our own wines?

問 ▶ 關於一般宴會活動專案，有贈送礦泉水或飲料嗎？自備酒類是否收取開瓶費？

A ▶ Each table is offered with two bottles of mineral water with no charges at all, or NT$700 per table is charged for coke or soda and is available to enjoy drinking without limitations. The corkage fee is NT$250 per bottle for either wines or other alcoholic drinks brought from somewhere else.

答 ▶ 每桌贈送兩瓶礦泉水完全免費，或每桌NT$700，可選擇可樂或汽水，無限暢飲。至於自備紅酒及其它酒精飲料，則要收每瓶NT$250開瓶費。

Q ▶ How many free parking coupons and parking hours are offered by the hotel? Any discounts for guests who want to stay in the hotel?

問 ▶ 免費停車　數量及可停幾個小時？另晚宴貴賓如要住宿，是否有折扣優惠？

A ▶ Free parking coupons are available for guests who park their cars in the hotel, each with a maximum of four hours. The hotel offers a 15% off room charge for those guests who need to stay in the hotel, but breakfasts are not included.

答 ▶ 停車券會發給有開車貴賓，每位最多可享有 4 小時免費停車。另貴賓如有需要住宿，房間費可打 85 折優惠，但不含早餐。

給力單字

1. **confirm** (*v.t.*)　肯定，確認
   Could you confirm the dates we discussed?
   你能確認我們討論的日期嗎？

2. **advise** (*v.t.*)　通知，告知
   Please advise us of any change in your plan.
   你們的計畫倘有變更，請告訴我們

3. **limitation** (*n.*)　限制，限制因素
   Every form of art has its limitations.
   每種藝術形式都有本身的侷限。

4. **arena** (*n.*)　表演場地
   The bull was led into the arena.
   公牛被帶進競技場

5. **napkin** (*n.*)　餐巾
   She handed him a napkin.
   她遞給他一條餐巾。

6. **decoration** (*n.*)　裝飾
The decoration of the house had taken months to complete.
裝修這所房子花了好幾個月的時間。

7. **corkage charges** (*n.*)　開瓶費
Corkage charges are paid in the restaurant if wine is brought from somewhere else.
如果從別處帶酒來此餐廳則要付開瓶費。

8. **alcoholic drinks** (*ph.*)　含酒精的飲料
Restaurants are not allowed to sell alcoholic drinks to teenagers.
餐廳不准賣含酒精的飲料給青少年。

9. **parking coupons** (*ph.*)　停車優待券
Parking coupons are available for guests in the hotel.
飯店有提供停車優待券給客人。

10. **15% off** (*ph.*)　打 85 折
The hotel offers a 15% off incentive for room reservation by the end of this month.
本月底前預約飯店房間，有打 85 折優惠。

Incentive Travel

給力句型

1. confirm　確認；證實
*confirm that

The hotel confirmed that the money had been paid for the banquet.
飯店確認宴會那筆錢已經支付。

2. advise　建議；通知

*advise sb on sth

He advises us on banquet service by the hotel.
他就飯店宴會服務問題向我們提供建議。

*advise sb of sth

We'll advise you of any changes in the banquet date.
宴會日期有任何改變，我們都會通知你。

*keep sb advised

Keep us advised of the developments.
請隨時告訴我們進展情況。

職場補給 **Place Consultation** 接洽場地

　　舉辦宴會或活動場地有很多種，例如飯店、教育訓練中心（education training centers）、或各地活動中心（activity center）等，以下一些共同的注意事項，可以做為選擇時參考：

1. 牌價（list price）與底價（floor price）：一般對外出借場地的營業組織，有所謂的「牌價」，但在價格方面在有些時段都會有彈性的。例如平日晚間時段的收費有時候是跟假日白天相同的。在租價場地時除了貨比三家外，不妨先殺價也許可拿到較低之價格。

2. 實地洽訪（on-site visit）：可事先上網搜尋場地有關信息，但最好還是實地洽訪。一方面確認場地是否適合，另一方面也與對方承辦人打個照面，所謂「見面三分情」。

3. 請務必確認哪些設備是包含在租金（rental included）底下的，有些訓練中心或飯店對設備收費是分得很清楚的，例如單槍投影機有些場地是算在租金內，有些則是要另外收費的，價格很高，請一定要留意！

4. 註明需要的座位佈置方式（layout）：如果您是向飯店、教育訓練中心等租借場地的話，通常會需要下確認單。內容包括租借日期及時段、地點、租金總額，其中可能會有一項「桌椅佈置型態」，這項就是要寫明貴單位桌椅要擺成什麼型態（這部分是算在租金內的，通常是一次免費）。如果還需變換桌型的話，則依各場地而收費不同。

5. 場地復原（return）。大部分在離開活動場地時事不用做復原動作，因為清潔、復原都已經算在租金內了。如果您今天是在飯店租場地，那麼幫忙復原場地一方面是幫您的公司或團體打公關形象，另一方面說不定下次有合作機會，再來借場地時的殺價空間會有幫助喔。

達人提點 Activity Rules 活動規定

在租借場地時，要對各項設備，例如音響，麥克風，投影機，或桌椅等先進行點交（hand over）動作。此舉可確保各項設施有正常使用功能，另在退場（check out）時，如數奉還，完璧歸趙。

確實掌握宴會或活動租借時段，含場地佈置及撤場時間。有些逾時未滿（over time but less than）一小時以一小時計，每小時又依各該時段收費標準比例計費。

有些場地費用不含餐飲，除非經出租單位事先同意，否則限用該單位內之餐飲。還有其它特殊規定（special regulations）也要事先問清楚，才會讓整個宴會或活動得以順利進行。

2-7 晚會節目設計 Party Program Designs

情境 1 Exquisite Display 精心呈現

情境設定

So many programs can be designed for a good party. To this end, two colleagues who are responsible for the party program initiated and probed into each of their ideas in the following dialogue：

許多節目可以設計在一場好的晚會裡。為此目的,兩位負責晚會節目之同事各自提出並探討他們的想法,如以下對話:

角色設定

Colleague A：承辦同事 A
Colleague B：承辦同事 B

情境對話

A ▶ What category of performance programs will be designed for the party? Which kind is superb：music, dancing, skills, or others?

承辦同事 A ▶ 本次晚會要設計什麼類別節目?哪種表演是最好的:音樂、舞蹈、技藝或是其它?

B ▶ It intimately connects with the main theme of party. Any kind of performance will be a good one if it is designed elaborately.

承辦同事 B ▶ 這跟晚會的主軸有密切地關聯。無論任何表演，只要經過精心地設計都會是很棒的演出。

A ▶ In my point of view, the program mainly contains performance contents and process of activities as its main part. With innovations, the performance and activity designs are expected to arouse the interest of participants.

承辦同事 A ▶ 以我個人淺見，節目最主要的部分就是包含表演內容以及活動流程。基本上表演要有創新，活動的設計也要激發參與者的興趣。

B ▶ In addition to the stage performance, other supplementary activities are suggested to take into consideration for the purpose of funs. For instance, every one is fond of drawing lots for prizes.

承辦同事 B ▶ 除舞台表演外，我建議可考慮一些附加的小活動，讓晚會變得更好玩。例如：每個人都喜歡抽獎活動。

A ▶ That's a good idea. Maybe we can design certain games for distinguished guests, making the party more joyful.

承辦同事 A ▶ 那也是一個好的想法。我們也許可以設計來賓參加某些遊戲活動，如此讓晚會更加具有趣味性。

B ▶ Stage performance, lottery drawing, and games should be combined during the party time. This will be full of surprises and joys, I

承辦同事 B ▶ 晚會進行時舞台表演、抽獎活動、遊戲應該相互組

Incentive Travel

believe.

合。我相信，這樣能讓
整場晚會充滿著驚奇與
喜悅。

A ▶ An emcee is the soul of party, and what about the foreign language capability of this guy?

承辦同事 A ▶ 晚會主持
人是一個很重要的靈魂
人物，這位老兄他的外
語能力如何？

B ▶ Our emcee is fluent in both Mandarin and Taiwanese, and can speak well of both English and Japanese. He will certainly make the party to life, leaving a good and unforgettable memory for each participant!

承辦同事 B ▶ 我們的主
持人國、台語流暢，也
通曉英、日語。他的帶
動能力確定會讓每個參
與者都能留下美好難忘
的回憶！

給力單字

1. **category** (*n.*)　種類；類目
   The category of party program has not yet been decided by the organizer.
   主辦單位尚未決定晚會節目將採用哪一種類別。

2. **superb** (*adj.*)　極好的，一流的
   The program acting in the party was superb.
   晚會裡的節目表演好極了。

3. **intimately** (*adv.*) 熟悉地；親切地
He knew the party program design intimately.
他非常熟悉晚會節目設計。

4. **elaborately** (*adv.*) 精心地；精巧地
Every program in the party was elaborately designed.
晚會裡的每個節目都精心設計過。

5. **contain** (*v.t.*) 包含；裝盛
The program design contained important details about the party.
這個節目設計包含有關晚會的重要細節。

6. **arouse** (*v.t.*) 喚起；使奮發
The party aroused the curiosity of guests.
晚會引起了來賓的好奇心。

7. **supplementary** (*adj.*) 補充的，附加的
There is a supplementary party design in case the main program is not popular.
如果主要節目設計不受歡迎，還有補充的計畫。

8. **fond** (*adj.*) 喜歡的；愛好的[（+of）]
Every guest is very fond of games in the party.
每位來賓都很喜歡晚會裡的遊戲。

9. **certain** (*adj.*) 某些；某個
Certain important customers will be invited to attend the company's party.
某些重要的客戶將被邀請來參加公司的晚會。

10. **joyful** (*adj.*) 高興的，充滿喜悅的
Imagine the joyful scene when the party is joined by the company and its guests.
想像公司與客戶團聚時的場面該有多麼歡樂。

Incentive Travel

11. **combine** (*v.t.*)　使結合；使聯合[（+with）]

Some party programs combine with games.

有些晚會節目把遊戲結合起來。

12. **full** (*adj.*)　滿的；充滿的[（+of）]

The party was full of people.

晚會內擠滿了人。

13. **emcee** (*n.*)　司儀；主持人

He proved to be a very competent emcee (master of ceremony) for the party.

他證明了是一個很稱職的晚會司儀(主持人)。

14. **capability** (*n.*)　能力，才能

He has the capability of hosting an important party.

他具有主持重要晚會的能力。

15. **fluent** (*adj.*)　流利的，流暢的[（+in）]

He hosts with fluent English in the party.

他用很流暢的英文主持晚會。

16. **unforgettable** (*adj.*)　難以忘懷的

It was an unforgettable party.

那是一個令人難忘的晚會。

給力句型

1. certain　某些

   *a certain

   There's a certain feature about the party program design.
   晚會的節目設計還是有些特色的。

   *to a certain extent/degree

   I agree with you to a certain extent but there are other factors to consider for the party program.
   對於晚會節目在某程度上我同意你的看法，但還有其他一些因素需要考慮。

2. capability　能力

   *capability to do sth

   A willingness and a capability to change are necessary to meet the party's needs.
   願意並能夠作出調整，這對於滿足晚會需求是很必要的。

   *beyond sb's capabilities

   He has a good knowledge of English, but simultaneous translation is beyond his capabilities in the party.
   他的英語不錯，但是在晚會裡做同步翻譯卻不是他能力所及的。

Incentive Travel

情境 2 Q&A on Program Designs 節目設計問與答

情境對話

Other Q&A about program designs：	其他有關晚會節目設計之問與答：

Q ▶ Please identify the purpose behind the party and its participants?	問 ▶ 可否請確認舉辦此晚會之目的，會有哪些參加者？

A ▶ It is celebrated for the 10th anniversary of the company with the participation of all employees. The company will invite valued clients and foreign guests.	答 ▶ 主要慶祝公司成立十週年，原則上所有員工都會出席。也會邀請一些重要客戶及國外來賓。

Q ▶ Where to take place the party, and in which type of operation?	問 ▶ 晚會在哪邊慶祝？會舉行哪一種活動型態？

A ▶ It supposes to hold the party at a five-star hotel but the operation type and details are yet to be finalized for the time being.	答 ▶ 猜想會在一家五星級舉辦，但其進行方式及相關細節目前尚待定案。

Q ▶ Do you have any suggestions regarding program designs, rehearsals, and backup plans?	問 ▶ 您在節目設計、彩排、或替代方案方面有何建議？

A ▶ Basically, the program design is very	答 ▶ 基本上，本次節目

innovative, and interesting. It is a must to pay attention to the safety, however.

設計非常有創意，也極具趣味性；可還要注意安全原則。

Q ▶ By the way, who is responsible for the entire program record such as photos or DVD films, and follow-up data treatment, including expenses and receipts?

問 ▶ 順便說說，誰負責整個節目成果記錄，例如活動照片/DVD 影片，還有後續資料處理以及經費收支明細工作？

A ▶ We have two professional photographers to take charge of photos and DVD fabrication and copies will be sent to each participant by e-mail. Relevant expenditures of the party will be reported to the finance department by the organizer, and this is an important work.

答 ▶ 我們有兩位專業攝影師將負責有關照片以及數位光碟製作，複製本會 e-mail 給參加晚會者。相關的消費支出另由承辦者呈報財務部，這個也是很重要的工作。

Incentive Travel

給力單字

1. **participant** (*n.*)　關係者；參與者[+in]
   Would participants in the next game come forward?
   下個遊戲參賽者請到前面來好嗎？

2. **celebrate** (*v.t.*)　慶祝
   We held a party to celebrate our success.
   我們舉行宴會慶祝我們的成功。

3. **valued** (*adj.*)　貴重的；寶貴的

Several valued guests confirmed their participations to attend the party.

有幾個重要來賓已經確認會來參加晚會。

4. **take place** (*ph.*)　舉行

The game will take place after the party.

晚會之後將舉行遊戲。

5. **suppose** (*v.t.*)　猜想，以為

I suppose the party to be a success.

我想晚會將會很圓滿成功。

6. **backup** (*adj.*)　備用的

We should always have a backup plan for the party.

對於晚會，我們應該總該要有一個備用的計畫。

7. **innovative** (*adj.*)　創新的

A young innovative program was presented in the party.

一個新且富有創意節目呈現在晚會中。

8. **record** (*v.t.*)　記載下來的; 正式記錄的

The program of party held recently was on record.

剛舉行的這個晚會節目已被記錄下來。

9. **expenditure** (*n.*)　支出額；經費

Expenditures for the party amount to $100,000.

晚會經費花了 10 萬元。

給力句型

1. celebrate　慶祝

   *celebrate sth

   The company is celebrating its 10th anniversary.
   公司正在慶祝它的 10 週年紀念。

   *celebrate anniversary/Christmas/Thanksgiving etc

   The company celebrates its anniversary each year.
   公司每年都會慶祝它的成立週年。

2. suppose　假設

   *supposed to

   The time for the party is not supposed to take too long.
   晚會舉行時間不可拖太久。

   *suppose (that)

   What makes you suppose the company is going to cancel the party?
   你憑甚麼認為公司準備取消該晚會？

   *be generally supposed

   The party was generally supposed to be cancelled due to unexpected factors.
   由於未預期之因素，一般認為晚會將會被取消。

Incentive Travel

職場補給 **Perfect Planning 完美規劃**

有很多所謂專業娛樂（entertainment）公司會代為規劃晚會節目，附帶有各式各樣表演（音樂、舞蹈、技藝等），甚或邀請知名藝人（entertainers）參加演出。如果與上述公司合作，在節目設計方面確實可省下很多瑣事，惟代辦收取費用一般都非常昂貴。

因此，近年來國內比較有規模之企業，每逢重大慶典如尾牙（annual banquet）、忘年晚會，包括目前很流行的『角色扮演（cosplay）』或『企業家庭日（enterprise family day）』等活動，均由內部員工自行規劃節目，並親自參與演出。除了動員各部門同仁參與表演外，有時也會邀請大老闆和一級主管等一起粉墨登場，眾人同樂。經由精心地規劃，加上全體同仁賣力演出，不但幫企業省下大筆委外費用，達到預期晚會節目效果，也讓大家留下美好難忘的回憶！

節目設計事先要蒐集資料及進行調查，有關內容要創新（innovation），勇於嘗試：最重要是激發參與者的意願與興趣。另外也要知道哪些人會參加？隨時注意晚會活動參與者之情緒控制，以免有違美意。

另活動安排首重安全原則，如在戶外（outdoors）舉行，更要有替代方案（如下雨天之備案）。最好事前知道有多少資源可運用，進行沙盤推演；如有安排表演節目，也需要預先進行 1~2 次彩排，期以達到盡善盡美之表現。

一個節目設計及執行成功，不會憑空而降，更是需要靠大家共同努力去贏得（to win with joint efforts）。

達人提點 **Epilogue** 後記

　　有關節目計畫，實施要點，及活動結果應該要請專人做紀錄與整理。並將完整的資料及成果報告列入檔案（files），以供爾後承辦者做為重要參考。

　　還有晚會活動結束時之場地恢復也是很重要，尤其要記得帶走所有垃圾。最好能將垃圾大致分類，為地球環境保護（environmental protection）略盡棉薄之力。

Incentive Travel

213

2-8 餐飲的安排
Food & Beverage Arrangements

情境 1 Conference Dining at Hotel 國際會議之飯店餐飲

情境設定

Making arrangements for food and beverages in a hotel's restaurant is required if the international conference is held there. See the dialogue between the guest and restaurant as it may become references when conducting such logistics.

果在飯店舉辦國際會議，則有需要跟裡面餐廳安排餐飲等事情。請看客人與餐廳之對話，也許可以做為在進行這些籌備工作時之參考。

角色設定

The Guest：客人
The Restaurant：餐廳

情境對話

The Guest ▶ How do you offer food and beverages for conference guests in the hotel, and which one is the popular dining style in your restaurant?

客人 ▶ 貴飯店如何提供餐飲給參加會議之來賓，哪一種用餐方式是比較受歡迎？

The Restaurant ▶ For your references, we can offer both buffet and table dining styles, including Chinese, western, or Muslim food.

餐廳 ▶ 謹供您參考，我們可以做自助餐及桌餐方式，包括中式、西式、或是回教食物。

The Guest ▶ Due to the close confinement in our budget, please explain the difference between the two dining styles?

客人 ▶ 因為我們預算有嚴格限制，請您解釋兩種用餐不同之處？

The Restaurant ▶ The buffet style is usually controlled by the meal coupons, which is more convenient for attendees to use. While the table style is complicated as it has to consider the number of guests for each table, the dining time, table seats, special food requirements, and other factors.

餐廳 ▶ 自助餐方式通常會用餐券來控管，比較方便來賓自行使用。如果採用桌餐方式會複雜些，因為要考慮每桌用餐人數、開飯時間、座位安排，特殊食物需求，以及其他因素。

The Guest ▶ What are your specialty dishes in the restaurant, and may I see the menu first?

客人 ▶ 貴餐廳拿手菜有哪些？我可以先看菜單嗎？

The Restaurant ▶ We are famous for both Hunan and Cantonese dishes, and our delicious Hong Kong style seafood is also popular, enabling to meet demands of clients.

餐廳 ▶ 我們以湘、粵菜聞名，另有各式精緻味美的港式海鮮料理也很受歡迎，能滿足客戶需求。

The Guest ▶ How do you charge your beverages and the payment for wines?

客人 ▶ 貴餐廳飲料如何收費，以及購酒之付費？

The Restaurant ▶ The beverage fees for mineral water and soft-drinks is covered in the dining budget, but individual guests have to pay their own wines, if ordered.

餐廳 ▶ 礦泉水及一般不含酒精飲料費用包含在晚餐預算內，如有個別來賓需要點酒，則須自行付費。

The Guest ▶ The sanitation question—do you offer insurance policy for food safety?

客人 ▶ 公共衛生方面疑問—你們餐廳是否有提供食物安全保險單？

The Restaurant ▶ As a restaurant in the international hotel, we are very concern about the food safety, and guests are welcomed to inspect our kitchen at any time. With a compensation amount of up to NT$10 million, we are liable for any death or causalities caused by food poisoning.

餐廳 ▶ 做為一個國際飯店裡的餐廳，我們非常關心食物安全問題，也歡迎來賓隨時檢查廚房。客人起因食物中毒而死亡或受傷，我們有責任賠償，最高可獲金額新台幣 1,000 萬元。

The Guest ▶ Meanwhile, we might need a cock-tail reception before the dinner. I would appreciate it very much if you combine the quotation of this part with the dining party?

客人 ▶ 同時，我們或許在晚餐前會需要一場雞尾酒歡迎會。我將會很感激您，請將這部分與晚宴一起報價。

The Restaurant ▶ No problem. A joint quotation with good price will soon be submitted for your approval.

餐廳 ▶ 沒問題。我會儘快呈報一份優惠之聯合報價單，並請求您的核准。

給力單字

1. **food and beverages** (*ph.*)　餐飲
The food and beverages of this restaurant are great but they are expensive, too.
這家餐廳的餐飲很好吃，可是也很貴。

2. **buffet** (*n.*)　自助餐，快餐
They had a buffet after the conference.
開完會後，他們吃自助餐。

3. **budget** (*n.*)　預算；經費[（+for）]
It is essential to balance the budget for expenditures.
平衡支出的預算是很重要的。

4. **meal coupons** (*ph.*)　餐券
It is a must to use meal coupons for food in the restaurant.
在餐廳用餐必須使用餐券。

5. **table style** (*ph.*)　桌餐
The restaurant only serves table style dishes.
該餐廳僅供應桌餐菜單。

6. **specialty dishes** (*ph.*)　拿手菜
The chef is famous for many specialty dishes.
該主廚有好幾道聞名拿手菜。

7. **menu** (*n.*)　菜單
Let us see what is on the menu today.
讓我們看看今天菜單上有些什麼菜。

8. **delicious** (*adj.*)　美味的；香噴噴的
The fried chicken is delicious.
這炸雞味道鮮美。

Incentive Travel

9. **charge** (*v.i.*)　索價；收費[（+for）]

The restaurant doesn't charge for delivery.

該餐廳免費外送。

10. **soft-drinks**　不含酒精的飲料

Different soft-drinks are offered in the restaurant, and they are self-served.

餐廳裡有供應多種不含酒精飲料，可自行取用。

11. **sanitation** (*n.*)　公共衛生，環境衛生

The sanitation is a very important issue for the restaurant.

公共衛生是餐廳一項非常重要的問題。

12. **insurance policy** (*ph.*)　保險合同；保險單

This restaurant has purchased insurance policies for its food.

這家餐廳有購買食物保險單。

13. **inspect** (*v.t.*)　檢查；審查

They inspected the restaurant for its food safety.

他們檢查了餐廳看它的食物是否安全。

14. **liable** (*adj.*)　負有法律責任的，有義務的[（+for）]

The restaurant will be liable for food safety.

該餐廳將對食物安全負責。

15. **quotation** (*n.*)　報價; 行情

Could you give me a quotation for dining at your restaurant?

你可以給我一個在貴餐廳用餐的報價嗎？

16. **approval** (*n.*)　批准；認可

The dinning plan had the approval of the organizer.

用餐計畫得到主辦單位的認可。

給力句型

1. payment 付費；付款

   *make a payment

   The food and beverages payments are made in cash or credit cards.
   餐飲付費可用現金或信用卡。

   *in payment of

   I enclose a cheque in full payment of food and beverages.
   我附上一張支付全部餐飲的支票。

   *on payment of

   The table can be reserved in the restaurant on payment of a small deposit.
   付一小筆訂金後就可以保留該餐廳用餐桌位。

2. liable 有責任的

   *liable [+for]

   The restaurant is liable for any safety in food.
   該餐廳對食物的任何安全都負有賠償責任。

   *liable [+to]

   Any sanitation problem is liable to a maximum fine of $10,000.
   任何公共衛生問題，最高可被罰款 10,000 美元。

Incentive Travel

情境 2 Additional Q&A 附加問答

情境設定

Additional Q&A references on food and beverage arrangements：
餐飲安排之附加 Q&A 參考：

情境對話

Q ▶ I would like to further understand details about your dinning service and the price of menu?

問 ▶ 我想進一步了解您們宴會餐飲提供方式，及菜單價錢方面之細節？

A： Of course. We are specialized in banquet services for wedding, birthday party, and large-scaled commercial activities. Take Chinese style table service for instance, the price is fixed at NT$15,000 for a 10-person table. (Wine and beverages are excluded.) As for the price of western-style buffet, we charge NT$1,000 each person with all beverages free and no service charges.

答 ▶ 當然。我們是專門做婚壽喜慶或商務聚餐等各種中大型餐飲活動。以中式桌餐 10 人座為例，固定的價格大約是 NT$15,000（酒水另計）。至於西式自助餐，每位費用則是 NT$1,000，含各式飲料及服務費免費。

Q ▶ Your menu is well-known in Jiang-zhe dishes, which are supposed to be yummy. Is that possible to add certain famous Taiwanese food, leaving good tastes for our foreign visitors?

問 ▶ 您們菜單內容以江浙菜聞名，應該是很好吃。但可否增加特定的台灣名菜，讓我們國外訪客留下一些好吃口味？

A ▶ Thank you for your compliments. Our chef can prepare his specialties with the local food as the "glory of Taiwan".

答 ▶ 感謝您的讚美。我們大廚也可用本地食材準備他的拿手菜，做為『台灣之光』。

Q ▶ Meanwhile, I have to change some of the seafood menu, and I hope this would not incur any surcharges for the banquet?

問 ▶ 另外，我要更換一部分海鮮菜單，希望不會因此帶來晚宴之額外費用？

A ▶ If you need to change seafood, we can offer another menu for your options, and try to control it within the budget.

答 ▶ 如果要更換海鮮，我們另有菜單可供挑選；並會儘量控制在預算內。

Q ▶ Do you offer specially made lunch boxes for member staff of conference, and how much each costs?

問 ▶ 您們是否也有訂製特別餐盒等給會議工作人員，每份要多少錢？

A ▶ You bet. Our meeting lunch boxes are very exquisite and popular. It costs NT$500 per unit.

答 ▶ 是的。我們的會議盒餐相當精緻，很受歡迎。每份 500 元。

Q ▶ How much do I need to pay for the deposit, and do you accept credit cards for the remaining sum?

問 ▶ 我需要先付多少訂金，餘額可用信用刷卡付費嗎？

A ▶ Please pay 10% for deposit in advance if this is convenient for you. Yes, we accept credit card.

答 ▶ 如果您方便的話，請預先付 10%訂金。是的，我們可接受信用卡付費。

Incentive Travel

221

給力單字

1. **price** (*n.*) 價格，價錢
The table dinner is much more expensive in price than that of buffet.
桌餐價格比自助餐貴。

2. **specialize** (*v.t.*) 專攻；專門從事[（+in）]
The restaurant specializes in Taiwanese stir-fry dishes.
這家餐館擅長台式熱炒菜。

3. **fixed** (*v.t.*) 固定的
Menu prices are fixed, plus a 10% charge on service.
菜單價格是固定的，另外加 10%服務費。

4. **yummy** (*n.*) 美味的東西；令人喜愛的東西
Most people like yummy food.
大多數人喜歡美味的東西。

5. **taste** (*n.*) 味道；體驗
The food has delicious taste.
這食物味道真好。

6. **compliment** (*n.*) 讚美的話；敬意
It's the nicest compliment I've ever had .
這是我聽到的最好的恭維話。

7. **surcharges** (*n.*) 附加費；額外費用
Some surcharges are levied for the restaurant services.
餐廳有時候在服務方面會徵收一些附加費用。

8. **option** (*n.*) 選擇
It is at your option to select a Chinese or Japanese style food.
你可自行選擇吃中式或日本料理。

9. **lunch box** (*ph.*)　餐盒；便當

The lunch box is specially prepared by the restaurant, and is very expensive, too.

該餐盒是由餐廳特別準備，而且也很非常貴。

10. **exquisite** (*adj.*)　細緻的

He has exquisite taste in various foods.

他對各類食物的品味很高雅。

11. **remaining sum** (*ph.*)　餘額

The remaining sum of the payment can be made by either credit card or checks.

餘額可以使用信用卡或支票付款。

12. **in advance** (*ph.*)　預先

He paid the deposit for the restaurant in advance.

他預先支付保證金給餐廳。

Incentive Travel

給力句型

1. price 價錢

   high/low price

   You can get good food in the restaurant at very low prices.
   在這家餐廳可以以很低的價錢吃到好食物。

   price increase/rise

   Some restaurants say that menu price rises will be gradual.
   有些餐廳說菜單價格將逐漸上漲。

   right price

   We should negotiate with the restaurant for the right price.
   我們應該與餐廳協議一個合適的價格。

2. taste 鑑賞力；口味

   have (good) taste

   She has good taste in all kinds of food.
   她對各種食物有不錯的鑑賞力。

   have a taste for

   I've always had a taste for Italian and Japanese foods.
   我一向喜愛義大利和日本料理。

   to sb's taste

   She had the whole menu reordered to her taste.
   她按照自己的口味重新點菜。

職場補給 **Importance on Foodstuff 民以食為天**

安排晚會餐飲相當重要，相關協調事項也極為繁鎖。所謂『民以食為天（Foodstuff is all important to the people）』，承辦人員必須花更多心血，如何挑選一個好菜單，讓大家吃得好、吃得飽，賓主盡歡，順利達成工作目標。

飯店餐廳推薦他們各種宴席或酒會菜單，因為由專業師傅（chefs）負責料理，加上美輪美奐之場地布置，一般都是採取固定報價，很少會給折扣。但也並不表示承辦單位都要全盤接受制式菜單，多半可經由雙方協商可更換比較合適之『客制化（customized）』菜色，且又控制在餐飲預算裡。

另如果餐飲人數達一定數量，也許可要求飯店餐廳贈送（complimentary）1~2 道菜，以增加菜單份量。飯店餐廳為了拿生意訂單，通常會爽快答應，同意給食蔬或菜類居多。

餐飲方面有時要考慮一些額外需求，例如有素食者（vegetarians）或宗教等可能影響因素，則另做安排。另如有國外賓客參加，可事前詢問他們的餐飲習慣或有否特別需求？並告知飯店餐飲服務人員先做好準備，以避免屆時招待不週。

中式宴客入座方式需要有座位表（seating chart）輔助，這部分也要先做好有關來賓入席號碼牌。現場招待人員須保持機動性作業，除協助客人入座外，並隨時處理突發狀況。

西式自助餐（Western buffet）宴客方式，賓客間彼此互動比較頻繁，但也需在劃定預留區域內進行，以免影響到其他單位之活動。西餐要搭配合適餐具使用，包括酒水杯子；提醒飯店餐廳注意這方面問題，尤其餐具、碗盤有缺口或破損等，不要出現在餐會中，避免讓賓客不小心遭到受傷。

有關宴席前酒會安排也需細心策畫，這方面菜單通常以開胃菜

（appetizer），小點心，小蛋糕居多，有時也會有一些燒烤食物。現場如有樂隊演奏或表演者，也要關心是否需要協助之處？

主人儘量控制好開席時間，並準時請所有賓客入席；並於預訂時間內完成所有活動及處理場地歸還動作。

達人提點 **Food Insurance** 食安保險

在餐飲方面安排首應注重衛生安全，除了用餐環境，可了解業者是否投保食物中毒責任保險（liability insurance）？台灣目前除大型觀光旅館外，其他餐飲業者投保的情形仍不普遍。

如果飯店餐廳菜單上附有中英文對照，要先看一下翻譯內容是否正確？把錯誤的菜單名稱放在桌上，外賓有時很難理解到底是什麼菜？如有安排翻譯人員陪坐同桌，可在旁協助翻譯，另顯現貼心待客之道。

另特別注意穿著服飾（attires）及基本用餐禮儀（table manners），尤其在國際性宴會及酒會等場合。

NOTE

Conferences

大會

3-1　開幕
Grand Opening

情境 1　歡迎詞及宣布開會 Opening Announcement

On the occasion of certain conferences or special events, the delivery of speeches is necessary, and prior preparations of such drafts, especially an English language version, have turned to be a must for this purpose. Short remarks or statements are generally used for different occasions, as mentioned below：

在某些會議或特殊場合裡都必須要發表演說，為此目的而事先準備之這類演講稿，尤其是英文版本，已成為是不可或缺的。經常會在不同場合中所使用的簡短致詞或談話例句，臚列如下：

例句 1

His Excellency, Mr. Chairman, Fellow Delegates, Ladies & Gentlemen：I would like to extend my warmest welcome for your participation in the conference of the year. Now, I declare the conference open!

總統閣下，主席先生，各位代表、女士們及先生們：我要以最熱烈的歡迎各位出席今年會議。現在，我宣布會議開始!

例句 2

Mr. President, Mr. Chairman, Distinguished Guests, Ladies & Gentlemen : I am very honored to announce this annual conference has formally opened!

總統先生，主席先生，各位貴賓，女士們及先生們：我非常榮幸宣佈本次年會已正式開始!

情境 2 來賓在開幕式上致詞 VIP Remarks on Opening

例句 1

Thank you very much for inviting me to deliver a speech in the conference. I appreciate efforts of your organization and my best wishes for the success of the conference.

非常感謝邀請本人在大會發表演講。我很欣賞貴單位所做的一切努力，並對大會圓滿成功致最大的祝福。

例句 2

It is my pleasure to be invited for a speech at the conference. I sincerely hope that efforts you made have paved the way for the success of the conference this year.

本人很榮幸受邀請在大會上發表演說。我真誠地希望由於貴單位所做的努力已為今年的大會成功鋪平道路。

Conferences

情境 3 主辦單位對參會者致詞 Remarks of the Organizer to Delegates

例句 1

As the chairman of the most important forum between Taiwan and the U.S. economic and trade ties, I extend my heartfelt gratitude for your attendance, and especially, His Excellency who personally attends the grand opening out of tight schedules.

以台灣-美國之間最重要經貿關係論壇理事長身份,我衷心感謝各位參加本次大會,尤其是總統閣下能在百忙之中撥冗親自出席開幕典禮。

例句 2

On behalf of the chairman of the Taiwan-U.S. Economic and Trade Forum, I appreciate it very much for your participation in the conference, the most important of its kind held annually by two sides

我代表台美經貿論壇理事長,非常感激各位出席雙方每年舉辦最重要之會議。

情境 4 參加者對主辦單位致詞 Remarks of Delegate to the Organizer

例句 1

As the official delegate to the conference, I would like to take this opportunity to appreciate the invitation, and all participants are thankful for the warm hospitality shown by the organizer.

以大會正式代表身份,我想趁此機會表達大會邀請,所有參與者也非常感謝主辦單位展現的熱情款待。

例句 2

All delegates thank you so much for the organizer's invitation and warm hospitality.

我們全體代表謝謝主辦單位的邀請和盛情的招待。

情境 5 介紹會議的背景、目的和期望 Meeting Background, Purpose, and Expectations

例句 1

Aiming at the strengthening of the two-way trade ties between Taiwan and the U.S, this forum was initiated by leading commercial and industrial businessmen after both nations severing diplomatic relations in 1978.

以加強台灣與美國雙邊經貿關係為目的，本論壇由雙方工商領導業者創始於 1978 年中美斷絕外交後。

例句 2

This annual conference is held alternatively in Taiwan or the U.S., with joint delegates totaling over 500 persons each year. The President of the local country is invited to deliver a speech; or instead, he will grant a written speech to the General Assembly for the celebration if he is unable to attend.

本年會輪流在台灣及美國舉辦，每年雙方代表達 500 多位。地主國總統如果有空，將會出席並發表演說；如未克出席，另致贈大會一篇書面講稿，以表慶賀。

Conferences

例句 3

Ministerial-level and ranking governmental officials of both sides are usually invited to attend the conference and represent as keynote speakers. Sometimes, the organizer invites senators of the U.S. to attend the conference as a honorable guest.

雙方部長級和高階政府官員通常會受邀出席並擔任大會專題主講人。有時後，大會也邀請美國參議員擔任特別嘉賓。

例句 4

The forum offers a platform for exchanges of trade issues, and opinions about the two-way investment are compiled and submitted to the government authorities as important policy references for the years to come.

該論壇就貿易問題提供一個交換平台，有關雙邊投資意見彙整、呈報有關政府部門作為來年施政參考。

情境 6 確認音響效果，燈光、展示幻燈片 To Check Stereo, Lighting, and Slides

例句 1

Please check and make sure that the stereo set system is in good function. We need two more wireless microphones for "question and answer" section, thank you.

請檢查並確認音響系統是否正常功能？我們另需要多兩支無線麥克風提供給『提問與答詢』小組使用，謝謝您。

例句 2

May I have your attention, please！ An electrical engineer should be on standby to ensure the function of stereo and lighting operations, and he is responsible to control the projector presentation. Thank you very much for your cooperation.

請注意！一位電器工程人員必須在現場待命，以確保音響及燈光操作功能，他也要負責幻燈機操作。謝謝您的合作。

給力單字

1. **participation** (*n.*)　參加；參與 [+in]
   We want more participation of delegates in the conference.
   我們想要有更多代表來參與會議。

2. **declare** (*v.t.*)　宣布
   I declare this conference open.
   我宣布會議開幕。

3. **announce** (*v.t.*)　宣布
   The vote was completed, and the chairman announced the result.
   投票完畢，主席宣布了結果。

4. **deliver a speech** (*ph.*)　發表演說
   The president was invited to deliver a speech in the grand opening of the conference.
   總統受邀在大會開幕時發表演說。

5. **pave the way for** (*ph.*)　為…鋪平道路
   The organizer had paved the way for success of the meeting.
   這個主辦者為會議成功鋪路。

Conferences

6. **gratitude** (*n.*)　感激
The chairman extended his gratitude for the participation of delegates.
主席對代表能來參加開會充滿感激。

7. **granding opening** (*ph.*)　開幕典禮
The grand opening will be started punctually.
開幕典禮預定準時舉行。

8. **on behalf of** (*ph.*)　代表，為了…的利益
The chairman presented himself to the meeting on behalf of his association.
理事長代表他的協會出席會議。

9. **delegate** (*n.*)　代表；代表團團員[（+to）]
We sent five delegates to the conference.
我們派了五個代表參加會議。

10. **hospitality** (*n.*)　好客；殷勤招待
Many thanks for the hospitality you showed me.
非常感謝你對我的款待。

11. **warm** (*adj.*)　熱情的；衷心的
All delegates were accepted with a warm reception by the conference.
所有與會代表均受到大會極為熱誠的接待。

12. **sever** (*v.t.*)　中斷
Taiwan severed its diplomatic ties with the U.S. in 1978.
台灣與美國在 1978 年時斷交

13. **alternatively** (*adv.*) 輪流的；間隔
The conference is held alternatively in the country or abroad per year.
本會議每年在國內或海外地區輪流舉行。

14. **the General Assembly** 大會；全體代表會議
The General Assembly is the highest policy-making unit of the conference.
全體代表大會為會議之最高決策單位。

15. **keynote speaker** 專題演講人
Most keynote speakers are university professors or ranking government officials.
大多數專題演講人為大學教授或是高階政府官員。

16. **honorable guest** (*ph.*) 特別嘉賓
Our honorable guests extend thanks for your hospitality.
我們的特別嘉賓感謝你的熱情款待。

17. **two-way investment** (*ph.*) 雙邊投資
The two-way investment between Taiwan and the U.S. decreased in recent years.
台灣與美國之雙邊投資近年已下降。

18. **stereo set** (*n.*) 音響設備
The stereo set happened to be malfunctioned in the conference.
音響設備在會議中碰巧發生故障。

19. **on standby** (*ph.*) 隨時待命
The conference has technicians to keep on standby for facility maintenances.
大會有請電工隨時待命修理有關設備。

Conferences

給力句型

1. announce　宣布，發布

   *announce (that)

   The chairman suddenly announced that the meeting was ended.
   主席突然宣布會議結束。

   *announce for

   He announced for the chairmanship.
   他宣布參加競選主席。

2. declare　正式宣布

   *declare that

   The chairman finally declared that the conference to be over.
   主席最終正式宣布大會即將結束。

   *declare sth a success/failure/unsafe, etc

   The chairman declared the conference a success.
   主席宣布大會圓滿成功。

3. delegate　代表

   *official delegate to

   He is an official delegate to the conference.
   他是一名大會正式代表。

   *delegate sb to do sth

   I've been delegated to organize the weekly meetings.
   我被指派組織每週的會議。

4. warm 熱烈的

*a warm welcome

Please give a warm welcome to our special guest!

請熱烈歡迎我們的嘉賓！

*warm up

The organizer is warming up before the conference.

主辦者在為大會做暖身準備。

Conferences

職場補給 Conference Agenda & Scenario 會議議程及演出劇本

　　國際會議正式開幕典禮，有時還要安排樂隊在現場演奏本國及與會代表國家之國歌，以示隆重。按照會議議程（agenda），大會主席及主要貴賓會先行上台，並就指定座位入座。主席致上簡短歡迎詞後，即可宣布大會正式開始。

　　大會如有邀請到總統或重要貴賓出席，承辦單位可能還需要編寫一套劇本（scenario），包括位置及動線等，以提供主席進行開幕時參考。例如，主席什麼時後邀請總統上台演講？何時請每位代表起立並鼓掌？與哪些陪賓需要恭送總統離開會場？以上這些有關禮儀都很重要，最好事先排練過，以表現出對國家元首尊重及大會待客之道。

　　遇有雙邊國家元首級與貴賓出席之會議，大會在各項準備工作方面更需周全及細膩。事先協調貴賓到場及離場時間，還有特殊配合事項；尤其元首級之安檢作業（security check）及進出動線方面都要預先規劃好，不能有任何失誤。

　　除大會開幕外，與會代表通常會選擇參加各項研討會（seminars）或小組討論（discussion sessions）活動。這些會議應分派主持人和主講人員，有關場地、設備、開會使用器材，例如幻燈機、活動螢幕、紅外線指示筆等，也需要事先準備妥善。最好每個會議室都有安排工作人員在旁待命；或有機動小組，隨時處理任何問題。

　　當今智慧手機流行 LINE 及 APP 軟體，運用到會議現場聯繫工作相當便利，遇有任何事情可立即拍照，傳遞訊息後立馬處理。對照以前會場工作人員彼此聯絡，主要專靠手提無線通話機（walky-talkies）或室內對講機（intercom），有時碰到緊急狀況又碰巧收訊不佳，急的像熱鍋螞蟻，已不可同日而語也。

達人提點 **Speech Draft & Meeting Facilities** 演講初稿與會場設施

有關重要貴賓講稿，主辦單位要先詢問是否準備演講者初稿（draft）？講稿內容須提供大會召開之背景及目的等，並事先送請貴賓之秘書處核備，以供卓參。有些貴賓自己單位有專人會撰寫講稿，主辦單位則負責講稿製作影印本即可。

大會新聞中心（press center）是媒體必拜訪之處，要負責現場報導或採訪功能。另也蒐集所有演講者之中/英文講稿，以提供媒體或各代表參用。現場最好另租用一台影印機，以備不時之需。

開幕儀式裡主席及來賓之講話過程最具代表及重要性，因此有關音響效果或燈光方面，一定要多加檢查以確認無誤。尤其麥克風，包括講台上還有無線麥克風、幻燈機遙控器（remote control）等，必須有專人在現場待命外，另也要安排備用品。

Conferences

3-2 主持報告會
To Preside Over a Presentation

情境設定

How to play a good role of chairman in the presentation? The chairman's speech, invitation sequence of VIPs (keynote speakers), time control, and relevant skills are essential of preparations. The sentence examples listed below may serve as references of the reader of this book.

如何在報告會議中稱職扮演主席的角色？主席致詞、邀約貴賓（引言人）致詞順序、時間掌控方面、及相關技巧等，都需要做好事前準備工作。以下列舉一些常用句型範例，或可供本書讀者援用參考：

情境 1 報告開始前 Before Presentation

討論會主席

It is my great pleasure to chair this panel discussion for economy and trade issues between Taiwan and the U.S. I hope that the conclusion to be made by this session would be valuable to future policy-making guidelines of both sides.

本人很榮幸主持本次台美經貿問題小組討論。我期望本會議最後所做之結論會很具有價值，並做為雙方在未來制定政策之指導方針。

Welcome to join our panel discussion! I am privileged to chair the session, and expect we can reach a resolution on the topic assigned by the Assembly in this afternoon.

歡迎來參加我們的小組討論會! 我有殊榮擔任本會主席,期望我們可以根據大會指派之題目,在今天下午做出決議。

 ## 主持報告 Chair a Presentation

情境 2

In this session, we have the honor to invite Mr. Kuan Chung-ming, chairman of the National Development Council of the Executive Yuan, to address on the topic ："Taiwan's Golden Ten Years". Let's applaud and welcome the keynote speaker!

在本次會裡,我們有幸邀請到行政院國家發展委員會管中閔主任委員,他將以:『台灣的黃金 10 年』為題目發表演講。請大家鼓掌歡迎此位專題演講者!

Following Chairman Kuan, we have Economic Minister Chang Chia-juch who will present his paper on "Taiwan's Free Economic Pilot Zone", the latest incentive to be offered by the government for foreign investors, in the second phase discussion. After his presentation, Minister Chang is pleased to discuss and answer any questions that you may have about his speech.

緊接在管主委後面,我們有請經濟部長張家祝在第二階段討論會裡,將提出『台灣自由經濟示範區』報告,這是我國最新吸引外資來台投資獎勵。在他演講結束後,張部長很樂意討論與回答有關此報告之任何問題。

The topic presented by Minister Chang is an important subject, offering new business opportunities in the two-way investment in the

Conferences

future. Our delegates could probe into this topic in the discussion later.

剛才張部長所報告的題目非常重要，也提供未來雙邊投資新商機。我們與會代表也可在後面小組會議裡就此議題作深入探討。

情境 3　報告後的討論 Discussions after Presentation

According to agenda, the session has two paper presentations with 40 minutes; and followed by Q&A discussions, with 30 minutes. Shall we now getting started the discussion from the first keynote speech?

依照議程，本會有兩個報告發表，時間為 40 分鐘：接在後面的是提問與答詢，討論時間為 30 分鐘。我們現在可否先從第一個專題報告開始進行討論？

Thank you for raising so many questions. Chairman Kuan is pleased to respond to more questions, if any?

非常感謝各位提出這麼多問題。管主委將會很樂意回覆更多問題，不知道還有沒？

情境 4　保持會場秩序與中場休息通知 Keeping Order and Notice of Breaking Time

If there are no more questions, this session is adjourned for 10 minutes. After taking a break, we will go on to the discussion on the second topic.

如果沒有其他問題，本會議暫停 10 分鐘。休息過後，我們將進行第二篇題目之討論。

Your attention, please! There is a 10-minute break between the discussion sessions.
大家請注意！每節討論會中間會有 10 分鐘休息。

Now, all delegates must return to their original panel discussions and be seated for the second session. Thank you very much for your cooperation.
現在，所有代表必須返回各原討論小組並就座，要準備進行第二次會議。非常謝謝大家的配合。

Conferences

情境 5 結束會議 The End of Presentation

We have reached so many resolutions in the discussion session this afternoon, and a summary report will be submitted to the Assembly as a research paper.
我們今天下午的討論已達成多項決議，將呈上大會一份總結報告做為學術論文。

The discussion is finished for the day. Thank you very much for your participation and time.
今天的討論到此為止。非常感謝大家參與及寶貴時間。

This session is completed now. Please proceed to the banquet room for the delegates' cock-tail reception.
本次討論會現在結束。請各位前進宴會廳參加歡迎各位代表的雞尾酒會。

給力單字

1. **chair** (*v.t.*)　主持；擔任主席
   I'd like you to chair the meeting.
   我想請你主持會議。
   He will chair the meeting.
   他將擔任該會議的主席。

2. **panel discussion** (*ph.*)　座談會；小組討論會
   There will be a panel discussion on economic and trade issues this morning.
   早上將有一場經貿的小組座談會。

3. **session** (*n.*)　會議，集會
   The committee held a session to discuss the proposed bill.
   委員會開會討論提出的議案。

4. **privilege** (*n.*)　恩典，殊榮
   It is a great privilege to know you.
   認識你真是莫大的榮幸。

5. **assign** (*v.t.*)　派定，指定[（+to/for）]
   He was assigned to the presentation of discussion group
   他被分配到分組討論報告會工作。

6. **National Development Council**　國家發展委員會
   The National Development Council is a cabinet-level authority of the Executive Yuan.
   國家發展委員會是隸屬行政院的一個內閣部會。

7. **keynote speaker** (*ph.*)　專題演講人
   He is a concurrently keynote speaker and economic minister of the nation.
   他是專題演講者也是我國之經濟部長。

8. **present** (*v.t.*)　提出，呈遞[（＋to）]
Some 300 papers were presented at the conference.
會上提出了大約三百篇論文。

9. **incentive** (*n.*)　獎勵；優惠
The government offers investment incentives to solicit foreign investors in Taiwan.
政府提供投資獎勵以吸引外國在台投資。

10. **business opportunities** (*ph.*)　商機
Business opportunities are expected to grow in the newly established free trade zone.
該新設之自由貿易區預期將增加許多商機。

11. **probe** (*v.t.*)　刺探；徹底調查
The chairman appointed a committee to probe the causes of the strike.
該主席委派一個委員會去徹底調查罷工的起因。

12. **agenda** (*n.*)　議程
So many discussion items have been listed on the agenda.
許多待討論事項已被列入議程。

13. **keynote speech** (*ph.*)　專題報告
Some keynote speeches were canceled, and submitted with written papers instead.
有部分專題報告被取消了，改用以書寫報告呈交。

14. **raise** (*v.t.*)　提出；發出
None of them raised any objection.
他們誰也沒提出反對意見。

Conferences

247

15. **respond** (*v.t.*) 以…回答

He responded no to the first question.

他對第一個問題的回答是否定的。

16. **adjourn** (*v.t.*) 暫停

The chairman has the power to adjourn the meeting at any time.

主席有隨時暫停會議的權力。

17. **break** (*n.*) 暫停；休息

There is a ten - minute break between the discussion panels.

小組討論中間有十分鐘休息時間。

18. **attention** (*n.*) 注意；專心

Let me have your attention!

請注意聽我講話！

19. **seated** (*adj.*) 就座的；有…座位的

Please be seated, the conference will open soon.

請大家就座，大會即將開始。

20. **summary** (*n.*) 總結，摘要[（+of）]

Please write a one - page summary of this report.

請給這份報告寫成一頁的摘要。

21. **research paper** (*ph.*) 研究報告

This research paper has to be delivered to each delegate of the conference.

這份研究報告必須發給每位參加會議之代表。

22. **finish** (*v.t.*) 結束；完成工作

What time does the presentation finish?

報告會什麼時候結束？

23. **proceed** (*v.t.*)　行進

The chairman got off the stage and proceeded to his own seat.

主席下了講台，走回他自己的座位。

給力句型

1. break　休息

   *have/take a break

   Let's take a ten minute break.

   讓我們休息十分鐘。

   *tea/coffee/lunch break

   It's time for a coffee break.

   該喝杯咖啡休息一下了。

   *without a break

   She had worked all day without a break.

   她一整天都在工作，沒有休息。

2. finish　完成

   *finish doing sth

   I finished typing the report just minutes before it was due.

   我在報告該交出前幾分鐘才打完它。

   *finish by doing sth

   She finished off her speech by thanking her sponsors.

   她以感謝贊助人結束了談話。

Conferences

*finish sth

You can't go anywhere until you finish your work.

沒完成工作前你哪兒也不能去。

職場補給 **Prologue & Host Presence 開場白與主持風采**

　　主席在主持報告前，開場白（opening remarks）會先簡單自我介紹並歡迎各代表專程參加會議等。另外最主要是介紹專題演講者及其學經歷背景（curriculum vitae），此部分 c.v.簡歷，一般在開會前主辦單位都會事先聯絡所邀請者之單位或其本人提供，再準備好後給主席於報告時卓參。藉此介紹，各參與會議代表當下可大略認識主持人及演講者身份，對於整個會議進行效果有很大幫助。

　　上述資料，主持人會請大會秘書單位將備份資料發給參加開會來賓，或現場採訪記者。各文件格式最好能一致，並以新聞稿方式（press release）發出，以表示對會議之尊重。

　　由於主講人是會議靈魂人物，關係著整場會議之成功與否。因此，在進行演講時，有關會議音響器材或幻燈機（over-head projector）輔助設備等，都須保持正常功能，以達成召開會議之目的。另現場有駐派專人維修會議有關電子設備，以防有任何突發狀況。

　　一個稱職的主持人要掌控好所有議程，讓整個會議得以順利進行。尤其在時間管控及現場秩序方面，更顯得重要。主持人有時也要製造愉快的會議氣氛，不致於讓開會者覺得太無聊。在國際會議中分組討論裡，有些會議室不斷傳出笑談聲音；但有些會議室裡則老是靜悄悄，主持人與大家沒什麼互動性（interaction）。

　　會議裡互相討論，表達不同看法或意見，大家發言機會均等。每位獲准提問發言者，主席必須尊重並給予充分發言時間；如因考慮到議程關係，有必要中斷（interrupt）太冗長發言，也需事先告知並致歉意。可建議個別有太多問題者，於中場休息時間，私下請教專題主講人，或另用書面（in written papers）方式補給主持人轉達意見即可。

達人提點 Documentations 報告資料

　　一般會議主講人的報告（paper）會先影印並裝訂成冊，特別要注意不要裝訂錯頁碼或漏頁。在主講人開講前幾分鐘即可同步發送資料給與會代表。另如有臨時性補充資料，負責會議工作同仁也要盡快送請影印，即時達成任務。

　　報告內容錯誤更正，這部分如果不是很嚴重之錯誤，主持人用口頭更正（oral correction）即可。如果主持人表示要很正式更正的話，工作人員則還是需要使命必達，以避免所謂『為山九仞，功虧一簣』。

Conferences

Exhibition

展覽會

4-1

參展前
Before Exhibition

情境設定

Exhibitions cost a lot but they serve as a valuable media between exhibitors and their potential buyers. The results of most exhibitions are successful if exhibitors are ready—including preparation works before exhibition, on the show, follow-ups, etc., as two exhibitors discussed in the following dialogue：

國際展覽費用很多，但它們在廠商和潛在買主間具有極大之媒介效果。大部分之展覽結果會是圓滿成功的，如果參展者有所準備好，包括參展前、展場中、或是參展後續等等工作，如同兩位參展者以下對話：

角色設定

Exhibitor A：參展廠商 A
Exhibitor B：參展廠商 B

情境 1 規劃活動 Activity Planning

情境對話

Exhibitor A ▶ It is reported that certain international machinery shows are so popular

參展廠商 A ▶ 據報導，有許多特定的國際機械

254

and they attract excessive exhibitors than expected. One good example is the Taipei International Machine Tools Show (TIMTOS), a largest exhibition of its kind for machinery and relevant parts held in Taiwan every two years.

展會非常搶手,每年都吸引超出預期之參展廠商。『台北國際工具機展』即是一個好例子,它是機械及相關零配件類之最大型展覽,每兩年在台灣舉辦一次。

Exhibitor B ▶ You are absolutely right. That's why my company decides to attend TIMTOS 2015, and we'll soon submit the entry form to the organizer.

參展廠商 B ▶ 您說得完全地正確。這就是為何本公司決定要參加『TIMTOS 2015』之原因,我們也即將繳交報名表給主辦單位。

Exhibitor A ▶ Do you know that the TIMTOS has been short of booths due to great demand in recent years and it is very hard to get extra space? Exhibitors are required to book their booths ahead of the show by about six months ago?

參展廠商 A ▶ 您知道『台北國際工具機展』這幾年因為大量需求之故,攤位一直很短缺,也很難求到多餘位置?參展廠商也必須於展會前半年左右就開始預約他們的攤位?

Exhibition

Exhibitor B ▶ The company applied for a total of 20 booths for the show, but it is said that the number may normally be cut by half. I hope that the organizer would grant us with the booth as needed.

參展廠商 B ▶ 本公司總共申請 20 個攤位,但據說該數目通常會被對半砍。我希望展會主辦單位能盡量核准我們所需求之攤位。

Exhibitor A ▶ Yes, it is. So, remember to send back the entry form and booth rentals at your earliest convenience. Too many exhibitors are still on the waiting list for approvals.

參展廠商 A ▶ 沒錯，它是這樣的。因此，務必記的儘快報名表格及攤位租金寄回。目前有許多參展者正在等待名單批核。

Exhibitor B ▶ Any idea about Chicago's IMTS and Hannover's EMO, two famous international machine tools exhibitions in the world? Would you mind making a brief introduction of the two specialized exhibitions?

參展廠商 B ▶ 您對於芝加哥國際工具機展以及漢諾威製造工業展，兩個世界知名工作母機設備大展，有無任何概念？您不介意對此兩檔專業展會做簡短介紹？

Exhibitor A ▶ IMTS is another popular machine tool exhibition aiming at the North American machinery market, compared that of EMO show for the European Union region. About 100,000 visitors and buyers are attracted to call on the shows each year.

參展廠商 A ▶ 芝加哥國際工具機展成為北美地區機械市場另一最熱門展會；然而漢諾威展則在歐盟地區。上述各展會每年吸引參觀人潮及買主大約 100,000 人次。

Exhibitor B ▶ Thank you for reminding me. As you suggested, my company should plan more exhibitions in the two shows mentioned above.

參展廠商 B ▶ 謝謝您的提醒。如您所建議，本公司應多規劃並參加上述兩個展會。

給力單字

1. **exhibitor** (*n.*) 展示者；參展者
All exhibitors displayed their best products.
所有參展者展示了他們的最好的產品

2. **exhibition** (*n.*) 展覽；展示會[（+of）]
We went to an exhibition of machine tools at the Taipei World Trade Center.
我們去台北世界貿易中心參觀工具機展。

3. **absolutely** (*adv.*) 完全地；絕對地
The exhibition is an absolutely successful marketing event in recent years.
此展會絕對是近年來最出色的一個行銷事件。

4. **entry form** (*ph.*) 報名表
The entry form for the machine tool show has to be submitted for registration.
必須繳交工具機展會報名表以便登記。

5. **booth** (*n.*) 攤位，攤檔
The organizer successfully sold out over 8,000 booths for the exhibition this year
今年主辦單位為此展會成功地銷售超過 8,000 個攤位。

6. **book** (*v.t.*) 預訂；預約
The company has booked 20 booths for the show to be held next year.
公司為明年即將舉行的展會已預訂了 20 個攤位。

Exhibition

7. **apply for** (*ph.*)　申請，請求
We have applied to the organizer for extra booths.
我們已向主辦單位申請多一些攤位。

8. **grant** (*v.t.*)　同意，准予
The organizer granted the company's booth request for the exhibition.
主辦單位同意該公司對展會攤位的要求。

9. **booth rentals** (*ph.*)　攤位租金
All booth rentals have to be paid before exhibition according to the organizer.
根據主辦者，所有攤位租金必須於展會前繳清。

10. **approval** (*n.*)　批准；認可
The booth application had the approval of the organizer.
攤位申請得到主辦單位的認可。

11. **machine tools** (*ph.*)　工作母機；工具機
Statistics shows that Taiwan ranks as the world's No.4 machine tool production.
數據顯示台灣是全世界第四大工具機製造國。

12. **European Union** (*ph.*)　歐洲聯盟；歐盟
European Union used to be the 2nd largest single economic market in the world.
歐盟曾經是全世界第二大單一經濟體市場。

13. **remind** (*v.t.*)　提醒；使記起[（+of）]
This exhibition reminds me of the one we attended in the U.S. last year.
這個展覽會使我想起去年我們在美國參加過的那一次。

給力句型

1. apply　申請

   *apply for

   He has applied for a booth in the exhibition.
   他已申請在展會中有一個攤位。

   *apply to

   The company applied to four exhibitions and was accepted by all of them.
   公司向四個國際展會提出了申請，都被接受了。

   *apply sth. to

   New technology is being applied to product displays in the exhibition.
   新技術正被應用到展會產品展示裡。

2. grant　允許

   *grant sb sth

   The consortium has been granted permission to rent a pavilion in the exhibition.
   該財團已獲准在展會中租用一整個展示館。

   *grant sb's request

   The company's request for exhibition benefit has been granted.
   該公司的展會補貼申請已經得到批准。

Exhibition

情境 2 控制預算 Budget Control

情境對話

A ▶ In comparison with other international exhibitions, the booth rental is reasonable for TIMTOS 2015, estimating at about NT$500,000 for a total of 20 booths, but this cost expects to exceed our budget. Is that possible we bargain with the organizer over the rental?

參展廠商 A ▶ 與其他國際性展會比較，雖然『2015 台北國際工具機展』之攤位租金比較合理，20 個攤位將近要 NT$500,000；但費用也已超出我們的預算。我們可以跟主辦單位協議租金嗎？

B ▶ As I know, the booth rental is a fixed price. However, the organizer offers a 5% early-bird discount as an incentive for exhibitors, and the government authorities have offered subsidies for certain exhibition.

參展廠商 B ▶ 就我所知，攤位租金係採用固定價格。主辦單位有提供 5%早鳥折扣優惠給參展廠商，而且政府有關單位已有提供某些特定參展之補貼。

A ▶ We still need to retrench expenditures regarding the booth decoration so as to meet the budget. The basic decoration fee costs about US$150 per square meter.

參展廠商 A ▶ 我們公司仍需要在攤位裝潢方面樽節開銷，以配合預算。基本裝潢費用每平方公尺大約要價美金 150 元。

B ▶ Compared with your company, we will focus on more product exposure in the exhibition, instead of only corporate image. The booth design in product display is cheaper due to less use of wood decorations.

參展廠商 B ▶ 與貴司比較，本公司將在本次展會中多做些產品曝光，而不只是企業形象。攤位設計在產品展示方面會比較便宜，因為需要木工裝潢較少。

給力單字

1. **rental** (n.)　租金；租金收入[C]
   The quarterly rental will be $ 50,000.
   每一季的租金為五萬元。

2. **bargain** (v.t.)　討價還價[（+with/over/about）]
   She bargained with the booth decoration designer over the price.
   她與攤位裝潢設計講價錢。

3. **early-bird discount** (ph.)　早鳥折扣（優惠）
   The early-bird discount has become a popular incentive package in many exhibitions.
   許多展會之早鳥優惠已成為受歡迎的獎勵方案。

4. **subsidy** (n.)　津貼；補助金
   The exhibition industry depends for its survival on government subsidies.
   展覽行業依靠政府津貼而得以維持。

Exhibition

5. **retrench** (*v.t.*)　緊縮；樽節

Due to financial difficulties, the company will retrench expenditures on exhibitions.

由於財政危機，該公司打算緊縮展覽費用。

6. **exposure** (*n.*)　陳列；曝光

Exhibitors make more product exposures through the attendance of exhibition.

參展廠商因展會而使產品得以多增加曝光。

7. **corporate image** (*ph.*)　企業形象

The corporate image of the company improves significantly in the exhibition.

該公司之企業形象透過參展而有顯著地改善。

給力句型

1. rental　租金

The booth rental is expensive in international exhibitions.
國際展覽會租金很貴。

£ 20 of this booth bill is for lighting rental.
這份攤位賬單上有 20 英鎊是電燈租用費。

*rental car

We had a rental car when we were on the period of exhibition.
我們在參展期間租了一輛車。

情境 3 邀請客戶 Invitation

情境對話

A ▸ It is a must to advise our customers about the TIMTOS exhibition next year, and invite potential buyers to visit our booth if they are available. And our invitation has to be sent to make appointments on their calendars in advance.

參展廠商 A ▸ 我們必須告知客戶有關明年台北國際工具機展，並邀請具有潛力買主是否有空來我們攤位拜訪。邀請函也必須提前寄出，讓客戶在他們的行事曆上預留拜會時間。

B ▸ Are we going to offer the airport pick-up and hotel accommodations for our important foreign buyers? This move has been done over the past few exhibitions, and customers are very satisfied with our services.

參展廠商 B ▸ 對於重要國外買主，我們通常會安排機場接機或飯店住宿事宜嗎？過去幾次展會都做此項措施，而且客戶非常滿意我們的服務。

A ▸ Instead of visiting exhibition, please make sure whether there are any clients who would like to pay courtesy calls to our factories. Some international buyers prefer the visit to the factory and have an on-site understanding of suppliers.

參展廠商 A ▸ 請確認是否有哪些國外訪客不去展場，反而有需要到工廠參訪者。有些國際買家比較喜歡直接拜訪工廠，以實地了解供應商情形。

Exhibition

263

B ▶ Of course, we also arrange a factory tour, but foreign buyers can first visit our booth in the exhibition. I am thinking that we are unable to receive them at the factory when most of our sales persons are assigned to the exhibition arena.

參展廠商 B ▶ 那是當然，我們也會安排客戶工廠參觀旅程，惟希望他們能夠先到攤位拜訪。我在想因為大多數業務人員都已指派去展會現場，無法在工廠接待。

給力單字

1. **advise** (*v.t.*)　通知，告知[（+of）]
   Please advise us of any change in your exhibition plan.
   你們的展會計畫倘有變更，請告訴我們。

2. **appointment** (*n.*)　約會[（+with）]
   I have an appointment with foreign buyers in the evening.
   今晚我與國外買主有個約會。

3. **move** (*n.*)　措施，對策[+to-v]
   The airport-up service is a friendly move to foreign buyers in exhibitions.
   展會去機場接機，對國外買主是一個很友善的措施。

4. **instead of**　代替；寧願
   He will go to the exhibition instead of you.
   他將代替你去參加展會。

5. **on-site** (*n.*)　現場
We set up an on-set service center in the exhibition.
我們在展會設立一個現場服務中心。

6. **tour** (*n.*)　參觀；巡視
Together with our foreign buyers, we made a half-day tour around the city.
我們與國外買主一起在該城市做了半日旅遊。

7. **receive** (*v.t.*)　接待，歡迎
They received us most cordially.
他們熱忱地接待了我們。

給力句型

1. appointment　約會

*appointment to do sth

I have an appointment to see the foreign buyer in exhibition.
我約好了在展會中與國外買主見面。

*make an appointment

Phone his secretary and make an appointment in the exhibition.
打電話給他的祕書約定時間在展會碰面。

*keep an appointment

If you fail to keep an appointment with the foreign buyer, you may lose the order.
如果你和國外買主約好時間但卻沒去，你可能會因此而失掉訂單。

Exhibition

情境 4 宣傳活動 Marketing Activity

情境對話

A ▶ The organizer offers a manual which introduces the exhibition layout and the booth number of exhibitors. It also designates more than one information counter for catalog displays of exhibitors.

參展廠商 A ▶ 主辦單位會提供一本大會手冊，包括一張展會地圖及所有參展者之攤位號碼。也會指定一個以上之諮詢櫃檯以提供給參展者放置公司型錄之用。

B ▶ Another important marketing channel is to insert advertising pages in the directory published by the association. For instance, the Taiwan Machine Tools Directory recruits about 400 advertisers per year and is the most popular and specialized publication of its kind in exhibition.

參展廠商 B ▶ 另一項重要宣傳管道是參加公會出版之總覽廣告。以『台灣工具機總覽』為例，它每年平均招攬約 400 家公司廣告，在展場上是最受歡迎及專業的刊物。

A ▶ It sounds like perfect product marketing in exhibition. Could you elaborate more details about the directory and its advertising effects?

參展廠商 A ▶ 聽起來像是不錯的展會產品宣傳。您可以再深入談一下該總覽之細節，以及它的廣告效益如何？

B ▶ Jointly published by both TAMI and Lets Media, the directory has become increasingly popular in international machinery exhibitions such as TIMTOS and among others. Through the directory's distribution, many local and international manufacturers have gained feedbacks through their exposures over 25 exhibitions each year.

參展廠商 B ▶ 該總覽是由機械公會與雷斯媒體共同出版，在台北國際工具機展及其他國際展會裡已逐漸成為熱門刊物。透過總覽的配送，許多國內及國際廠商透過每年超過 25 檔展會中曝光，並獲得相當回饋。

給力單字

1. **manual** (*n.*)　手冊，簡介
The exhibition manual made by the organizer is very handy for visitors.
主辦單位所製作的大會手冊對參觀者非常方面使用。

2. **catalog** (*n.*)　目錄；目錄冊
Company catalogs are an important marketing tool in exhibition.
公司型錄在展會中是一項很重要之工具商。

3. **directory** (*n.*)　工商名錄；電話簿等
The exhibition directory is sold at the price of US$40 per copy.
大會參展手冊每份售價 40 美元。

4. **advertising** (*n.*)　廣告
The magazine contains a great deal of advertising.
這本雜誌裡有大量廣告。

Exhibition

5. **increasingly** (*adv.*)　不斷增加地，越來越多地

Exhibitions have become increasingly full in the world over the past five years.

在過去的五年中，全世界展會越來越多。

給力句型

1. recruit　招募；吸收

   We're having difficulty recruiting qualified staff for exhibitions.
   →We encounter difficulties in finding qualified staff for the exhibition work.
   →It is hard for the company to find qualified staff for exhibitions.
   我們很難招募到合格職員去作展會工作。

   *recruit sb to do sth

   The company recruited two employees to handle everything in exhibition.
   公司動員了兩名員工去處理所有的展會工作。

2. distribution　分配；銷售

   They could not agree about the distribution of the exhibition work.
   他們無法就展會工作分配一事達成協議。

   We have a good product but our distribution is bad in exhibition.
   我們的產品很好，但在展會的銷售情況不佳。

攤位佈置 Booth Decoration

情境對話

A ▶ The organization has confirmed the booth layout for the exhibition, and the decoration plan should be conducted soon. I need to know the budget set for the decoration.

B ▶ As we have spent too much money on the booths, I am afraid that our decoration budget is limited to somewhat extent. It looks like we only highlight the decoration of both product display and negotiation areas but less on the image pavilion.

A ▶ Are you acquainted with the organizer's regulations about exhibitor decoration, and what should be noticed? Is that possible to locate our own booth designer or it has to be working with the decoration company designated by the exhibition?

B ▶ There are regulations made public in the service manual of the exhibition. Refer your question to the organizer to see whether you can find your own designer or not.

參展廠商 A ▶ 主辦單位已確認我們展會攤位平面圖，應該即刻進行裝潢規劃。我必須知道有準備好多少裝潢預算。

參展廠商 B ▶ 由於我們已花了許多錢在攤位部分，我擔心裝潢預算多少會受到限制。看來我們只會強調產品展示與洽談區裝潢，形象展示館部分則會較少著墨。

參展廠商 A ▶ 您熟悉有關參展者裝潢規定嗎，有哪些重要事情需注意？我們可以自己找攤位設計師或者一定要使用大會指定之裝潢公司？

參展廠商 B ▶ 大會服務手冊裡有公告有關展會裝潢規定。請將問題提交主辦單位並了解是否可自己找攤位設計師。

Exhibition

269

給力單字

1. **confirm** 證實;確認

   The organizer has confirmed the booth reservation of exhibitor.

   主辦者已確認參展者之攤位預約。

2. **set for** 準備好的[(+for)]

   The company was set for the exhibition.

   公司已為展會做好準備。

3. **highlight** (*v.t.*) 使顯著,使突出

   The booth decoration highlighted the company's products in exhibition.

   攤位裝潢讓公司的產品在展會中顯得非常突出。

4. **image pavilion** (*ph.*) 形象館

   There are several national image pavilions in this international machinery show.

   本次國際機械展裡設有許多國家形象館。.

5. **designate** (*v.t.*) 標出;表明

   Booth numbers of exhibitors are designated on the manual of exhibition.

   展會手冊上標出參展廠商之攤位號碼。

6. **make public** (*ph.*) 公佈

   Technical seminars held in line with the exhibition are made public.

   配合展會所舉辦之技術研討會已經被公布。

7. **refer** (*v.t.*) 將…提交,交付[(+to)]

   We referred the proposal to the organizer of exhibition.

   我們把這一建議提交展會主辦單位處理。

給力句型

1. acquaint　認識

   *be fully acquainted with sth

   All our employees are fully acquainted with exhibition affairs.
   我們所有的員工都十分熟悉展會事務。

   *get/become acquainted

   You can get better acquainted with exhibitions if you ever participated in.
   如果你曾經參加過展會，你可以有更多了解。

2. designate　指定；指派

   *designate sth as/for

   We're going to designate this space as a negotiation area.
   我們準備把這個空間指定為洽談區。

   *designate sb to do sth

   He has been designated to take over the organizer of exhibition.
   他被選派接任展會主辦者的職位

Exhibition

情境 6　製作型錄、海報、名片 Production of Catalogues, Posters, Name Cards

情境對話

A ▶ It is necessary to reproduce the product catalogues, business cards, posters, and premiums for the exhibition to come. What are your comments on these?

B ▶ The sales department needs 500 copies of new brochures for the exhibition, and this budget has been approved. As for the fabrication of name cards, posters, and premiums, the deadline is set on one month ahead of the exhibition.

A ▶ My company also plans to make premiums which are useful in daily life, and are convenient for visitors to carry in the exhibition.

B ▶ That is a very good idea, especially on small gifts and the budget. We will discuss this issue in the 2nd phase preparatory meeting of the exhibition slated next month.

參展廠商 A ▶ 本次展會需要重新製作公司產品型錄、名片、海報、及小贈品於會場中發送。您對此有何高見？

參展廠商 B ▶ 業務單位展會要用 500 本新小冊子，這部分預算已核准。至於有關名片、海報、及小贈品等製作，截止完成日期訂於展會前一個月前。

參展廠商 A ▶ 我們公司也計畫製作一些日常生活有用的小贈品，也非常方便展會參訪者攜帶。

參展廠商 B ▶ 那是很好的想法，尤其針對小禮物及預算方面。我們在下個月排訂之第二階段展會準備會議中再另洽談。

給力單字

1. **catalogue** (*n.*)　目錄，一覽表
The company catalogue lubricates sales in the exhibition.
公司目錄在展會銷售有潤滑作用。

2. **premium** (*n.*)　優惠；附贈禮品
If you buy three you get a premium of one more, free.
如果你買三個，可以再免費多送你一個。

3. **brochure** (*n.*)　宣傳小冊子
The company presented glossy brochures to those visitors to the booth.
公司贈送精美宣傳小冊子給來攤位拜訪之客人。

4. **fabrication** (*n.*)　製造，生產
The fabrication of these posters is expensive.
這些海報製造成本很昂貴。

5. **convenient** (*adj.*)
It is very convenient to take MRT to the exhibition.
搭乘捷運到展場非常方便。

6. **slate** (*v.t.*)　預定；選定[（+for）]
The exhibition is slated to kick off at 10 o'clock this morning.
展會已定於早上十點鐘開始。

Exhibition

給力句型

1. slate　預定

*be slated for

The new exhibition buildings are slated for construction next year.
這些新展覽會大樓定於明年開始建設。

*be slated to be/do sth

New exhibition halls are slated to start the construction soon.
新展覽館即將開始建造。

情境 7　展品物流 Product Logistics

情境對話

A ▸ We have entrusted a sea transportation company for the shipment of our products in the U.S. exhibition. Please pay close attention to the shipping date and prepare all packaging works in due time.

參展廠商 A ▸ 我們已委請一家海運公司負責美國展會產品托運。請密切注意裝船日期，並於適當時間準備好包裝工作。

B ▸ The packaging will be completed as soon as article descriptions for the shipping are printed out. I will contact with the sea transportation company for the delivery.

參展廠商 B ▸ 等船舶麥頭印好後，即可完成包裝工作。我會與海運公司聯繫有關托運事情。

A ▸ We still need to prepare our product

參展廠商 A ▸ 我們還需

documents, including patent rights and certification of origin. These documents have to be carried for the customs clearances.

要準備有關產品文件，包括專利證書、原產地證明等。需要攜帶這些文件，以便通關之用。

B ▶ You bet. I will rule out any influences on the delivery, and make sure our products can reach the exhibition destination with no delays.

參展廠商 B ▶ 當然。我會排除任何影響托運問題，並確保我們的產品不會延誤抵達展會目的地。

給力單字

1. **sea transportation** (*ph.*)　船運
   The sea transportation is arranged about one month ahead of the exhibition.
   船運工作需要在展會大約一個月前即安排好。

2. **packaging** (*n.*)　包裝；打包
   Displayed products should be prepared in good packaging to avoid damages.
   展示用產品要預先包裝好以避免損害。

3. **article descriptions** (*ph.*)　嘜頭；物品說明
   The article descriptions are made in both Chinese and English languages.
   物品說明使用中英文語言。

Exhibition

4. **delivery** (*n.*)　運輸

Please ensure that the product delivery is punctual for the exhibition.

請務必保證產品運輸必須準時抵達展場。

5. **patent rights** (*ph.*)　專利權

Our products have obtained patent rights in Taiwan and abroad.

我們的產品在台灣及國外均獲得專利權。

6. **certification of origin** (*ph.*)　原產地證明

All products are earmarked with certification of origins.

所有產品都標示原產地證明。

7. **customs clearances** (*ph.*)　通關

The procedures of customs clearances are strict in the U.S.

美國海關通關手續很嚴格。

8. **you bet**　的確；當然

"Will your company to attend this exhibition next year?" "You bet!"

「貴公司明年會再參加這個展會嗎？」「當然！」

9. **rule out**　把…排除在外，排除…的可能性

The company ruled out the possibility of attending the show in the U.S.

該公司完全排除到美國參加展會之可能性。

給力句型

1. delivery　發送的東西

Deliveries to the exhibition should be made at the back entrance.

貨物應該送到展場後門口。

*take delivery of sth.

When can we take delivery of the product for exhibition?
我們什麼時候才能收到展會用產品?

*special delivery

We used special delivery for our products in exhibition.
我們使用限時專送寄展會產品。

職場補給 Exhibition Sidelights 展會花絮

規劃參加展會牽涉範圍很廣,舉例以必須或如何參加哪幾檔展會而言,就是一門學問。許多知名專業國際展會,因為在業界深具代表及重要性,國內外重量級(heavyweight)廠商早已列入公司重點行銷場所,每年必定報名參加,藉此推廣公司產品,更爭買主訂單。因此,在『僧多粥少』情況下,大會總攤位數量往往供不應求,更遑論要拿到好地點或多爭取 1~2 格攤位?

一般大會在報名參展方面,都會有一些『潛規則』(hidden rules),例如,前提要先具有該主辦公會之會員身份,另年營業額或外銷實績(export records)要達一定金額以上,最少會保障一個基本攤位數量。國際與本國廠商之報名方式及費用也不盡然相同,因為有政策上及特定單位參展補助款等考量,這些有關事項在規劃報名參展時,承辦人員最好能掌握所有資訊,以利進行報名相關展會及攤位之申請工作。

由於展會報名費用多半很昂貴,尤其在歐、美地區更是高的嚇人;以一格 3 x 3 平方公尺標準攤位計算,收費大約落在 NT$120,000~NT$150,000 價位,平均展會期間僅六~七天左右。再加上攤位佈置、機票、住宿及人員出差(business travel)等費用,因此必須先控制好相關預算,另評估展會

Exhibition

277

可能帶來之效益及回收? 如果是首度參展『大拜拜』或僅是試水溫（test the water），就極有可能『摃龜』而不會接到訂單，廠商要先有心理準備。

　　相對有些廠商早已在當地設有代理（agent）或經銷商（distributor），一旦決定去參展時，一定會請他們幫忙；包括申請攤位、佈置等工作。參展廠商也會提前打電話及寫信告知現有及鄰近國家地區客戶，邀請他們屆時來會場攤位見面，充當攤位人氣；也趁此展會熱絡情誼，奠定未來商機。

　　針對現場洽商需求，目前很多資深廠商在攤位佈置時，會保留比較多空間做為會客及洽談區（negotiation areas）用途，產品區則比較少空間；配合此需求，可能要多租一組桌椅或增加咖啡機及飲水設備即可。有些世界級廠商會場攤位佈置華麗，甚至設有吧檯與廚師伺候；這些攤位上經常高朋滿座，也達到預定宣傳效果。

　　相對上，國內展會場地佈置比較簡單。一般標準攤位上方僅貼上公司中英文名字，再加後面幾片隔板（panels）並掛上海報等，屬『陽春型』設計，費用低。國際級展會佈置，每個攤位裡外都鋪長毛軟地毯，有些隔間也會使用布慢，整體看起來很優雅及舒敞，但這些裝潢費用比較高。如臨時有需要設計一張海報，可能要報價上萬元台幣。

　　參加展會前，事先準備有關公司產品型錄/紀念品等，提供有潛力客戶（potential clients），以加深對公司印象。一個製作完美得型錄，有時會加強客戶採購意願。另外，負責參展業務人員也要寄的多帶一些名片到會場，以備不時之需。針對各不同市場，名片上除中/英文對照外，也可考慮另外製作加印有當地語言之名片，以增加客戶之親切感，有時候說不定會因此舉而小兵立大功。

　　有關託運參展產品等，如屬大型機器設備或樣品，在包裝上都要很小心，必須確保產品不會受到任何損壞，並如期抵達會場。最好跟託運公司事先談妥有關作業要點，並準備好相關文件，還要加上運輸保險（transportation insurance），以免造成公司損失。

　　參展人員儘可能提前至會場，除了協助堆高機等進場搬運作業，也要作好測試（test run）等工作，才會讓展會期間順利進行。撤展時亦同，一般大會有關機械進出原則：先進場者後離場，要依照大會排定間表進行作業尚可。切忌擅自行動，引起無謂紛爭，甚至鬧出國際笑話。

達人提點 Anti-burglaries 防竊之道

　　廠商在前一天佈展時，要特別注意自己隨身物品（personal belongings），尤其是背包及重要證件等，務必隨身攜帶或保持高度警戒。許多佈置工作在展會前一天，現場還是如火如荼在進行裝潢中或收尾工作，兵荒馬亂，危機四伏。有些初次出國參展人員一時大意，將貴重東西隨便「藏放」在攤位裡，自己以為很安全；殊不知早已被宵小盯上，瞬時不翼而飛，損失慘重，時有所聞。

　　展會開跑後，失竊（burglary）問題則比較少。因為這時候每家攤位上都有負責人，一般訪客不太敢隨便進入空攤位「參觀」，但參展人員自己也是要小心。如果預算可以的話，最好建議公司至少同時派兩人參展，比較可互相照應。

　　國際大展期間，旅館住宿（hotel accommodations）也會出現水漲船高情形，自己定行程有可能會被安排住到離會場較遠之飯店，如此每天往返會場交通時間佔太久。如果是透過旅行社安排行程，這個問題較小；因為是團客，飯店會有優惠和讓步。且進出有專人專車負責，負責參展人員可以專心展出，全力拼業務；不必擔心交通食宿等雜事，以上這些因素及效益可列為規劃參展時之重要評估。

Exhibition

4-2 在展場 At the Exhibition

情境設定

As exhibitors are busy with reception of buyers at the exhibition, their skill of salesmanship becomes a vital process to get on-the-spot orders from buyers. In the process of exhibition, an experienced salesman is responsible for marketing and publicity as well as crisis management, if needed.

 展廠商在展會期間忙碌接待買主，他們的銷售技巧成為在爭取買主現場訂單中的一個重要過程。有經驗的業務人員在展場中要負責行銷宣傳，也包括危機處理，如果有需要的話。

角色設定

The Salesman：公司業務員
The Buyer：買主

情境 1 介紹公司與產品 Company and Product Briefs

情境對話

The Salesman ▶ It's my pleasure to brief my company's products to you. With over 30

公司業務員 ▶ 我很榮幸簡報敝公司產品給您認

years of expertise, we are now a leading manufacturer in the machine tools industry in Taiwan with a full production line of CNC machines, including latest five-axis machining center models.

識。我們是來自台灣一家擁有超過 30 年專業的機械廠,目前在工具機製造方面居於領導地位,生產線有能力製造全系列電腦數位輔助控制機械,包括最新型五軸綜合加工機型。

The Buyer ▶ It is very nice to meet you. I am very interested in Taiwan-made machine tools and my company has solicited many supply sources from your country over the past decade.

買主 ▶ 很高興能與您認識。本人對台灣製造工具機非常感興趣,我們公司在過去十餘年來也從貴國徵求過許多供應來源。

The Salesman ▶ So you are an old Taiwan-hand. My company has ventured into foreign markets and fared well in both Europe and the U.S. in recent years.

公司業務員 ▶ 那您應該是一位台灣通。我們公司近年才冒險進入國外市場,在歐洲及美國銷售還頗有進展。

The Buyer ▶ Indeed. I also noticed that your company is a regular exhibitor in several international machinery exhibitions, occupying many booths with fantastic decorations.

買主 ▶ 確實。我也注意到貴司最近幾年在國際機械展會上已成為一名參展常客,租用許多攤位而且佈置地極佳。

The Salesman ▶ My company participates in major machine tool exhibitions held both

公司業務員 ▶ 我們公司每年參加國內外舉辦之

Exhibition

281

home and abroad each year, and we expect to increase our exports and sales in this regard. By the way, would you like to see a demonstration of our CNC machining center?

工具機展會，期望能增加外銷方面生意。順便問一下，您願意看我們的機器操作示範？

The Buyer ▶ I appreciate it very much for your presentation and time, and may I pick up a complimentary copy of your brochures? For an assessment purpose, please send me more information after the exhibition.

買主 ▶ 非常謝謝您的報告與時間，我可以帶走一份公司免費贈送之產品型錄嗎？也請您在展會結束後寄多送一些資料給我，做為評估用途。

The Salesman ▶ Thank you for your visiting. I'll offer you a quotation with best prices by e-mail soon.

公司業務員 ▶ 謝謝您的來訪。我會儘快用電子郵件提供您一份優惠報價單。

The Buyer ▶ Please do that, and use the e-mail address of my business card. I expect to locate more supply sources from your esteemed company in the future.

買主 ▶ 請就按照那樣吧，用我名片上之電子郵件地址即可。我希望未來能從貴公司發掘更多供應資源。

給力單字

1. **brief** (*v.t.*)　簡報
The exhibitor briefed the buyer the company's products displayed at the exhibition.
該參展廠商向買主簡報其公司在會場中展示的產品。

2. **production line** (*ph.*)　生產線
The manufacturer has now specialized in full machine production lines.
該製造廠目前專門從事全系列機械生產線。

3. **solicit** (*v.t.*)　請求；徵求[（+for）]
Exhibitors are busy soliciting foreign orders at the exhibition.
參展廠商正忙著在展會中爭取國外訂單。

4. **old hand** (*ph.*)　老手；有經驗者
He is an old hand in displaying products.
他是一個陳列商品方面的老手。

5. **fare** (*v.t.*)　遭遇；進展
His company fared better in exports to the world marketplace.
他公司在全球外銷市場上頗有進展。

6. **indeed** (*adv.*)　真正地，確實
A friend in need is a friend indeed.
患難之交才是真正的朋友。

7. **demonstration** (*n.*)　示範；論證
The demonstration of machine operations and functions is necessary at the exhibition.
在展會中示範機械操作及功能是有其必要的。

Exhibition

8. **complimentary** (*adj.*)　贈送的

I've got two complimentary gifts for the exhibitor.

我獲贈兩份參展者送的禮物。

9. **quotation** (*n.*)　報價; 行情

Could you give us a quotation with relevant specifications of this machine type?

你能提供給我們本機型以及有關規格的報價嗎？

10. **business card** (*ph.*)　名片：商務名片

I exchanged business cards with many buyers in the exhibition.

我與許多買主在展會中交換了名片。

11. **locate** (*v.t.*)　探出，找出

The foreign buyer is trying to locate new supply sources from Taiwan.

該國外買主正設法從台灣找到新供應商。

給力句型

1. demonstration　示範

*give a demonstration

He gave a demonstration of how the machinery works.

他作示範來說明這個機械是如何運作的。

*break up a demonstration

Hong Kong police used tear gas and pepper to break up the demonstration.

香港警察使用催淚彈和胡椒粉來驅散示威者。

2. locate　找出位置：座落

We couldn't locate the source of new exhibitions.
我們無法確定新展覽會的來源。

*be located in/by/near etc

The exhibitor is located right in the center of exhibition hall.
該參展廠商正好位於展覽館之中心。

情境 2 掌握買家資訊 **To Command Buyer's Information**

情境對話

The Salesman ▶ May I present you latest CNC machining centers from my company? Our machines are featured with high precision and high quality, which are suitable for high precision metal cutting and processing.

公司業務員 ▶ 我可以向您報告本公司最新型綜合加工機？我們的機器擁有高精密及高品質特色，非常適合做各種高精密之金屬切削及加工。

The Buyer ▶ Could you explain other functions on CNC machining centers, and the prices for the latest model of your company? I am looking for different machine types, and conducting procurements in the exhibition.

買主 ▶ 您可否進一步說明其他的功能，及貴公司最新型之機台價格？我正在尋找不同機型，要在展會中進行採購。

The Salesman ▶ Our machines are good in quality but priced reasonably, compared with

公司業務員 ▶ 與日本或歐洲屬同類型機種，我

Exhibition

285

counterparts from either Japan or Europe. We offer a total solution package service, and make quotations only after a better understanding your requirements.

們公司的機器品質優良但價格卻很合理。我們提供一套全面性解決方案服務，會再進一步了解您們需求之後才報價。

The Buyer ▶ It sounds fair to me. I will offer specifications and special purposes of the machine to be purchased by my company.

買主 ▶ 我聽起來很公平。我會提供我們即將採購之機器規格及特殊需求。

The Salesman ▶ In this case, we are able to provide you with machine function details immediately, plus the summary of both delivery and payment terms. I hope to become your trusted partner soon!

公司業務員 ▶ 既然這樣，我們可以馬上提供機器功能細節，外加運送及付款條件等摘要。我希望不久將來能成為您值得信任的夥伴!

The Buyer ▶ How is your guarantee policy? Could you dispatch technicians abroad to fix up any problems that may occur within the effective period?

買主 ▶ 您們有何品質擔保政策？在有效期間如果有發生任何問題，可以派遣技師到海外維修嗎？

The Salesman ▶ Normally, we guarantee the machine for a formal running of at least one year, and allow an extension of another year period, depending on different situations, however. Yes, technicians are sent to foreign

司業務員 ▶ 正常而言，公司保證機器可正式運轉一年，並視不同狀況允許再延長一年期限。是的，如果有必要的

countries for the repairing purpose, if necessary.

話，技師可被派出國做維修。

The Buyer ▶ That would be a nice deal. I will review your quotation and we might contract with you soon.

買主 ▶ 那將會是一個好交易。在檢視您們的報價後，我們也許可以很快與您簽約。

給力單字

1. **feature** (*n.*)　特徵，特色[（+of）]
   This is a key feature of our machine.
   這是我們機械的一個主要特色。

2. **suitable** (*ad.*)　適當的；合適的[（+to/for）]
   He was suitable for the job of salesman.
   他適合幹業務員工作。

3. **type** (*n.*)　類型，型式[（+of）]
   What type of machine would you prefer to purchase?
   你喜愛採購哪一類機器？

4. **procurement** (*n.*)　採購
   A government procurement package was revealed in an exhibition seminar.
   一項政府採購方案在展覽研討會中被揭示。

5. **counterpart** (*n.*)　極相像的人或物
   The two machines are exact counterparts in make, model, and color.
   這兩部機器的式樣、型號和顏色完全一樣。

Exhibition

6. **solution** (*n.*) 解答；解決[（+to/of/for）]
It may take a long time to find a solution to the machine.
也許要花很長時間才能找到解決這個機器的辦法。

7. **specification** (*n.*) 規格；明細單[（+for）]
The engineer can't start working without the specification for the design.
沒有關於設計的詳細計畫，工程師無法開工。

8. **guarantee** (*n.*) 品質保證；保證書
The machine has a year's guarantee.
這機器有一年的保修期。

9. **dispatch** (*v.t.*) 派遣；發送[（+to）]
The company dispatched an experienced engineer to repair the damage.
公司派遣一個有經驗的工程師去修理損壞的地方。

10. **formal running** (*ph.*) 正式運轉
It takes about half hour to get formal running of the machine.
大約需要半小時機器才能正式運轉。

11. **technician** (*n.*) 技術人員，技師
He is a machinery technician by profession.
他的職業是機器技術人員。

12. **review** (*v.t.*) 再檢查，重新探討
The buyer may review quotations of the new machine.
該買主可以再檢討新機器的報價。

13. **contract** (*v.i.*) 訂契約[（+with）]
We contracted with a Japanese firm for the purchase of CNC machines.
我們與一家日本公司簽約購買電腦數位控制機器。

給力句型

1. guarantee　擔保期

   *be under guarantee

   Your machine will be repaired free if it's still under guarantee.
   你的機器在保用期內可享受免費修理。

   *give sb a guarantee (that)

   Can you give me a guarantee that the work will be finished on time?
   你能向我保證工作會按時完成嗎？

2. review　審查

   *under review

   The new machine systems are currently under review.
   新機器系統目前正接受審查。

   *come up for review

   The company's procurement policy came up for review recently.
   該公司的採購政策最近應該進行審查。

3. contract　合約；合同

   *sign a contract

   Read the contract carefully before you sign it.
   簽署合同以前要仔細閱讀。

   *enter into a contract

   They have just entered into a contract with a machinery company.
   他們剛剛與一家機械廠訂立了一份契約。

Exhibition

情境 3 吸引攤位人氣 Booth Popularity

情境對話

Sales ▶ Welcome to my booth. May I help you?

業務 ▶ 歡迎至本攤位。有需要我幫忙嗎？

Customer ▶ Yes, I am looking for certain cutting tools that are used for lathes and milling machine. I am very interested in tungsten and carbide steel types.

客戶 ▶ 是的，我正在找特定切削刀具供車床及銑床使用。有興趣看看鎢鋼或碳化鋼材製造刀具類。

Sales ▶ For the first exhibition, special offers only for today, with a discount of up to 50% off. Buy one and get one free.

業務 ▶ 配合我們首度參展，僅限今日有特價供應，折扣高達五成。買一送一。

Customer ▶ That's awesome. What are your most popular items at the exhibition?

客戶 ▶ 那真是太棒了。本次展會中您們哪些產品項目最受歡迎？

Sales ▶ My company has specialized in the manufacture of a wide variety of cutting tools, including throw-away types. You may find some good sellers in this booth.

業務 ▶ 本公司為專業製造廠，生產多種不同切削刀具，包括拋棄式的。您可以在攤位上看到這些熱銷貨。

Customer ▶ I am sure that you are expert in

客戶 ▶ 我確信您們是有

cutting tools, but what I concern is product reliabilities and supplying capability of your company in this region.

經驗的刀具廠商，不過我關心的是產品可靠性以及貴公司在本地區之供貨能力。

Sales ▶ For your information, our cutting tools are adopted by leading machine tool makers in the world since we ventured into the line 10 years ago, and we have seldom received customer complaints in the past. Our local distributors are now in a better position to meet individual requirements if orders and payments are confirmed.

業務 ▶ 不妨告訴您，從 10 年前我們冒險進入本行業以來，我們的刀具產品已經獲得世界主要工具機大廠廣泛採用，過去很少接到有客戶抱怨。只要訂單和付款經確認後，我們目前當地經銷商都可以配合個別不同需求。

Customer ▶ The agreement should be reached under the company's purchasing procedures. Before this, I would place orders on trial for some of your products.

客戶 ▶ 協議需要遵照公司的採購程序。在這合約之前，我會先下一些試用性訂單。

Exhibition

給力單字

1. **welcome to** (*ph.*)　歡迎到

   "Welcome to my booth," the exhibitor said.
   「歡迎來本公司攤位，」參展廠商說。

2. **tungsten** (*n.*)　鎢鋼

New generation tungsten cutting tools are now displayed at the exhibition.

新一代鎢鋼刀具正在會場裡展示中。

3. **special offer** (*ph.*)　特價供應

Special offers are usually available in the last day of exhibition.

在展會最後一天通常會有特價供應品。

4. **awesome** (*adj.*)　很好的，了不起的

This international machinery exhibition was really awesome.

這個國際性的機器展會真不錯。

5. **good sellers** (*ph.*)　熱銷貨

This machine is a good seller.

這種機器賣得很好。

6. **expert** (*adj.*)　熟練的，有經驗的[（+at/in/on）]

He became an expert machinery salesman.

他成了一個有經驗的機器業務員。

7. **reliability** (*n.*)　可靠；可信賴性

His reliability is unmatched.

無人比他更可靠。

8. **venture** (*v.t.*)　使冒險；拿…冒險

They ventured their businesses in the new machinery development.

他們冒險去開發新機種的生意。

9. **complaint** (*n.*)　抱怨；抗議

There is no real reason for complaint.

沒有什麼可抱怨的理由。

10. **on trial** (*ph.*)　試驗性的

    Take the machine on trial and then, if you like it, buy it.

    請試用這部機器, 如果你喜歡再買。

給力句型

1. venture　冒險；冒險事業

   They started a commercial venture in the manufacture of machinery.

   他們開始從事製造機械之商業冒險。

   *joint venture

   They had a joint venture in sales of machinery.

   他們合夥作銷售機械之生意。

2. complaint　抱怨

   *have/receive a complaint

   The company received a stream of complaints about its machinery quality.

   該公司收到許多投訴關於它的機械品質。

   *file/lodge/submit a complaint

   I wish to lodge an official complaint.

   我要提出正式投訴。

Exhibition

情境 4 展場危機處理 On-site Crisis Management

情境對話

A ▶ Do you know how to claim to the organizer about the poster we lost in the booth? Will the organizer be responsible for the loss and pay for it?

A ▶ 我們攤位裡遺失了海報，您知道如何向主辦單位要求認領？主辦單位會負責損失並賠償嗎？

B ▶ First, you have to fill out a "lost and found" form and hand it over to the organizer of the exhibition. Secondly, you may claim for the loss if the poster is not found during the exhibition period.

B ▶ 首先，您必須先填寫一張『失物招領』表格，並交給展會主辦單位。接下來，如果在展會期間仍未尋回海報，您就有可能獲得賠償。

A ▶ I am thinking to change the spotlight's direction on the booth because it is harsh to my eyes. Can I do it myself or should I file for an application to the organizer?

A ▶ 我想把攤位上的聚光燈改變方向，因為光線太刺眼睛。我可以自己更換它或是要向主辦單位提出申請？

B ▶ In consideration of the safety reason, any transformation in the booth, especially in electrical items, is done after gaining approvals from the organizer, according to the exhibitors' manual. Thus, you'd better report the problem to the organizer ASAP,

B ▶ 根據參展者手冊，任何攤位變更，尤其有關電力項目，考慮安全理由，必須先取得承辦單位同意始可進行之。因此，您最好儘快告知

and they will send plumbers over the booth to handle this issue.

主辦單位，他們會派水電工過來攤位處理此問題。

A ▶ I found some large-sized signboards which are illegally displayed on the booth, and this may probably cause injuries to visitors at the exhibition. We have to stop this situation before it's too late.

A ▶ 我發現一些大型公司招牌違規放在攤位上面，這樣極有可能會導致展會參觀者因此受傷。我們必須阻止這種情形，以免太遲。

B ▶ Better late than never.

B ▶ 遲做總比不做好。

給力單字

1. **claim** (*v.t.*)　要求；認領
   Do you know how to claim for consumption to the organizer?
   您知道如何向主辦單位索賠嗎?

2. **fill out** (*ph.*)　填寫
   He has to fill a form out.
   他必須填好一張表格。

3. **file** (*v.i.*)　提出申請；提起訴訟[（+for）]
   She decided to file for burglary at the exhibition.
   她決意對展會之竊盜案申請訴訟。

Exhibition

295

4. **transformation** (*n.*)　變化；轉變

The exhibition industry has undergone a complete transformation in recent years.

展覽會行業近年來經歷了重大的轉型。

5. **signboard** (*n.*)　招牌

Too many illegal signboards are hung at the exhibition.

展會中掛了許多違規招牌。

6. **late** (*adj.*)　遲的；[（+for）]

He was late for the grand opening of exhibition this morning.

早上展會正式開幕時候他遲到了。

給力句型

1. stop　停止

*stop sth

You'll have to stop the machine, its generator is overheating .

你得把機器停下來，它的發電機過熱了。

*stop doing sth

He's trying to stop operating the machine.

他正試圖停止操作機器。

*stop and do sth

He stopped the machine operation and waited for further instructions.

他將機器停止操作並等待進一步指示。

*stop that/it

Stop it ! You're breaking the machine.
住手！你要把機器弄壞了。

2. late　遲的；最近的
   *late in August/the evening/1995

   The exhibition took place late in May.
   展會在五月底舉行。

   *of late

   We've not seen the exhibitor's participation at the exhibition of late.
   我們最近沒見過該廠商來參加展會。

情境 5　現場臨時工作人員 On-site Helpers

情境對話

A ▶ As an attempt to strengthen our service, the company decides to hire two young and beautiful lady helpers for the exhibition. Each with US$150 per day, the cost is just the same as we paid last year.

A ▶ 為了加強我們在會場的服務，公司已決定要僱用兩名年輕美麗女助手。每人每天美金 150 元，跟去年我們所付費用一樣。

B ▶ What are their assignments at the exhibition, and are these assistants really

B ▶ 她們會場有分配哪些任務，這些助理對您

297

helpful to your business?

A ▶ With a bilingual capability, these helpers are mainly assigned to distribute catalogues in front of the booth, trying to allure more buyers to visit. And this move usually works!

B ▶ So it is very helpful. That's why your booths are overcrowded with visitors, compared with other exhibitors in the exhibition.

A ▶ Meanwhile, our helpers have the job description to include the collection of visitor's name cards, and footnoting individual requirement at the same time. This is important for follow-up sales contacts and even orders.

B ▶ It is very organized of your helpers, and its function deserves my company to emulate. Perhaps, I expect to enlist the helper into the budget of next exhibition.

們生意能真正地幫上忙嗎？

A ▶ 這些助理通曉兩種語言，主要是在攤位前分發公司型錄，以吸引客人拜訪。這個方法通常會有用!

B ▶ 那倒是很有幫助。難怪相較其他參展廠商，您們攤位上擠滿了訪客。

A ▶ 同時，我們助理工作職責也包括收集訪客名片並同時註記個別需求。這對於業務後續接洽，甚至訂單都非常重要。

B ▶ 您們助手人員非常有組織，其功能頗值得我們仿效。或許，我可以將助手這部分納入明年展會徵招預算裡。

給力單字

1. **helper** (*n.*)　幫手；助手
   She's a good helper at the booth of exhibition.
   她是一個展會攤位好助手。

2. **cost** (*n.*)　費用；成本
   We must reduce the cost for the exhibition.
   我們必須降低展會的成本。

3. **assignment** (*n.*)　任務；工作
   She gladly accepted the assignment as an assistant.
   她高興地接下作助理的工作。

4. **bilingual** (*adj.*)　會說兩種語言的
   Some exhibitors are completely bilingual.
   有些參展廠商能流利地說兩種語言。

5. **allure** (*v.t.*)　引誘，誘惑
   The fine weather allures many visitors to the exhibition.
   晴朗的天氣吸引許多訪客來到展會裡。

6. **overcrowded** (*adj.*)　使過度擁擠[（+with）]
   Too many visitors are overcrowded in the exhibition halls.
   太多訪客造成展覽館擁擠不堪。

7. **job description** (*ph.*)　工作職責說明
   She is qualified for to do job description of exhibition.
   她可勝任展會的工作職責。

8. **footnote** (*v.t.*)　給…作腳註，給…作註釋
   I have not yet footnoted special requirements of customers.
   我還沒有給客戶的特別需求加上腳註。

Exhibition

9. **organized** (*adj.*)　有序的，有組織[條理]的

You can be sure the conference will be well organized if he is in charge.

如果由他來負責，你可以肯定大會將組織得有條不紊。

10. **enlist** (*v.t.*)　徵募，使入伍

We must enlist more show girls as our helpers at the show.

我們必須招更多的展會小姐來當展會助手。

給力句型

1. distribute　分發

*distribute sth among/to

Catalogues and presents have been distributed among the visitors.

已經向訪客分發了型錄和紀念禮物。

The security banned a man distributing leaflets to visitors in the exhibition.

保全禁止一名男子派發傳單給展會訪客。

2. organize　組織

*highly organized

The organizer is famous for being highly organized in the exhibition.

該主辦單位以高度組織展會而聞名。

*get organized

I have to get organized and get some things done.

我得讓自己清醒一下，然後去完成一些事情。

職場補給 Sales Challenge 業績大挑戰

如何在一場國際展會中成功地將自家產品介紹給買主認識，甚至讓買主當場同意下訂單？此深具挑戰性任務，乃是業務人員對公司之貢獻與自我成就感（egocentric achievements）。

要達成上述任務，有許多前置性工作必須準備妥善，所謂『工欲善其事，必先利其器』。當然，現場人員如何掌握買主、洽商業務、以及主導助理在攤位上幫忙拉台人氣（popularity）、招呼客人；每一環節都非常重要，缺一不可。

參觀國際展會之訪客，多半屬專業買主，很少有閒雜人士。攤位負責人員必須在最短時間內分辨出，以最誠懇之態度，專注精神，提供服務給真正潛在客戶。不必擔心參觀人潮之多寡，最重要是有多少專業訪客會來您的攤位拜訪，自己也要在短短幾天展期中，發揮參加展會之最大綜效（combined effects）。

主要國際展覽會館，設備新穎，動線流暢，燈光明亮。參展廠商攤位設計一定要依照大會相關規定，切莫私自作主，以免違反規定，造成無謂困擾；情節重大者，有可能會被取消參展資格，不可不慎。另也須注意當地或有『特殊規定』（local rules），入境隨俗即可。

Exhibition

達人提點 Hidden Rules? 潛規則?

參展費用高，每天早上攤位要準時開張，所謂早起鳥兒有蟲吃（the early bird gets the worm）。下午打烊時間也要儘量以大會指定展覽時間為準，切忌提前唱空城計，因為訂單通常會在下班前幾分鐘敲定。如果此時恰巧有買主來訪未遇，失之交臂，豈不扼腕?在展會中整天守株待兔雖然無奈、無聊，但上述經驗也算是『撇步』。因為老天不負苦心人，戲棚下站久，就會是您的了!

目前國外會場臨時工作人員，廠商大多會聘用當地華僑（overseas Chinese）子女或留學生（student studying abroad）。每個攤位事先洽妥 1~2 位即可，太多人有時反而幫不上忙。有關這部分費用及付費方式，要先問清楚有無『潛規則』？有些展會現場臨時工作人員會透過仲介公司代為聘用，則此費用要先交給該仲介，再由該公司另轉給來幫忙的人。

4-3

參展後
After Exhibition

情境設定

Follow-up works aim at building up a good relation with clients and offering the opportunity to sign up orders. It seems like these things are trivial but they are steps taken to ensure success, as some dialogues excerpted in the following：

參 展後續工作主要為建立與客戶之良好關係，也有機會因此拿到訂單合約。相關之事項也許看似瑣細，但在邁向成功之路卻是極其重要之步驟，如以下對話摘要：

角色設定

Colleague A：公司同事 A
Colleague B：公司同事 B

Exhibition

情境 1 後續追蹤與答謝函 Follow-ups and Thank-you Letters

情境對話

A ▶ The exhibition closed last week was a success as we received many foreign buyers than expected at the exhibition. Most of all,

公司同事 A ▶ 本公司在上週剛結束的展會相當成功，因為我們在展會

303

we've gained trial orders, and expect more follow-up orders for the year.

接待的國外買主比預期多。最重要的是，我們也獲得試用訂單，並且期望今年會有許多後續訂單。

B ▶ As a token of appreciation, it is necessary to write thank-you letters to those visitors in the exhibition. This increases the built up of a close relationship in the future.

公司同事 B ▶ 為了象徵感激之意，有必要寫一些答謝函給那些來展會之訪客。這樣做會增加未來更緊密的客情。

A ▶ Yes, an U.S. buyer placed a trial order and requested quotations for follow-up orders. He hoped to enter into negotiations for the best price this week.

公司同事 A ▶ 是的，有一位美國買主已下了試用訂單也希望我們給他後續報價。他希望再本週內能協商出一個好價位。

B ▶ For a secured business transaction, the trade information should be relayed to our distributors in the U.S., who are very experienced in new clients?

公司同事 B ▶ 為確保此買賣進行，本交易是否應該轉交美國經銷商，他們對於新客戶很有經驗？

A ▶ I am afraid that we have to handle this trade by ourselves this time. Besides, the U.S. distributors are now occupied in Chicago's IMTS show.

公司同事 A ▶ 我擔心我們這次必須自己處理此項交易。況且，美國經銷商正忙碌於芝加哥 IMTS 展覽而分身乏術。

B ▶ That is fine for me. After all, the company has to become independent in handling exhibition and foreign orders in the future!

公司同事 B ▶ 對我而言沒什麼差別。畢竟我們公司在處理展會及國外訂單方面以後更要獨立作業了!

給力單字

1. **gain** (*v.t.*)　獲得,得到[(+from)]
   We gained several foreign orders from the exhibition.
   我們從這次展會中獲得許多國外訂單。

2. **token** (*n.*)　標記;象徵
   I sent thank-you letters to customers as a token of my appreciation.
   我給客戶寄去感謝函以表示感激之意。

3. **negotiation** (*n.*)　談判,協商
   Trade negotiations are still going on.
   貿易談判仍在進行。

4. **transaction** (*n.*)　交易;買賣
   A record is kept of all the firm's transactions.
   公司的一切交易都有記載。

5. **occupy** (*v.t.*)　使忙碌,使從事[(+in/with)]
   She is occupied in coping with follow-up works of the exhibition.
   她正忙處理展覽的後續工作。

Exhibition

6. **independent** (*adj.*)　獨立的；自立的

The company has now become independent in handling foreign orders.

公司現在處理國外訂單方面都可獨立作業了。

給力句型

1. gain　得到

   *gain experience/support/a reputation etc

   You'll gain useful experience in follow-up works .

   在後續工作的過程中，您會得到有用的經驗。

   *gain currency

   These kinds of exhibitions have gained currency in recent years.

   這些種類之展覽會近幾年已變得很流行。

   *stand to gain

   Who could possibly stand to gain from these exhibitions?

   誰真正能從這些展會中受益？

2. negotiation　協商

   *be open to negotiation

   The terms of the contract are still open to negotiation.

   合同條款仍可協商。

   *enter into negotiation

   Sitting down, representatives of two parties entered into negotiation.

   坐下來後，雙方代表展開談判。

3. occupy　占用

*be occupied with

She was fully occupied with follow-up matters.
她因後續工作纏身。

*keep sb occupied

Too many follow-up works will keep me occupied for days.
太多後續工作將讓我忙上好幾天。

 情境 2　客戶資料與建檔 Creating Customer Database

情境對話

A ▶ How many business name cards had been received by you from the exhibition, and how will you create a database of these documentations?

公司同事 A ▶ 您在展會中收到多少張客戶名片，這些資料要準備如何建檔？

B ▶ Over 100 visitors crowded into the booth during the five-day period exhibition but I received only 50 name cards with most having new data. I'll file it carefully by using our "client relation management (CRM)" system.

公司同事 B ▶ 在五天展會裡，有超過 100 位訪客湧入攤位，但我只收到 50 張名片，而且大部分是新客戶資料。我會利用我們的"客戶關係管理"系統，仔細建檔。

Exhibition

307

A ▶ Certainly, my company spent a lot of money for the CRM last year. This new system deserves several functions to offer, especially in the field of sales and management.

公司同事 A ▶ 當然可以，我的公司去年為了『客戶關係管理系統』花了許多錢。新系統值得提供許多功能，尤其針對業務及管理領域方面。

B ▶ It is worthy of spending two days to key in new data. After a new database is completed, the company's potential clients are expected to grow significantly.

公司同事 B ▶ 值得花兩天時間鍵入新增資料。等新資料庫完成後，公司之潛在客戶將會明顯地增加。

給力單字

1. **database** (*n.*)　資料庫
   Put the new customers on the database.
   把新客戶的資料輸入數據庫。

2. **crowd into** (*ph.*)　大批湧入
   Visitors crowded through the gates into the exhibition.
   訪客擠過大門，湧入展會場。

3. **client relation management** (*ph.*)　客戶關係管理
   The new client relation management favors sales of the company.
   新客戶關係管理對公司業務有利。

4. **function** (*n.*)　官能；功能
The new CRM has so many functions to offer.
新客戶關係管理有許多功能。

5. **field** (*n.*)　領域；專業
He is a prominent expert in the field of customer management.
他是客戶管理方面的傑出專者。

6. **potential clients** (*ph.*)　潛在客戶
The company was eager to impress potential clients.
這家公司急於給潛在客戶留下深刻的印象。

給力句型

1. file　檔案
   *keep a file on

   The company keeps a file on new customers.
   公司保存着新開發客戶的檔案。

   *file sth away

   The new database will be filed away in my office.
   新資料庫將歸檔存放在我的辦公室。

2. field　領域
   *in his/her field

   He is a leading expert in his field.
   在他的研究領域裡他是其中最傑出的專家。

*lead/be ahead of the field

The company is already way ahead of the rest of the field.
該公司已經遙遙領先於其他同類公司。

3. potential 潛力

*achieve/fulfill/realize your potential

The company wants each colleague to realize their full potential.
公司想讓每位同事的潛力發揮到極致。

*have/show potential

She has sales potential, but she needs training.
她有業務潛力，但需要訓練。

 情境 3 安排洽訪潛在客戶 **Call on a Potential Client**

角色設定

Sales Manager：業務經理，
The Secretary：秘書，
The Chairman：董事長

情境對話

Sales Manager (on telephone) ▶ I would like to have an appointment with the Chairman on next Monday morning. Could you make it at ten o'clock?

業務經理（（電話上） ▶ 我想下星期一上午與董事長會面。請可否安排在上午 10 點？

The Secretary (on telephone) ▶ The Chairman will be presiding over a regular meeting until 10:30 on each Monday morning, but I can make a reservation at 11:00 a.m. Are you available for the time?

秘書（電話上） ▶ 我們董事長每週一上午都要主持一個固定會議到 10:30，但是我可以幫您預訂 11 點。這個時間對您方便嗎？

Sales Manager (on telephone) ▶ Thank you for your kind attention. The Chairman visited my booth in a machinery exhibition held last week in the U.S., and we agreed to meet again for a business transaction between our two parties.

業務經理（電話上） ▶ 感謝妳體貼的關注。貴司董事長上週在美國機械展會中有到過我們公司攤位拜訪，我們同意再另約談雙方一樁交易。

The Secretary (on telephone) ▶ I think the Chairman would be pleased to meet you in his office on schedule. Thank you for your calling.

秘書（電話上） ▶ 我想董事長會很樂於與您準時見面。謝謝您的來電。

Sales Manager (in the office) ▶ Hi, I have an appointment with the Chairman at 11:00. Would you please report my arrival to him?

業務經理（在辦公室） ▶ 妳好，我與貴司董事長 11：00 有會面見面。可否請妳通報董事長我已經抵達？

The Secretary (in the office) ▶ Yes, Sir. Please have a seat and tea, and the Chairman will be seeing you in a minute.

秘書（在辦公室） ▶ 是的，先生。請先就坐並喝杯茶，董事長立刻會接見您。

Exhibition

311

Sales Manager (in the meeting) ▶ Mr. Chairman, it was a fruitful meeting with you, and we made three important decisions. I am sure of a better understanding of your company if you allow me to look around the factory after the meeting.

業務經理（在會議中）▶ 董事長先生，這是非常有成效的會議，我們做了三個重大決議。等開完會後，如果您同意讓我看一下工廠，相信對貴司會有更進一步了解。

The Chairman (in the meeting) ▶ For confidential reason and among other things, our factory is not open to the general public in most of the office time. But as a courtesy call, I will bring you to the reception room and arrange a factory tour for your presence only.

董事長（在會議中）▶ 除了機密因素還有其它事情，我們工廠大部分上班時間是不對外開放的。但基於禮貌拜訪，我會帶您到接待室並為您專程安排一趟參觀之旅。

Sales Manager (in reception room) ▶ I appreciate it very much for your kind consideration. I will call your secretary to check the arrangement of our next meeting, and I expect to see you again soon.

業務經理（在接待室）▶ 非常感激董事長如此周到考慮。我會另外打電話給您的秘書並確認我們下次會議的安排，並期待儘快再與您見面。

給力單字

1. **appointment** (*n.*) 與某人約會
I've made an appointment with Mr. chairman.
我已與董事長先生有約會。

2. **preside** (*v.t.*) 擔任會議主席，主持
The chairman presided at the meeting.
董事長主持了會議。

3. **reservation** (*n.*) 預訂；預訂的房間
We have made reservation for a meeting room at the hotel.
我們已在這個旅館預訂了一個會議室。

4. **attention** (*n.*) 關心，關注
She was flattered by all the attention he was giving her.
他對她很關心，她感到受寵若驚。

5. **transaction** (*n.*) 交易；買賣
A record is kept of all the firm's transactions.
公司的一切交易都有保存紀錄。

6. **on schedule** (*ph.*) 準時
The guest arrived on schedule.
客人準時來到。

7. **arrival** (*n.*) 到達；到來
We waited for the arrival of our guests.
我們等著客人的到來。

8. **in a minute** (*ph.*) 馬上；立刻
Our guests will be here in a minute!
我們的客人馬上就到!

Exhibition

9. **fruitful** (*adj.*)　富有成效的
Today's meeting proved more fruitful than last week's.
今天的會議證明比上星期的有成效。

10. **look around** (*ph.*)　四下環顧
He looked around the factory with great interest.
他懷著很大的興趣四下環顧工廠。

11. **courtesy call** (*ph.*)　禮貌拜訪
The sales manager paid a courtesy call to the chairman.
該業務經理對董事長作了一個禮貌性拜訪。

12. **appreciate** (*v.t.*)　感謝，感激
They deeply appreciated his kindness.
他們對他的好意深表感謝。

給力句型

1. preside　擔任會議主席，主持
   *preside at

   The general manager presided at the meeting.
   總經理主持了會議。

   *preside over

   The manager presides over the business of this store.
   經理主管本店的業務。

2. attention　注意

*hold/keep sb's attention

He keeps the reader's attention throughout the book.
他的書從頭到尾都吸引着讀者的興趣。

*give sth attention

The press has given the story a lot of attention.
新聞界對這個報導給予很大關注。

*the focus of attention

The focus of attention has shifted away from domestic issues.
人們關注的焦點已不再是國內問題。

情境 4 簽訂合約 **Signing a Contract**

情境對話

Party A ▶ This is the contract of the trial order for your perusal. To be valid of the contract, please put your signature on the blank underlined.

甲方 ▶ 這是一份試用訂單合約書，請您詳閱後。於空白劃線處簽名，合約即生效。

Party B ▶ I reconfirmed the price and the payment terms. The contract has to be endorsed by the legal department, however.

乙方 ▶ 我已重新確認過價格及付款條件。但是本合約也要經由法務部門簽署認可。

Party A ▶ Please note that the 5% value

甲方 ▶ 請注意 5%增值

Exhibition

315

added tax will be waived by your party, which was promised by the Chairman in the previous meeting. My company's financial department will send you an invoice after conducting this transaction.

稅會由貴方放棄，這部分董事長在上次會議中已經答應好此事。我們財務部門在交易進行後，也會另寄發票給貴方。

Party B ▶ This tax issue in the contract will be identified and obeyed by my company, according to the instruction of the Chairman. He also appreciates it very much for your consideration.

乙方 ▶ 我們董座指示，有關稅的問題經確認後，公司會遵照合約進行。董事長也非常感激您們的考量。

給力單字

1. **perusal** (*n.*)　細讀；閱讀
   That contract deserves careful perusal.
   那個合約值得細讀。

2. **valid** (*adj.*)　合法的；經正當手續的
   The contract is valid for one year.
   這張合約一年內有效。

3. **signature** (*n.*)　簽名，簽署
   This contract needs signatures of both sides.
   本合約需要雙方簽名。

4. **endorse** (*v.t.*)　在背面簽名，背書
   She has already endorsed the contract.
   她已在這合約上背書。

5. **value-added tax** (*ph.*)　增值稅

   The contract requires a 5% value-added tax.

   合約需要多加 5%增值稅。

6. **waive** (*v.t.*)　放棄，取消

   She waived her right to the contract

   她放棄了該合約的權利

7. **invoice** (*n.*)　發票; 發貨清單

   Please send me invoice for the payment approval.

   請寄給我發票以利請款。

8. **obey** (*v.t.*)　服從；聽從

   You didn't obey the manager's instructions.

   你沒有執行經理的指示。

給力句型

1. valid　合法的；有效的

   *a valid contract

   This is a valid contract with an effectiveness date of one year.

   本具有法律效力的合同在一年期內有效。

   *sth. is valid

   His point about contract shortcomings was a valid one.

   他的關於合約缺點的看法是有根據的。

Exhibition

2. obey　服從

*obey the law/laws/rules

You'll have to obey the rules of the contract.
你要遵守合約的規定。

*obey an order/command

Obey the order of your boss or you will be fired.
服從你上司的命令，否則你會被解僱。

職場補給　**Thank-you Letters 感謝函**

　　後續追蹤是展會最後一項重要之階段，所謂『好的開始，是成功的一半。』（A well begun is half done）主管及同仁在這方面更要全力以赴，以期完成交辦任務；因此與客戶建立良好關係，幫公司爭取更多客源。

　　答謝函最好在展會剛結束後第一週裡即配合名片公司資訊，盡快寄出。自己接待的客戶，最好是由自己親自寫感謝函，每一封信內容儘量不要太過制式化（too formulated），可親切地（cordially）提起展會中雙方交談事項，以增加客戶對您或公司之印象。有些比較重要客戶也必須再用電話追蹤，詢問是否需要另提供樣品或相關服務，甚至藉此安排洽訪潛在客戶機會。

　　建立電腦資料檔是基本功（essential），但也要用心做好，不可發生誤植客戶資料，甚至張冠李戴，切記! 有關展會初見面、與客戶洽談或有關該行業一些事情，建議可用重點方式紀錄寫下來，等下次與客戶見面時順便提起，增加洽商題材。客戶會很感激您的關心，說不定會增加成交機會?

　　勤跑客戶，建立客群，是做業務人員自我要求。與客戶約訪要準時，最好提前 10 分鐘抵達公司地點；如有特殊情形，也要事先告知必須延誤原因，請客戶諒解並等您見面。現在大家都很忙，客戶如有答應洽訪，一定要加以把握，可能有機會拿到訂單。另見面三分情，也是超級業務業績長紅之『眉角』（tricks）。

達人提點 Contract Trap 合約陷阱

簽訂合約前要先仔細核對所有條款，尤其是雙方協議後總金額部分，另外有無涉及特別注意事項，簽約前必須釐清，方可簽名並蓋章（sealed）。

一般公司對外簽約，合約內容可請法務部門同事先行過目，看各條文有無問題或陷阱，而不致影響公司權益等。有些大公司雖然在商場打滾多年，有時在合約書卻也栽跟斗，以致蒙受重大損失；還要再花一筆費用聘請律師，處理跨國官司（lawsuit），良有以也。

Exhibition

Leader 008

Just the One～會展英語
MICE English

作　　者　陳志達
發 行 人　周瑞德
企劃編輯　劉俞青
執行編輯　陳欣慧
封面設計　高鍾琪
內文排版　菩薩蠻數位文化有限公司
校　　對　饒美君、陳韋佑

印　　製　大亞彩色印刷製版股份有限公司
初　　版　2014 年 12 月
出　　版　力得文化
電　　話　(02) 2351-2007
傳　　真　(02) 2351-0887
地　　址　100 台北市中正區福州街 1 號 10 樓之 2
E - m a i l　best.books.service@gmail.com
定　　價　新台幣 360 元

港澳地區總經銷　泛華發行代理有限公司
地　　　　址　香港筲箕灣東旺道 3 號星島新聞集團大廈 3 樓
電　　　　話　(852) 2798-2323
傳　　　　真　(852) 2796-5471

國家圖書館出版品預行編目(CIP)資料

會展英語 / 陳志達著. -- 初版. -- 臺北市：力
得文化, 2014.12
　面；　公分. -- (Leader；8)
ISBN 978-986-90759-7-8(平裝)

1.商業英文 2.讀本

805.18　　　　　　　103022771